to the other side of the road when she appeared. Others bought her story that she and her husband were sacrifices to victor's justice and greeted her silently with a quick glance, a cautious smile, a knowing nod.

During sun-filled summers Maria remembered her as the tired, dark-haired lady in the thatched villa who loved to hand out hot chocolate and cakes to the children at the beach. She would always give Maria the largest piece of cake and serve her first, even if other darker-haired children with different coloured eyes to her blue ones were ahead of her in the queue.

Peter had been a member of the Nazi youth movement during the War, as was required of all young people. But his father, however, had demonstrated considerable courage in his own convictions by speaking bluntly and openly about the "folly" of conducting a war on two fronts. "Anyone can see this is not going to work!" That was not the right talk for the time. Those zealously in favour of the new regime stopped buying in the König store and took pains to shun him at the frequent social events. After the War, he would describe those same zealots gleefully as "this tall, including their hats," holding the palm of his hand barely above the surface of the table to indicate how timid they had become.

For some, resentments had festered and deepened as they despairingly hoped an old order which had shown so much potential would re-establish itself. Others welcomed the passing of a regime that they claimed they had always known was doomed. Still others felt these questions were now all irrelevant and looked only to the future and in particular the business opportunities

rushing toward them from the mainland across the new island bridge. Many of the younger generation could only look at their parents aghast at what they had done.

Maria's father was quick to build on the small corner shop he had inherited, and his visionary foresight had reaped great rewards for his family. The shop grew as he bought neighbouring plot after plot to create an ever-larger store. Recognizing a potential competitor on the other side of the market square, he was quick to block the threat by secretly buying the piece of land that represented the only space his competitor could use to grow.

His success generated envy, but it also brought power and respect. Where once the family had worked their store themselves, now others worked for them. The family moved from their cosy flat above the shop to a large, far more respectable house with two floors, cellar, garden, and garage where Peter was soon parking his Mercedes limousine.

However, Maria's family successes created problems for her at school. Her special eye-contact and trust didn't help her with her classmates. She did not understand why she was not liked at school. She tried her best to make friends, remembering to greet everyone as she had been taught by her parents. Instead, she found herself the butt of nasty jokes, hurtful exclusions and sometimes painful pinches that left angry red weals. The other children were releasing their own parent's envy and confusion at the rapidly shifting sands of the island's society on her.

Mitya New – **Beyond Mount Kailash**

Mitya New

Beyond Mount Kailash

Novel

PalmArtPress
Berlin

Bibliografische Information der Deutschen Nationalbibliothek
Die Deutsche Nationalbibliothek verzeichnet diese Publikation in der Deutschen Nationalbibliografie; detaillierte bibliografische Daten sind im Internet über http://www.dnb.de abrufbar.

ISBN: 978-3-96258-210-4

First Edition, 2025 PalmArtPress, Berlin

Cover Design: Catharine J. Nicely
Layout: NicelyMedia
Editor: Michael Lederer, Paul Dinas
Printed in Europe

Ganz im Sinne der Nachhaltigkeit wurde diese Publikation auf FSC-zertifiziertem Papier klimaneutral gedruckt.

PalmArtPress
Pfalzburger Str. 69, 10719 Berlin
Publisher: Catharine J. Nicely
www.palmartpress.com

for

MARTINA

Chapter 1

The dull, muffled thud through the wooden plank at the rear of the rowing boat shook Maria from her sleepiness. The two oarsmen turned to each other with expressions of guilt and unease. As their oars hung suddenly motionless in mid-air, glistening and dripping, they looked furtively over their shoulders for guidance from Samir, the young tour guide she had commissioned the evening before for this pre-dawn boat trip.

At this time of morning, the river was somnolent. Although Maria had visited Varanasi, India's holiest city, frequently enough to know life never ceased on the river, in these earliest moments of the day the atmosphere was still dark, illuminated only by a few burning fires on the shore and the occasional chime of a cow's bell. Maria always loved this hour for its peacefulness. It was the moment that brought her some relief after an exhausting night of fear and wakefulness—before the onslaught of a new day.

"Big fish, Madam," Samir said, flashing a confident smile.

Maria looked at him uncertainly.

Then, a series of smaller bumps sounded beneath the keel, indicating the boat was now floating over a large object. There was a moment of pregnant silence, then a splash and perceptible sinking of the boat's stern into the water. Maria grasped the gunwales quickly, fearing the dark dirty water might flow in over the sides. An object bounced to the surface and started to float away in the boat's wake.

The expressions of the two oarsmen turned to horror. Then she saw it. The bright saffron-coloured sari in the water, the bloated face almost white, the eyes wide open and tongue too large for the mouth, lolling out grotesquely between two sets of decayed, uneven and missing teeth. With a sharp cry and shudder, Maria jerked her head away. The oarsmen immediately plunged their oars back into the water and urgently resumed their rhythmic movement to gain distance as quickly as possible from the corpse.

"Poor family, Madam," Samir said now. "No money for cremation. Bury in river."

"I see," she said as the body receded into the gloom. "Can nobody help them?"

Samir smiled politely but said nothing.

As the first golden rays of the rising sun broke the horizon, illuminating the higher walls of the *ghats*, she wondered why the sight of the body had upset her so much. She had come to Varanasi many times since moving to India as a married woman. Her Indian friends in Mumbai accepted her fascination for the city with a mixture of amused respect, unsure whether to feel embarrassment that she should have to endure the stench and filth of the city's streets, or pride that she could identify with its heritage and religious importance.

"You are more Indian than we are, Maria," said Deepa Thani, one of her closest Bombay friends, a prominent talk show host and newsreader, a few weeks earlier. They had been waiting for their banana leaf plates to be replaced at one of the many dining tables of a large Tamil outdoor wedding reception.

"We Hindus go to Varanasi to bathe in the holy Ganges only. Some of us hope to die there, you know. To escape *samsara*, the cycle of reincarnation, and to achieve *moksha*, which for us is like you going to heaven. But you are almost living there."

The evening before the boat trip, Maria had mustered the courage to take off her shoes and step down the long stone steps below the Bachraj Ghat to immerse her bare feet in the lapping waters of the Ganges for the first time in the dozen or so visits she had made to Varanasi. An elderly couple paused to watch her. As she turned to look at them, she saw their white clothes and face masks and realized that this was the *ghat* for the minority Jain religion. She knew that their masks weren't to avoid infection, but to guard against inadvertently causing harm to insects that might fly into their open mouths.

Maria tried to forget the stories of corpses, defecation, body washing and other horrors her foreign friends always warned her of whenever she mentioned she was going to Varanasi.

"Whatever you do, don't go near the river. It's disgusting! You can get ill just looking at it," Susan Wader, the Australian wife of a managing director at a foreign bank, had warned her one afternoon as they sat by a tree-shaded pool at the exclusive Willingdon Club in central Mumbai. "The Indians have different immune systems to us. They can swim in it, drink it, brush their teeth in it without getting sick."

As she hesitated to take another step, she heard the woman of the Jain couple say: "Mother Ganges cleans herself, Madam."

Maria marvelled that Indians could sense the emotional state of those around them so much more quickly than Westerners. It was one of the first things she had noticed when she first arrived in India. It allowed them to adjust their behaviour, thoughts, words, even feelings toward others so quickly. It made her feel so much more comfortable in India, reassuring her that others were not going to challenge, test, judge or embarrass her. Rather, they were going to accommodate her feelings in an endless series of enigmatic compromises with a willingness to learn from life rather than try to control it.

The sun continued to rise. The *ghats* lost their hazy softness and shifted into sharp relief. Maria remembered reading in a guidebook that the *ghats* had been built by benevolent local rulers to allow their subjects' access to the river for religious ceremonies—the washing of bodies and clothes, in some cases, cremations.

Suddenly the river seemed to come to life. Several boats with loud engines started up. Two *sadhus*, clad in long saffron robes and recognizable with the spiritual mark of three thick, white ash stripes across their foreheads, appeared from the old city's narrow streets and sat cross-legged on a cloth with their backs to a yellowing stone wall. At the river's edge, two young boys practiced somersaults from a small ferry pier into the water.

“Madam, Manikarnika Ghat!” Samir pointed.

Maria shivered. She always felt a sense of foreboding mixed with fascination when she reached this part of the river. Manikarnika Ghat was the largest of the open-air cremation zones, where some said 100 Hindus a day were cremated. Ahead she could see a few fires still burning, while other sites, already reduced to piles of ash, were being readied for the next ceremony. At an upper level, the white-clad men of a mourning family were gathering for the next cremation. Only men—according to Hindu tradition, women were excluded from attending cremations.

She saw a family's male elder, his head freshly shaven, step down from a large pyre erected on a stone podium that highlighted their wealth, while the flames, barely visible at first, began to lick serpent-like around the kindling and heavier wood piled beneath the body. Foreign friends she had brought to Varanasi on earlier visits invariably looked away in disgust, some even gasped in horror. Others were physically sick.

But as Maria watched, she felt an explicable mixture of excitement and terror as if the flames were caressing her. When the fire surged with a sudden roar, like a tower around and above the body wrapped in white cotton and garlanded with flowers, she could feel the spirit leaving the body. Sometimes she sensed the exact moment—a sudden lightness, when, with a loud *pop*, the heat of the fire exploded the skull.

Occasionally, it happened later when the male elder would take a long pole and fold the extremities of the body back over itself into the centre of the pyre where the heat and flames were stronger, and the torso had already disintegrated. The smoke rising into the hot still air, the distinct smell of burnt hair, and then the faint sickly cloying odour of burning flesh mixed with combustible melted ghee would cling to her own hair and clothes long after.

Initially, Maria had worried that her fascination with cremation was morbid. Susan Wader had described it as "macabre." But rather than feeling disgust, Maria felt a great sense of calm and serenity at the pragmatic confrontation with death that the stoic untouchable Dalits displayed, as they kept back the roaming dogs and cleared each site of ashes and remains in search of jewellery or gold fillings after the fire had run its course.

Samir motioned the boatmen, now sweating profusely in the growing morning heat, to ship oars. The boat continued to make its way closer to the shore. With a sudden shift in the breeze a wave of smoke from one of the pyres enveloped them, then just as quickly blew away.

As they drew near, Maria stared into the flames rising from the site. This pyre was large, taller than the surrounding family members and the small group of Dalits waiting to be tipped for their work after the cremation was over. She felt herself mesmerized by the colours, as if the flames were talking to her, inviting her in, pulling her toward them to join the warmth of the fire. As if they were telling her to have confidence, not to be afraid, but instead to embrace the release. She could hear her own voice telling her to have courage, to take that last step that would set her free.

She could also hear Bhavana Guruji, his soft gentle words in that deep voice, rising from within his large chest. "Remember the answers to your questions, and the solutions to your problems, are only within you."

Maria felt her mind ascending, leaving her body behind on the rough wooden planks of the boat seat. Now she saw the pyre from above, blurred through the thickening white smoke, recognizing her own face and body lying on top of the ungainly tower of bundled sandalwood. She sensed a wonderful release. Her muscles relaxing, her breathing slowing, she closed her eyes, embracing the deep calm and peace she so desperately craved.

Chapter 2

Maria's earliest childhood memory was of the broad, cobbled road that passed through the town's market square and its imposing red-brick town hall on the German island located just off the coast in the North Sea. She was always worried when walking along this main road that she would not be able to follow her mother's strict instructions to greet all family and friends politely. Maria knew she would never be able to recall the names of all the friends, not to mention the wider family of cousins, aunts and uncles who also lived in the small town or elsewhere on the island. The best solution was simply to greet everyone she encountered politely, regardless of whether they were family, friends, or others.

She had sun-bleached blond hair and a warm, friendly, cheerful smile with a gaze that lingered openly and trustingly in the eyes of all she met. They might be strangers on the main street, or in the small corner shop opposite the town hall which her parents owned and ran. It didn't matter. While others would often just turn away disinterested or unwilling to engage, she would connect directly with everyone, looking into the eyes of each person, radiating a natural care that few could ignore.

"Maria's eyes are so unusual," she once heard her mother's friend Anneliese Balstedt say. "Her face is so open. And her blue eyes make you feel warm."

Maria could see her mother was pleased hearing that, although for a different reason. "Always look into people's eyes," she had told Maria and her younger brother Karl. "It shows you are confident."

Maria enjoyed looking into people's eyes. Fear, happiness, disappointments, all right there to be discovered if you took the time and had the interest to look for them. In the split second it took to glance into someone's eyes, you might understand their life-story. The excitement of the local pharmacist on his way to pick up his daughter from school; the sadness of the young jewellery shop assistant whose boyfriend was not meeting her for the cinema that evening. Eyes were a window to the soul.

It was only when she was older that Maria discovered how her eyes affected others. People always seemed to smile back at her. Even the angriest of faces softened when she looked at them, however briefly. For Maria, an answering smile was like a little conversation. She felt in that moment that she and the other person were connected. Years later, one admirer described a look from Maria as being "like the caress of the sun."

The island's social geography was divided between the upper-class of long-established wealthy or gentry farmer families known as "natives" and a smaller group of enterprising tradesmen and entrepreneurs. who hoped to be accepted into established society during their, or at least their children's, lifetimes.

Maria's family was in the wrong category, on both counts. Her father, Peter, belonged to the entrepreneurial class. He had inherited the family business, a small corner shop selling shoes and furs and called König after the family name, when his father broke his neck falling down the stairs from their flat above the shop.

Peter became one of the louder entrepreneurial voices in the town, and indeed on the island. He argued that big changes were coming and must be embraced. Plans to construct a bridge connecting it to the mainland would transform the sleepy provincial backwater irreversibly. Some of the natives described the island almost proudly, if a bit tongue-in-cheek, as the world's eighth continent claiming its isolation from the mainland made it unique. But for Peter that was all irrelevant. He was focused on the wave of visitors and business the new bridge was going to bring.

In loud debates, sometimes fuelled by alcohol and always by fear of change, he had for years often found himself shouted down. There were many who resisted the construction of the bridge in favour of the cosy car and passenger ferry boat that had kept the paradise sufficiently separate from the mainland. Peter was already several steps ahead, and in quiet moments would shake his head in consternation at the inability of his fellow islanders to appreciate the scale of opportunity just waiting to be grasped. It was in those heady days that he coined a phrase he would use frequently and confidently in later years when proof of his prescience was evident in his wealth. "Money is lying on the streets. You just need to know how to gather it up."

Although Maria's father was in the wrong professional class, he had at least been born on the island and could claim a local family tree of several generations.

Ordinarily, that would have secured him grudging respect and conditional entry into the inner circle of natives. However, any credit he might have accrued on that account had instantly evaporated when he married Johanna, Maria's mother. She was a refugee from the mainland, whose parents and siblings had fled the Soviet forces occupying Germany from the east, and she came without a convincing story about her family provenance and, in particular, of their activities before and during the War.

As everywhere in Germany at this time, the War was wordlessly present—stuffed into everyone's bottom drawer behind a veil of silence concealing a collective horror, shame, embarrassment, regret, mixed with the pragmatic recognition that new winds were now blowing. But while never mentioned, the War was clearly visible like a patch hastily sewn on to cover a hole in well-worn clothes. And as across the country, it had riven the social fabric asunder and left the inhabitants to re-assemble their community as best they could.

All on the island knew the story of the former mayor. A submarine hero before the War, he had refused to raise the new Nazi flag in front of the town hall to celebrate the day Germany's new political power had ascended to power, arguing that the flagpole was reserved for the national flag and not to be used for party symbols. He was soon eased out of office by islanders more sympathetic to the new national socialist movement, then shunned, shoved and abused on the street near his home and finally found dead in a ditch, very possibly by his own hand.

Several years after the War, town archivists noted that the pages in the town hall's Golden Book for the period in which the National Socialist government was in power, had been neatly cut out, including the handwritten greeting and expression of thanks by one of Adolf Hitler's inner circle during a visit to the island as a guest of honour. The official story was that a pot of ink had inadvertently been spilt on these entries, requiring their removal, but most islanders knew the truth.

But perhaps the biggest mountain for society to climb on the War was the widow of the chief designer of the Nazi government's final solution for "the Jewish problem." Before the War, she had shone brightly in society, having married a rising star of the new political movement. Her husband, who was not from the island, had arm-twisted a fawning local administration into side-stepping existing regulations and selling the newly married couple one of the finest plots on the beach of the island's picturesque southern coast as a holiday home.

After the War, she had returned to the charming, thatched villa she and her husband had built there and turned it into a hotel. It was whispered that she entertained former members of the Nazi party there with weekend dinners of roasted local wild boar. The lights were on late into the night and strangers coming and going at all hours. Some suspected she was part of a secretive organization known as Silent Help, which financed the escape of prominent members of the former regime to South America.

As an upper-class native, she presented a social problem. Some on the island chose to go so far as cross

Maria began to develop a new social skill of adjusting chameleon-like to others around her. If she felt someone wanted her to be lively and cheeky, she would put on that behaviour. If she sensed someone preferred an intimate and confidential conversation, she would at once become sensitive in her tone and expression. These were not just acts of theatre. Whatever behaviour she displayed, at that moment she honestly felt and believed in completely. But despite her efforts she still felt excluded and could not help overhearing the angry half-whispered phrases about 'those Königs'. Increasingly, she just gave up and found it better to avoid looking at anyone in the school to avoid confrontations.

Maria had noticed another girl in the school suffering a similar fate to her own. Katrin Hudrich was the granddaughter of the controversial widow in the thatched villa hotel on the south shore beach. Maria did everything she could to attract the attention of Katrin. She would follow her around the school yard as she, too, sought to avoid the bullying attention of the toughs. She would offer to help Katrin hang up her coat when they arrived at class in the morning. She would offer Katrin half the snack the König's new housekeeper had packed into a paper bag in the morning.

However, Katrin just ignored her. When Maria did nevertheless succeed in making eye contact with her, even briefly, she detected a deep and forlorn inherited shame within her that left Maria feeling exhausted merely by sensing it.

Maria was never the best of pupils, partly because she was busy avoiding the taunting of the other children, but also because she was convinced she could not understand the subjects she was taught. She avoided asking or answering questions. So, she was surprised one morning when her German teacher, a young left-leaning failed author who always wore unwashed jeans with frayed bottoms, entered the class and addressed her directly.

Like most children in her class on the cusp of their teens, Maria had no way of understanding the ideological forces sweeping through Germany at this time. A young generation of left-wing intellectuals were not willing to let bygones be bygones. They had determined the War—the dirty laundry so carefully hidden by almost everyone—should be discussed openly rather than buried and ignored. Since many who had mastered previous political waters had now adapted their skills to succeed again, the young intellectuals felt justified labelling those who were successful with the mark of collaboration. Or at the least, of like-minded thinking. Perhaps lost on them were lessons so recently learned, not to label whole swaths of people in one broad stroke of a brush.

"König, stand up!" the teacher barked from the front of the classroom.

It was rare for any pupil to be asked to stand and even rarer for Maria to be the focus of any teacher's attention. The class fell silent. Many of the children wondered if Maria, now the daughter of the most upwardly mobile family on the island, was about to receive an award, or some other accolade.

Maria forgot her usual caution, stood, raised her head and looked into the red angry eyes of the teacher. He was short and she precociously tall, so that their eyes met across the children's heads at the same level. As she looked, she felt something ominous and cold in his heart. She shuddered. In his eyes, she saw a furious hate. Resentment built on bitterness, provincial envy and a vicious desire for revenge.

Speaking slowly, deliberately, in a loud voice, he said: "König, you capitalist swine! Why has your father parked his fat, corrupt Mercedes in the parking space for my modest, proletarian Volkswagen Beetle?"

You could have heard a pin drop. Maria felt physically unable to move. She was sure she was going to throw up. She did not know what to do or say. She was not even sure she understood what *capitalist* and *proletarian* meant. Her first thought was that she must have done something wrong, and that her parents would be angry or, to be more precise, her mother would be angry. Maria's mother was very black-and-white about who was in the right and who was in the wrong. It was quite simple. The school and teachers were always in the right. Maria was always in the wrong.

Quietly and slowly, she sat back down in her chair. The rest of the class seemed stunned as well at this unprovoked, unprecedented attack on what for them had been a legitimate playground target, but otherwise not worth much attention. Maria could tell from the smirks and whispered comments that new interest had been aroused, and a line crossed.

On the short walk home at lunchtime, she tried to put the incident out of her mind. As she sat down in the kitchen to the meal prepared by the new house-keeper, she heard voices shouting outside through the kitchen window. Roughly ten boys and girls from her class, came to a stop on the street outside her house. Then almost like a choir, as if they had practiced, they sang out: “Maria König is a capitalist swine! She is an ugly muck and looks like a duck!”

Tears streamed down Maria's cheeks. Covering her face with her hands, as she looked out between her fin-gers, she saw Katrin Hudrich at the front of the group. She even seemed to be the one egging them on. Inspired by the angry teacher, and the bullying she had experi-enced herself, Katrin must have recognised a sudden opportunity to win favour at Maria's expense.

“Don't make such a fuss. It's your own fault for being so shy,” the housekeeper, an elderly woman from one of the town's native but working-class families, had said dismissively when she came into the kitchen. But Maria had barely heard.

Luckily, her parents were not home. Maria did not tell her mother or father what had happened in school and outside their home, nor fortunately did the housekeeper. She could already see her mother's furrowed brow and silent look into the distance that was impossible to interpret and always left her feeling so worthless. Her mother had an unpredictable and terrifying capacity to explode in anger so powerful that to Maria it felt like being hit physically. On those occasions, when it was often impossible to fathom what was upsetting her mother, it was senseless to do anything but sit there and wait until the rage had passed. Johanna would not accept any different point of view.

As Maria grew older, she perfected what she called the 'tightrope walk' making sure any conversation with her mother did not venture into territory that could drive her mother 'over the cliff.' It required constantly being on guard, selecting carefully what to tell her, always embellishing it to meet her expectations.

Maria knew from bitter experience that school was a potential 'over the cliff' subject. She knew her mother's conviction that teachers were always right was unshakeable. She would have dismissed Maria's account of the teacher's behaviour as a distortion and not even have listened to Maria's feelings about the cruelty of her classmates.

But occasionally, when Maria looked into her mother's eyes, she would see softness and gentleness. She particularly enjoyed those times after dinner when her mother took a plate full of oranges, expertly sliced and peeled them, and handed her the juicy segments while the tower of orange peels on the plate grew higher. At such moments, her mother seemed calm and would listen with sincere interest to Maria's stories of friends or other happenings from her day. She marvelled at how quickly her mother could comprehend a complex situation. But even in those moments, Maria could not help fearing that something might spark an unanticipated flash, the serenity overturned at once and replaced with unbearable fury.

In many ways, Maria was similar to her father. She had inherited his winning smile a sudden wide crease of the lips that would fill his face with a beaming contagious positivity that would quickly win over all but the bitterest of enemies. Maria particularly liked his habit of dropping home-spun proverbs into his daily conversation that seemed to offer simple ways out of complex problems. He was drawn to people and loved to see them happy. As his wealth grew, his generosity grew with it. Often to the despair and sometimes furious rebukes of his wife, he would shower munificence on waiters, porters, sales ladies at the store, and really anyone he felt had in some way touched him, or whom he felt sorry for because they had been less fortunate than himself.

Within the family, this came to be known as the 'watering can principle.' The almost random and generous sharing of money with people around him in the hope, perhaps, that they would like him for it.

When Maria looked deeply into her father's blue eyes, she saw the same desire to be loved that she also felt, and the same unhappiness at rejection she feared. She knew instinctively that were her father to hear of the teacher's comments to her in class, the implicit rejection by the islander's society would hurt him even more than it had hurt her. And that was something she was determined to prevent at all costs.

Chapter 3

Maria stepped from the wobbling boat, guided and supported by Samir's helping hand. She offered the two-handed prayer-like *namaste* gesture of greeting and parting and a quiet *dhanyavaad* of thanks together with some welcome banknotes to each of the boatmen. On shore she looked at the now loud and bustling crowds of people on Varanasi's main Dashashwamedh Ghat. She briefly caught the eye of a destitute, barely clothed beggar sitting on one of the steps and was rewarded with a smile of mutual understanding from behind the dark-skinned mask of misery.

Making her way through the narrow streets between the centuries-old decaying structures of Varanasi, she noticed a sudden commotion ahead. A bull with large horns almost the width of the tight alley was ambling indifferently towards her, forcing the crowds of people to make way. She quickly stepped into a doorway but missed her footing. Her sandalled foot sank into a warm soft mass. She had no time to recover. Pressing her back against the door, she flattened herself as much as possible as the huge animal passed slowly by.

Ahead of her, the alley widened into a street with small shops bursting with merchandise on both sides out onto the crumbling paving stones of the sidewalk. Cars, motorcycles, bicycles and people tussled for right of way. At a street corner, another more passive cow had entered head-first into a small jewellery shop and was calmly chewing its cud just above a showcase of gold earrings and bracelets. The shop assistants sitting behind the display cases seemed unperturbed, chatting calmly amongst themselves. They accepted the beast as much as it accepted them. She would be relying on this quality when in a few moments she reached her destination, she thought to herself.

From the street, she turned back into the narrow alleys of the old city. In the tight passages between buildings, she had to give way to frequent processions of men carrying biers on their shoulders bound for the river cremation grounds. Beneath the many coloured scarves and shrouds wrapped loosely around the bodies Maria could often make out the head and the features under the tightly wound first binding of cloth, white for men and saffron or red for women. Ahead of her, the wide majestic expanse of the Ganges re-appeared as she came out at a different ghat. Immediately to her right was a small inconspicuous doorway in an old building marked by a grimy smeared sign in English: *Kamal & Sons—Best Quality Burning Woods.*

She pushed open the old heavy wooden door, remembering from her last visit to lift it, since it had long settled in its hinges and marked a groove in the stone floor. From the door, she crossed a dimly lit low-ceilinged room to a narrow and steep stone spiral staircase. She climbed and reached a floor with wide empty gaps in place of walls and windows, and a full open view down onto the Manikarnika cremation ghat below. She felt a light warm breeze caress her moist skin as she came to another door. She took a deep breath before knocking, then entered.

Sitting at a vast desk strewn with papers, sat a portly, middle-aged man with slick, oily black hair combed back without a parting from his brow. Behind thickly framed glasses, his eyes were alert. His skin was very dark, almost pitch black, adding to an overall mildly sinister appearance. Maria wondered briefly why so many untouchables had such dark skin. A name plate on a small, worn pyramid-shaped wooden block on his desk announced his name.

She had met Kamal on one of her earliest visits to the ghats. One of his young sons had seen her observing a cremation and had approached to ask her to donate money to an elderly woman who had come to Varanasi to die but could not afford the wood for her own pyre. Suspicious of being fleeced, Maria challenged the boy to show her the woman. He led her to a small, bare room at the top of one of the old dome-tipped towers overlooking Manikarnika Ghat. In the gloom, Maria initially saw what looked like a pile of rags on the stone floor. But as her eyes adjusted, she had to stifle a cry. She saw protruding legs and ankles so thin and a contorted, wizened face with eye sockets so deep they looked black. As she stared, something in the sockets moved, the dark pupils slowly tracking her from her face down to her feet. She was not sure whether she was more horrified or enraged by the terrible neglect she could see in front of her. Without hesitation, she opened her handbag and pulled out a wad of banknotes. Not stopping to count them, she pushed them all into the boy's hands. The old woman attempted a toothless smile of gratitude. The boy had led Maria back down the narrow staircase, then without asking her up another to his father's office where she had met Kamal for the first time.

From his desk Kamal looked up.

"Good morning, Madam Maria," he called out effusively, standing quickly.

"Good morning, Mr. Kamal."

"Please," he gestured to the chair. "Some tea, perhaps?"

"Thank you." Maria took the seat opposite him. A few minutes later, as they exchanged pleasantries about the weather and her journey, a bare-footed adolescent boy entered the room, wearing a white T-shirt emblazoned in bright red letters with the words *See Varanasi and burn*. He carried a small metal tray cradle in which two clay cups were suspended and placed them on the table.

"Have you thought some more about my proposal," Maria asked after each had taken a sip from their cups.

Behind his thickly framed glasses, Kamal's eyes were alert, but studiously avoided direct contact with hers.

"Very difficult, Madam. Very difficult," he said slow-ly. "You are not Hindu. You are foreigner. Why not you cremate at *Harishchandra* Ghat, then no problem, non-Hindu can cremate there."

"I know that, but I want to be cremated at Manikarnika." Maria said. "I am willing to increase my offer. I could give two of your sons the financial support they would need to get through college. This could change their lives and help them prepare for a better karma in the next life."

Kamal licked his lips nervously. Maria could see her offer had surprised him and was appealing. Perhaps more appealing than it needed to be, but she wanted to move forward. She had made up her mind.

"But every cremation is being registered—we will get very, very bad trouble if the authority is discovering."

Maria was excited. In principle, Kamal had just agreed. His resistance now was a final ritual dance to see if he could better the terms any further.

"For you we will be needing minimum 400 kilogrammes of wood. Perhaps you are taking sandalwood, Madam? Brings good luck for you and is burning well," Kamal said, clearly having decided to accept her proposal.

Sandalwood was the most expensive cremation wood available and usually selected only by the wealthiest to display their status. The less fortunate relied on cheaper wood types or leaves and even cow dung. She suspected Kamal was probably inflating the amount of wood needed to try and maximize his profits.

Strangely, at this moment she suddenly thought of her mother who had always insisted on not compromising on quality. She recalled how, whenever she took her shopping in Hamburg, she would always insist on visiting the most exclusive and expensive boutiques in the city.

"It does not make sense to save on quality in the long run," she had told her. "Quality shows who you are and in addition will last longer."

"Fine then. Sandalwood and 400 kilogrammes." Maria said.

She could see in his eyes he was surprised she had not offered more resistance.

"As we discussed and agreed, my body will be in the room at midnight, of course facing south, in a small apartment near the top of the Manikarnika Ghat. I will give you the address later. I do not have my wedding dress, but there will be a red cloth to wrap me in. I have arranged for the priest to organize the body washing and to read from the Vedas. The only jewellery I will be wearing will be a pair of white pearl earrings. Your people cannot, under any circumstances, remove those from my ears before the cremation. That is very important.

"Your people must prepare the body, cover it in ghee, and carry it down. Please put some sacred water in my mouth, and also remember to immerse me once in the river. I want to be on the first pyre as the sun rises. Also, please do not put me face-down but on my back. I want to face the sun."

Kamal looked up startled at that final, unconventional request. Maria knew tradition held that women should be cremated face-down. But he remained silent.

"The priest will be there to take care that you do everything according to my instructions. If you do not, you will not be paid."

"But Madam, how you will die? You are looking most healthy, and …" Kamal hesitated before adding, "according to our tradition we cannot cremate … suicide people. Your karma for next life will be becoming very bad."

Maria had expected this question, knew it was sensitive and could yet undermine her plans. Although almost anything was negotiable in India, this was something that was not. She was prepared with an answer.

"I have been told by my doctor I have a terminal illness. A blood disease. The doctor has told me to make all necessary preparations. He expects I have only a few months to live."

She was amazed at how smoothly and convincingly she told the lie. It was a skill honed dealing with her mother's volatile emotions. What made it easier was that she felt as if she did have a terminal disease. The months of sleeplessness; the struggle to get through every day filled with constant doubts and indecisiveness; the complete loss of energy or desire for anything. This must be what it felt like to have a terminal disease. Her life was nothing more than a mute existence, rising in the morning to pass the time in meaningless and joyless activities until it was dark again and time to sleep.

Sometimes over the last couple of months during the act of dressing in the morning she would pause and wonder what she was doing, why it even mattered. She took no pleasure in what little food she ate just to stay alive. The only way out, the only possible escape, was to end this life and pass on. That suddenly had given her a sense of purpose she hadn't felt for many months.

Kamal responded to her explanation with that most Indian of movements, his head oscillating from side to side in a gesture Maria had always interpreted as no more than an acknowledgement of having listened and understood without agreement, resistance or judgement.

She marvelled at how in this place of the dead, terminal disease and dying could trigger so little of the outward displays of despair she had experienced at grim funerals during her childhood. She recalled standing in line as a child the day after her grandmother had died peacefully in her sleep. They stood beside an open gaping grave in the cemetery of the town church during the bitter cold of an island winter, receiving the mumbled condolences of a seemingly unending procession of black-clothed men, women and children. Each of them had looked into her face with expressions that had horrified and scared Maria much more than the death of her grandmother. The adolescent son of one close family friend had bawled uncontrollably much to the discomfort of his parents. Between sobs he had clasped Maria to his chest in a way she had found uncomfortable, almost painful.

There seemed nothing left to say. But Kamal gave no indication the meeting was over. Swilling the dregs of tea in his red clay cup, he looked out the single window of his office into the blue, cloudless sky above the Ganges. Flecks of white and grey ash swirled lazily on the hot air outside the glass.

At last he put down his cup and, clearing his throat, leaned forward over his desk.

"Madam, I am sorry to asking, but why you are trying for cremation?"

Maria was surprised Kamal spoke to her in this familiar way.

"This life has run its course, and I need to find my inner peace. My *shanti*," Maria answered. "I don't want to come back for another life. I am ready to achieve my *moksha*."

She could tell from Kamal's face that he was pleased and impressed at her familiarity with Hindu religious concepts.

"Maybe this life not finished for you, Madam. You are good person, Madam, but maybe your life has challenges now. Could be you need help only, not next life."

Maria was surprised. She had always regarded Kamal as an opportunistic businessman. She had accepted he was a necessary part of the system but had never believed he looked beyond his own profit.

"I am seeing your face many times now when you come Varanasi. I am thinking Madam Maria is good woman, but Madam unhappy person. Your *atman*, your inner soul, is good but too many disturbances, too many challenges outside."

So clearly, he had not believed her lie of a terminal illness.

"It's not your concern," was all she could say.

"I like you meet my friend. He is my guru. Maybe he helps you."

Kamal wrote out an address and a telephone number. Then standing, he folded the paper and pressed it into Maria's palm.

Back down in the little alley, Maria opened Kamal's note. Written there were directions and a phone number for *Bhavana Guruji Ashram* in Varanasi.

Chapter 4

Maria's mother occasionally recalled her childhood memories from the end of the War when her family had slept under the horse cart they used to escape advancing Soviet Armies by passing through German and British lines. Johanna's father, a high-ranking *Nazi* party member and local government figure, had sent them on ahead on their own. The flight had taken three weeks. Johanna, the third of five children and only seven years old at the time, dimly remembered her own mother weeping at night as the roar of artillery, grenades and machine guns reverberated around them.

She recalled how one night three huge, evil-smelling Russians had broken into a dilapidated barn where they were hiding and started dragging her mother away, pawing like animals at her blouse and dress. She sprung up and grabbed hold of one of the Russian's legs and refused to let go, screaming: "*Svin'ja! Svin'ja!*" until an officer appeared and barked a command, and immediately the Russians let her mother go and ran out.

Eventually, a few weeks after the War had finally ended, her mother found a farmer behind British lines willing to let the family stay in an empty chicken coop at the back of his farmyard. No heat, only two small rooms, a mechanical pump in the centre of the yard the only source of water. How cold that water was in winter. In exchange for shelter and food, they had to work around the farm. This meant that they all had to get up well before down to complete a long list of chores.

Johanna still recalled with embarrassment the wooden clogs for shoes they all had to wear that, even in the spartan modesty of post-War Germany, still triggered titters and pitying looks from her schoolmates at the local school where the children were now all enrolled.

For her and her siblings, beyond the limited education they received, the local school offered one major advantage: heat and hot water. Johanna took to skipping some lessons at the school every day to wash herself with the warm water that steamed from the faucets in the girls' bathroom.

Her father had joined them a year after the War had ended. Johanna's mother had sent word to family relations, who had decided to risk staying in the Soviet zone, to let him know where they were. One evening he had simply appeared at the door of the chicken coop, exhausted and gaunt but alive. Johanna's mother screamed when she saw him, then burst into tears, while the children jumped from their beer crate chairs to hug him. Even in his threadbare rags, he was still a large, tall and strong man. She dimly remembered him from the time before their flight, with his imposing presence in his impressive brown shirt uniform and long, brightly polished boots.

A few days later, sick and home from school with a fever, she overheard her father and mother speaking with raised voices in the next room.

"It's done. It's all over," she heard her father say. "There is no trace. I have collected it all. Nobody will ever know. You can relax."

They were arguing about money and gold, her mother pleading with her father to dispose of something rather than keep it as her father seemed to want to do.

This was unusual, as normally her father was an authority whom all in the family obeyed without question.

"We lost everything once. We can't risk it again. This is our only chance," her mother cried. "Without that we'll be nothing."

She heard her father leaving the room and walking out into the yard.

That night, Johanna woke with a start, shaking from the same nightmare she had so often. She was in the stables of their large home where they had lived before fleeing. Unable to sleep she had gone out in her nightdress, eager to cuddle a new-born lamb. As she came around the corner, she was surprised to see her father kneeling on the dirt ground outside the stables, digging a hole. Next to him were a large wooden chest and several canvas bags. His back was turned to her, so he did not see her. Afraid he would be angry she was up at this time, and not wanting to disturb him, she stood still and said nothing, just watching. After several minutes, she began to shiver, then could not stifle a sneeze.

Her father wheeled around his features so contorted, the eyes piercing, almost threatening. She turned and ran. He quickly caught her and knelt in front of her.

"Forget that you saw me here, Johanna," he said shaking her. "Don't ever tell anyone! No one, do you hear me? If you tell anyone, anyone at all, we'll all die."

At that point, as always, she had woken from her dream. She lay in bed, her heart racing and could not go back to sleep. She rarely had nightmares, but since they had fled to the chicken coop it seemed to be happening more and more often. This dream seemed to recur the most.

After her father's return, the family's fortunes quickly turned a corner. They were able to move from the chicken coop to a nearby modest farmhouse. There, her father began cultivating a new variety of potatoes that proved highly profitable at the local and then regional markets. Their living situation improved further as she and her siblings were now allowed one set of real shoes, instead of wooden clogs, and nicer clothes. Even better, their new house had a wood-fired water heating system, so on Sundays all could enjoy the luxury of a warm bath, something they had forgotten from the time before they fled.

It was a nice house, but so different from their previous home from before their flight. The large rooms, the bright reflected light of the crystal chandeliers, the polished silverware on the tables, the uniformed staff. And the frequent, often uniformed visitors arriving in cars that came up the long drive, their drivers waiting respectfully until her father had finished talking to them.

With the memories of her struggles in mind, Johanna was determined to do everything in her power to ensure her children not only had a better start in life than her own, but also might recover her family's earlier social status. Once Maria reached her 15th birthday, she and her brother Karl were sent to a prestigious boarding school several hours drive from home.

Set on the coast in a beautiful old hunting lodge, gifted in the nineteenth century to the mistress of a member of the Brandenburg Prussian Hohenzollern family, the school was a small paradise and much favoured for the children of the German aristocracy.

After weekends at home, the students of the school arrived each Monday in sleek limousines driven by chauffeurs wearing uniforms and peaked caps. Some even arrived by helicopter. Maria understood quickly that amongst this upper class of nobility, she was among a tolerated sprinkling of children from the nouveaux riches in German society. On the island, she had suffered the bitter envy of her schoolmates for being at the top of the social pile. Here, she quickly realized she was very much at the bottom. If she had ever doubted her mother's insistence on projecting confidence by looking into people's eyes when greeting and speaking to them, at this school the advice could not have been more prescient. Although Maria understood this she was unnerved by the direct gaze of self-assurance in return.

Although well intentioned, her move to the boarding school gave her a huge mountain to climb. Maria was struck by a crisis of self-confidence, overwhelmed by the sense of entitlement of the other pupils. Her attempts to befriend her room-mate in the two-bedded dorm room were disdainfully ignored.

One evening she had come back early and gone to bed. She was awoken in the middle of the night by groans and moans and whispered words of a male voice along with those of her room-mate.

"Stop it!" Maria had screamed toward the other bed, where the cover was bouncing up and down like a trampoline.

The bouncing stopped for a moment. Hushed voices muttered something, giggling then the bouncing resumed even more furiously than before.

Maria gathered up her pillow and covers and stumbled out of the room, slamming the door behind her. She lay down in the corridor to sleep.

Although being kept clearly at arms' length, Maria found comfort in knowing that her classmates would not gang up and terrorize her in the way the island school children had, mainly because she came from a family that was simply too socially insignificant. The occasional rolling of the eyes, or deep sighs or the semi-stifled groans when she appeared with a bright and cheerful smile to join a clique of other girls, smoking rolled-up cigarettes and champagne from plastic cups was something she would have to live with.

One of these cliques was led by a tall, gangly and forbidding girl called Sabine Streng, who, in Maria's eyes, appeared to excel at everything. Not only was she beautiful and popular, but she was the top of the class, able to engage the teachers in rigorous debate and quoting freely from classical and other texts. She even understood the text of Jean-Paul Sartre that Maria had read ten times and could still not get straight in her mind. She was never at a loss when it came to deciding what to do on a weekend or choosing which rule-bending activity to select at night.

Maria lived in awe of Sabine and had been surprised that Sabine was willing to spend time with her, sometimes in smaller groups and occasionally even with just the two of them. Maria began to hope that perhaps at long last she had found a friend. However, the more Maria showed her affection the more irritated Sabine seemed to become. Once Maria picked up a pencil that had fallen from Sabine's desk. Sabine looked at her in irritation as she grabbed the pencil back from her. "I'm perfectly capable of managing my writing instruments on my own, thank you." If Maria saved a place next to her at lunch, Sabine would deliberately walk past that space and sit elsewhere.

But just when Maria was about to lose heart, Sabine would show a sympathetic side. Once she came up to her after classes were over for the day and asked Maria to join her on a forest walk. On another occasion, she asked Maria to come back to her dorm room and listen to her reading Schiller's poetry. Maria's heart was beating so fast as she watched Sabine recite with great seriousness, her nostrils flaring as she emphasized the words in the dramatic moments.

Later Maria walked out of Sabine's dorm believing she could take on anyone and anything. As she crossed the large, manicured lawn in front of the school buildings with an unusually confident stride, she noticed the heir to one of the country's most elite family names coming in the opposite direction. He was two school years older and had never even acknowledged her existence.

"My word," he said stopping briefly, "you are positively radiant! You must be having a good day."

Maria nodded her thanks shyly and continued on, but she could barely restrain herself from shouting out with happiness.

But the next day, it was if she had imagined it all. Sabine was her same steely, distant, remote self again and seemed to have completely forgotten the previous shared intimacy. For Maria the roller coaster of emotions was increasingly difficult to bear. She found herself spending much of her free time under the huge oak not far from her room. Its branches spread at least ten paces either side of the massive trunk, the tree stood isolated at the brow of the gently sloping incline that rose from her dormitory. She had noticed the tree through the window on her first day at school and felt at once drawn to it.

Often, she got up early and climbed the hill to sit at the base of the trunk and feel the rough bark scratching the back of her neck and head. She found this comforting before facing the gauntlet of the day's interaction with her fellow students. Sometimes she closed her eyes to listen to the wind rustling through the leaves, and believed she could hear the voices of people who had come and sat and talked to the tree before her.

She began to ask her tree the questions that she was unable to ask anyone else at the school.

"What have I done wrong to make Sabine angry? Why is she treating me in this way?" she whispered quietly one early morning following a day in which Sabine had ignored her completely.

She listened to the tree and closing her eyes imagined each one of the leaves listening to her separately and answering her question. She heard many voices, all of them friendly, and although when she rose to go back down the hill for breakfast, she could not recall a single word, she felt more relaxed and calmer.

Then one day she and Sabine happened to be walking back from a class to the dormitory building. While she was trying to avoid gaps of conversation by chatting excitedly about the latest gossip on Carsten Ramlow, one of the school's most eligible aristocratic bachelors, Maria suddenly felt Sabine's hand brush gently against her own. Maria noticed a tingling in her arm and, when a moment later, their forearms brushed again, she felt a wave of emotion engulf her. Her face felt warm and when she snatched a glance to her right, she thought she saw a red flush on Sabine's cheeks. They continued wordlessly to the dormitory building and with a curt "See you later" each went to their rooms.

For the following couple of days Maria thought she saw Sabine looking at her more frequently and intensely than before.

Whenever she saw Sabine she felt herself becoming breathless and her mouth dry. She would watch her from across the dining-room, in the sports hall or outdoors and immediately look away when their eyes met. It was almost like a game. Maria soon recognised that as much as she was watching Sabine, she was also watching her. Their eyes would connect fleetingly before each looked away.

Then once, while they were out on the pier watching the boys prepare a sailing boat, they both held each other's gaze and did not look away. Maria felt as if her chest was caught in a vice, but still she could not look away. Finally, Sabine gave her a gentle, beautiful, vulnerable smile. Maria's cheeks softened, and she smiled back.

The day after they had exchanged smiles on the pier Maria found herself walking to Sabine's dormitory in early evening after dinner. She had no clear idea what she was going to do there, but she felt unable to resist the need to see her as she knocked on her door. After a few moments, the door opened.

"Hi, nice of you to ..." Sabine smiled. Would you ... would you like to come in?"

"I ... thank you."

Maria had never seen Sabine like this. Her eyelids were trembling and her lips quivering. Her usual self-assurance seemed to have deserted her.

Maria felt powerless to speak. She sensed that by stepping inside the room she was making a commitment, but she had no idea to what. It was a step into the unknown and although she felt terrified, she knew she had to find the courage because in some indefinable way it felt right.

"Would you like to sit down?"

And as Maria looked around her, Sabine laughed, gesturing at the bed, desk and chair that made up the standard furnishing of all dorm rooms.

"I guess there isn't much choice."

Maria sat down on the bed and looked at Sabine.

"I liked your smile yesterday on the pier," she said cautiously.

Sabine's eyes, usually so steely, softened and she sat down gingerly on the bed next to Maria. Their legs were so close they were almost touching, and Maria gradually let her thigh edge closer until the skin below both their shorts was pressing against each other. Both of them were uncomfortable. The only sound that Maria could hear was her own breathing which had never seemed so loud. She felt Sabine's hand move up to hold the side of her face and turn it towards her and suddenly Sabine's lips were on hers pressing firmer and firmer until it almost felt like they were crushing her mouth. Then, she felt Sabine's tongue force its way between her lips and she jerked her head away. Sabine seemed transformed. She was panting and trying to force her face and mouth closer to Maria's.

"No, No, … I don't want to," Maria shouted, pushing her away.

She stood up and moved towards the door. "I can't. I don't know what we're doing."

Suddenly the spell seemed broken. Sabine's face, only moments earlier softened by her smile, had become firm and determined again.

"You better leave," she said and stood up to hold the door open.

"Wait, I am sorry … it was just too fast," Maria blurted out, suddenly unsure whether she was making a big mistake.

"I really think you should leave."

Maria's head was spinning. She walked immediately up the slope to her tree and sat at the trunk letting the gentle rustle of the wind in the leaves calm her beating heart. She could still feel the taste of Sabine's mouth in hers.

After that, Maria felt as if she was living two lives—the life of daily routine, sleeping, eating meals, going to classes and a second life in which she was powerless unable to resist a force of nature that had taken control of her.

Over the next few days, they avoided each other. Sabine looked the other way whenever Maria was near and made sure they were not on their own but always in company. Although initially Maria was relieved because she would not have known what to say, as the days passed and her sleep at night remained fitful, she decided she wanted to talk to her. Whatever had happened could be explained. It had all been so new and so sudden. Perhaps if they tried again, it might feel better.

Above all, Maria felt the curtain had been pulled back on a side of Sabine she had never seen before, something that was hidden not only from all around her, but also from Sabine herself. In those few moments Sabine had shown a courage that Maria could understand and also had herself. If she could find that again, perhaps they could find a way to be close again.

About a week later an opportunity suddenly appeared. Maria came into an English lesson early and found Sabine already there on her own. Surprising herself, Maria walked directly up to her.

"Why are you avoiding me?"

"I am not."

"You are acting as if nothing happened."

"It was a moment of weakness. But now there is nothing to discuss."

Maria felt as if the ground had suddenly opened up beneath her feet and she was falling precipitously. Had she imagined everything? Was the gentle, trusting smile that had flashed so fleetingly on Sabine's face not the genuine person but just a 'moment of weakness'?

"It's just as Brecht said. We need to make sure we think rather than get confused by feelings."

"But how can we ignore our true feelings? They are the most important thing we have."

"I don't think we need to continue this conversation," Sabine said with an impatient shrug of her head. "You simply don't understand. And if you don't understand I can't explain it to you." And turning her back on Maria she moved closer to a crowd of other students who had now entered the classroom.

Maria's ears were ringing and the blood rushing through her head. Were the emotions that overwhelmed her so often just weaknesses? She sat down quietly at her desk and pretended to be looking through her exercise book while trying to hold back her tears. She did not hear a word the English teacher said and once the bell rang rushed out of the classroom and straight to the oak tree, where she sat for a long time, her head bouncing rhythmically against the trunk until she felt blood trickling down the nape of her neck.

Whatever hopes Maria may have had for a friendship with Sabine were now lost and she felt even more alone. Sabine had probably ridiculed her to others because it seemed as if everyone was deliberately avoiding her. When she sat down at the lunch or dinner table in the cavernous hall, embellished with large stuffed heads of deer hanging over the chattering students, everyone at the table was so busy talking to each other that they ignored her completely. Out of the corner of her eye, she saw Sabine in the centre of her clique who all seemed to be listening with bated breath to her every word.

Adding to her unhappiness was the looming final graduation examinations. Maria knew that she was not a talented student. She studied hard but, with the exception of English which seemed to come naturally to her, still could not do well on the regular tests. In general, she expected not to know the answer to a teacher's question and would, whenever possible, hide at the back of the class to escape attention. Maria began to perfect a range of subterfuges concealing answers on inner arms, palms of hands, insides of thighs and, her most ingenious yet, on the skin of an apple which students were permitted to eat during the tests.

But despite her well-honed skills in getting by, she found the challenge of the *Abitur*—the final school graduation diploma—the worst of all. She soon realized that she would not be able to slip through the exams with some skilful sleight of hand as she had done in the past.

A memory that kept recurring and would not leave her in peace was a childhood scene on the island. Maria had been part of a children's contest in which each child had to arrange as quickly as possible a series of domino-like stones with different words and numbers on them in a sequence that answered a question written on the board. Whoever finished first should raise their hand. Maria had focused totally and within about five minutes completed the task and raised her arm. All around her she saw heads bowed as the other children tried to solve the riddle. Convinced that she couldn't possibly have solved the challenge and won, Maria brought her hand down again and broke up the pattern of pieces she had arranged and started again. A minute or two later another child shouted out joyously and after a brief check by their teacher was confirmed the winner and applauded by all. A little later Maria went up to the child's desk and glanced at her domino stones—as she had feared, and had never forgotten, the pieces were arranged exactly as she had set them several minutes earlier.

She had told her mother the story of the contest, hoping for sympathy. Instead, she got a cold response.

"It's your own fault for not raising your hand … you have to have confidence to win if you want to be the best."

Maria found herself becoming increasingly frantic and worried as the exam dates approached. Teachers and her friends noticed her increasingly pale and gaunt appearance. Her room-mate told friends that Maria didn't seem to be sleeping at all and barely eating.

In desperation, Maria went to the head of the school, a kindly spinster duchess who had seemed to like her, and asked for advice.

"Why don't you spend some time studying and preparing instead of worrying and avoiding," the duchess suggested. "I am sure you are much more intelligent than you think you are."

"I'm not, I'm not ..." Maria had almost shrieked back hysterically. "I don't understand, I can't remember, it's too difficult for me ..." She hadn't meant to raise her voice but couldn't help herself.

Sitting in front of the duchess, she had felt ashamed. "I'm sorry," she mumbled, "I always make the wrong choice ..."

"Whatever do you mean?" the duchess asked. "There are no wrong choices, only opportunities to learn. Whatever decision or choice you made and whenever you made it, you were not yet ready to make a different decision—maybe next time you will be."

Maria was stunned by the duchess' words. No one had ever spoken to her with such tolerance and treated her as an adult in this way.

"Thank you."

"I wish you good luck. Try to trust and believe more in yourself."

Despite this advice the tension of the *Abitur* remained. Her toughest examination was German language and literature. She had started a programme of preparation for assessment under the guidance of the German teacher who, perhaps triggered by the duchess' concern at her complete lack of self-confidence, had offered some remedial support.

Her final exam was a German *viva voce* in front of a panel of three teachers and the duchess herself. Maria did not sleep a wink the night before and walked into the examination room not even fully aware where she was. She answered the questions as best she understood them and based on what she thought she knew. Once she had given her last answer and the teachers withdrew into a huddle to consider the final grade, Maria thought she saw a grimace cross the duchess' face during the discussion. Maria could not take any more. She jumped out of her chair and rushed out of the room into the warm spring sunshine next to the lake.

The duchess found her there several hours later, head in hands, disconsolate on the lawn. Gathering her up, "Why are you crying?" the duchess asked.

"I know I failed the test. I couldn't finish. I ..."

"No. You have passed, you have passed ... Congratulations!"

"What?" she said between sobs.

"You have passed!"

Gradually Maria's sobs turned to giggles, then laughs, then cries of joy.

Chapter 5

Maria associated finishing school with a sense of escape. She was relieved that she had avoided the shame to her family of failing the *Abitur*, but she was not fully convinced that she had passed her diploma legitimately. She had a vague memory of being surprised to see her father coming out of the duchess' office at some point in the semester and a week or two later the teachers had made much of a brand new school bus that had been delivered to replace the old rickety and rusting one.

When years later Maria did finally ask her mother about this, her mother denied it emphatically.

"Wherever did you get that story from? That is nonsense, we would never have done that."

But her doubts that she could have achieved this on her own stayed with her.

"The first thing you need is a good vocational training," her father announced at the family dinner table one evening a few weeks after Maria had moved back home from school. "Something in the textiles area would be best. You could even work in the store."

"We have quite a business reputation now in this region," Johanna chimed in.

Maria had not devoted much thought to her future. But when fleeting daydreams had passed through her mind, she had always seen herself in elegant, beautiful, luxurious surroundings.

She recalled one conversation on one of the forest walks with Sabine before their relationship ended. They had imagined travelling around the world to exotic locations. Sabine had laughingly described how she would move from luxurious hotel to hotel, working as a banquet manager, or in some other role responsible for guest contentment, and enjoying the surroundings and company of glamorous and important international people. The image had stayed with Maria, seeing herself in far off locations surrounded by unusual scents, scenes, sounds and people.

"I think I would like to go into the hotel business," she said enthusiastically.

In her enthusiasm, she did not immediately notice the dead silence and aghast looks that fell over her parents.

"Hospitality industry? That's nothing but hard work. You would never have time for a family," her mother said with a dismissive shake of her head.

Nothing more was said of her future career development, until a week later when her father surprised a sleepy Maria at the family breakfast table with the news that he would like her to run a small fashion shop he had purchased some years ago and nestled next door to the now imposing König department store.

"But I am not sure I want to do that," Maria said. "Let me think about it."

"Nonsense. You'll love it. I have already told them you are starting soon. We will both be here to help you if you need assistance."

A few days later, Maria was installed in the boutique with two elderly sales ladies looking at their new boss with a mixture of respect, envy and fear. Maria was also terrified, but for a different reason. Although she had a good sense for clothing—both in terms of quality and fashion trend—and an impeccable sense of elegance after the years spent amongst the children of the highest echelons of German society, she had none of the self-righteous confidence of leadership that the two indifferent sales ladies, who had spent their entire lives steeped in the strict social hierarchy of the island, expected and needed.

Maria knew that the quality of the fashion in the boutique, despite its provincial clientele was superb. A large part of the meteoric success of the department store was attributable to Johanna's detailed and perfectionist approach to fashion, and the extensive knowledge she had amassed from the regional trade fairs she and Peter had attended regularly as the business had grown. The boutique had also profited from her attention.

Her family's position in society on the island had surged while Maria had been at boarding school. Maria's childhood memories were steeped in the struggles of her parents striving to win social acceptance despite their early business success. However, their current wealth had grown to such a degree that the family name was now more likely to strike fear for its influence, rather than trigger the mere envy of earlier.

Maria enjoyed their new status. Now others felt it important to catch her attention and greet her as her mother had always instructed her to do. Although she still sought people's eyes to see into their inner selves, she also revelled in the head-turning, muffled whispering and conversation-stopping effect when she walked through a crowd during Wednesday's weekly market day or at other events and festivities. After the suffering, the ridicule and isolation of her childhood it was like balm to her soul. Occasionally, some of the greetings felt forced and sycophantic, but Maria didn't care.

"My parents achieved this reputation, and I am benefiting," she once told Stefanie, an older friend of hers, an unconventional left-wing journalist from a nearby town. They had met at a dinner dance that her mother had encouraged her to attend in the island's largest hotel.

"You are wrong if you think it is your family's name that attracts people's attention to you," Stefanie said. "Actually, I think it is more because you really look stunning."

"Looks have nothing to do with it. At most they are looking at me because I am tall."

But even Maria could sense that this was disingenuous. She took great care in her dress and physical appearance. She had inherited the extraordinary blonde beauty of her mother. And her casual elegance, even though she did not feel it, made her presence even more arresting.

She did not care where her elevated status came from. She enjoyed being looked up to rather than down on. Increasingly, as the months and then a year or two went by, she found her self-confidence growing in the boutique and she would speak with authority to the sales assistants on how best to design the display window and even, when her mother happened by and inevitably had a suggestion on how to improve its appearance, talking her down. But much as she enjoyed this new-found success, she was often lonely.

"Nobody is really my friend on the island," she confided to Stefanie one Saturday evening over dinner.

"That's because I don't think you belong there," Stefanie said, placing her hand comfortingly on Maria's arm. You speak such good English. I think what would suit you is a tall handsome stranger from a foreign land who could take you away, perhaps an English aristocrat … "

Maria laughed, but inside she felt a warm glow of pride and was already dreaming.

Chapter 6

Maria was very inexperienced in relationships with men. On the island, the local boys had paid little attention to her. In boarding school, when an adolescent boy had looked her way or spoke with her, her stomach would tighten, and she would find a way to disengage quickly. The only intimate contact with anyone, that she felt she could admit to, had been that fleeting moment with Sabine.

Then there was the experience that disgusted her now, and which she had tried as hard as she could, but unsuccessfully, to erase from her mind. It had been soon after she started running the boutique. She was on a day trip to Hamburg, the closest large city to the island. At a small coffee shop in the elegant shopping district, a handsome man had started up a conversation with her. When they finished their coffee, he had invited her to see his apartment and not knowing how to decline politely, she limply accepted his invitation. The man, a part-time surfing school instructor, had led her to his small flat not far from the coffee shop. When they arrived, she had barely had time to put down her handbag before he was tearing at her clothes and hungrily kissing her all over her face and neck as he loosened his trousers and pulled up her skirt. She was paralyzed with shock and fear, not knowing what to do, feeling a sharp pain between her hips and then out of somewhere deep a guttural scream and with strength she had no idea she possessed, she pushed him away. He fell to the floor. As she grabbed her handbag and stumbled to the door, she caught an image of the man sprawled on the floor, his trousers around his knees, his erection visible.

As she staggered down the stairs, ignoring the wide-eyed stare of a woman and daughter coming up, she felt how the elastic on her panties had snapped, were sliding down her hips, and a wetness between her legs.

After waiting quite a few weeks, she had gathered the courage to tell her mother one evening while Peter was away on a business trip. She burst into tears describing the story while Johanna sat listening wordlessly, her eyes turning into an increasingly stony stare.

"When was your last period?" she had asked finally breaking the silence.

"I … don't … I don't know. About eight weeks, I think."

The next morning her mother bundled Maria into the car. She drove Maria to a gynaecologist on the mainland, in a small town Maria had never even heard of. As she was dressing after the lengthy and quite painful examination, which had felt more like some kind of medical procedure, she saw her mother and the doctor speaking earnestly in the next room through the half-open door. Johanna had reached into her handbag and pressed a bundle of banknotes into the doctor's hands.

"Do not say anything to your father," she said to Maria, her face set in a tight grimace on the way home.

"He would not understand, and it is better if you don't worry him with this."

Maria needed several days to recover. She slept only fitfully and, as her mother had demanded, said nothing to her father. However, somehow, he discovered the truth anyway. Perhaps Johanna had changed her mind. Some weeks later, he confronted Maria one evening after dinner.

"Now you will never have your own children," he said to her with eyes Maria believed she had never seen so furious.

She had just begun to recover from the experience and was almost sleeping normally again, but now suddenly felt all the guilt and shame return. Only this was worse.

Several weeks later when she was back at the boutique, where Maria's mother had filled in for her, her brother had mentioned a disco on the mainland where there was a hot new show. According to Karl, this was a show not to be missed with a new leading-edge disc jockey promoting a new aggressive form of music from London. Karl was going with a group of his friends that Friday and invited her to join them. He said that the disco and jockey were attracting rave reviews and party goers from all over Germany. Maria did not really feel up to going and feared the men she might be forced to meet. But on the enthusiastic encouragement of her mother, and even more excited entreaties of Karl, she succumbed.

As always, she took great care to choose the right outfit and make up. Despite her natural beauty, she had never felt attractive enough and now was even more unsure than before. While getting ready, she asked her mother repeatedly how she looked.

"The same as you did two minutes ago," she replied. "Don't be so vain."

The show was in a large, abandoned barn. Maria wondered whether it was the odour of farm animals that she identified as they walked in but then was not sure whether what she was actually smelling was a mixture of human perspiration and spilt alcohol and wrinkled her nose in distaste. Karl walked ahead with his friends, who had already been drinking on the trip there. The group whooped in excitement at the loud music and the gyrating dancers under the strobe lights on the floor. Almost immediately they had disappeared into the crowd on the dance floor.

Maria stood to one side, feeling uncomfortable as she watched the sea of people moving wildly to the beat of the music. The black leather, chains with padlocks, lank unwashed hair and black lipstick and fingernails on some women, made Maria aware of how inappropriate her own clothes and appearance must look. The whole place seemed to be powered by a frenzy of alcohol and sexual energy. In the dimly lit corners, on sofas, or on piles of clothes and blankets on the floor, Maria noticed pairs contorted in embraces.

At one end there was a makeshift bar with some bar stools made of empty wooden crates and a cushion on top for comfort. Maria noticed a young man sitting on one of the crates drinking a beer, also dressed in a way that made him look as out of place as she felt. At that moment the man turned his head and looked directly at her, catching her gaze before she could hurriedly avert her eyes.

A moment later the man was standing next to her. He was a little taller than her with dark full brown hair. Maria noticed how his eyes seemed to soften as he looked at her and his features somehow looked gentle as well. He introduced himself and extended his hand, Maria could not help but notice his perfectly manicured fingers and hands.

"Stockton, Paulus Stockton is my name. Do you feel as awkward here as I do?" he asked with a faint smile.

"Oh hello … My name is Maria König," she managed to stumble out after a short pause. "Yes, I feel out of place. I am probably not dressed right for this evening."

"But you do look wonderful … and very attractive."

Maria felt herself redden. She was grateful for the comparative darkness and the loud music that forced a natural pause in the conversation. She could feel her heart pounding.

"Would you like to dance?" he asked, holding out his hand.

"I don't …, I'm not really …"

"Come on. We can't just sit around here. It'll be fun."

"Okay."

They danced apart at first, then closer and then, almost with unspoken agreement, together with a variety of increasingly complex steps and moves. Maria could see and feel that Paulus was a confident dancer, and she was increasingly comfortable to rely on his lead and to allow the rest of the dance floor to recede into a whirl of colours and faces and then almost not to be there at all. Suddenly, they were dancing in the centre of the floor surrounded by other dancers watching them.

Finally, when the music ended, Paulus now sweating, suggested a break. As they walked from the floor toward the bar, she noticed a few admiring looks incongruously from mostly leather-clad and spiky-haired women, and a few even applauded lightly.

Maria was glowing with content and satisfaction.

"What can I offer you to drink?" he asked.

"A whisky sour, please."

"Oh … that sounds like it's a favourite of yours."

Maria giggled. "It was my favourite at boarding school."

And there it was again, the gentle softening of the face, starting deep within the eyes and spreading across his mouth and cheeks.

"I think I will have a gin tonic. I love all things British."

As he shouted to the bartender, Maria noticed how handsome he was.

"I was sent to boarding school as well in Switzerland."

"How did you like it?" he asked. "I was quite unhappy at mine."

And suddenly Maria found herself sharing all her struggles and unhappiness at the school and her relief and sense of escape when she graduated.

He was listening intently. When their eyes met, Maria felt he was accepting what she said exactly as she meant it.

"I left home early," Paulus said. "My father abandoned us, and my mother sacrificed everything to make sure I got a good education. She couldn't really afford the boarding school, but somehow she made it happen." Paulus paused and looked into the distance. "I couldn't tell my mother how much I disliked the school. It would have broken her heart. I think just about everyone bullied me there, even the teachers."

"I'm sorry."

As he spoke Maria wondered whether her stories of school hardship were quite as bad as she always made out. Perhaps in future she should just keep them to herself and stop complaining.

It was almost as if he could divine her thoughts:

"I am not comparing your experiences to mine," she said. "I know you suffered a lot as well. I just want you to know who I am."

Suddenly, Karl burst in on the two of them, swaying slightly.

"Well, who has my sister met?"

"My name is Paulus Stockton," he said, standing up immediately from the crate and offering his hand.

"Karl."

"Your sister is a wonderful dancer ..." then, after a pause "and a very interesting person to talk to."

"Yes, she is." He turned to Maria. "We were thinking of going back now ... things seem to be closing up here."

Maria looked around and noticed that he was right. The disc jockey was packing up and had been replaced by recorded music, the dance floor was emptying, and the lights had been raised slightly.

"It was nice to meet you," Paulus said to Maria. "Perhaps we could keep in touch?" He jotted down his address on a bar napkin.

When she saw his address was in Geneva, her heart sunk. The spell had been broken. But she smiled and accepted it. They stood and rather formally shook hands.

"Thank you for a nice evening," she said.

Maria followed her brother and his friends out of the barn, suppressing the tears that she felt rising.

* * *

"How was the show?" her mother asked the next morning at breakfast.

"Fun. Maria even met some guy," Karl had blurted out. "He was Swedish, wasn't he?"

"He was Swiss actually, from Geneva," Maria said quietly.

"What does he do?" her mother asked.

"I don't know. He was nice. "

"A pity he does not live closer," Johanna said almost to herself.

"Everyone is the smith of his own fortune," her father mumbled from behind the daily paper he was reading at the breakfast table.

Maria didn't comment. She didn't want to talk at all.

What she wanted was to remember the sound of Paulus' voice, the softness of his eyes. And the way his hand and felt as he led her onto the dance floor and the assured firmness of his arms as they danced.

For several weeks, Maria's thoughts were consumed by how she might see Paulus again. She would work every day in the boutique, serve customers, monitor the sales ladies, greet family acquaintances on the streets and go home in the evening. But it all seemed so irrelevant and unimportant to her now. She grew more and more distracted. She slept fitfully and often would open her eyes in the middle of the night thinking of Paulus. Was he also struggling to sleep, she hoped? Or had he forgotten her already? Did he perhaps already have a girlfriend? Was he married? Did he even think of her?

Apart from occasional trips to Hamburg, family holidays and the time spent at boarding school, Maria had barely travelled beyond the island and hardly ever on her own. Her parents had only consented to her taking day trips to Hamburg, but that had stopped abruptly following that experience with the surf instructor.

She would take long walks along the coastal cliff paths on the east of the island with only the squalling seagulls for company. She imagined strolling hand-in-hand along the narrow path, telling Paulus about the island and her life on it, or walking together through the fields of sunflowers or rape that transformed the fields into yellow carpets every spring. She would dream of lying in his strong arms in the sand dunes and staring into those soft and gentle eyes of his. She visualised introducing him to acquaintances as her 'boyfriend', sitting in one of the coffee shops on the main square and perhaps even presenting him to her parents.

Both Johanna and Peter noticed how distracted she had become and said nothing to her. Then one early evening, looking out over the North Sea in the southerly direction toward Switzerland while on one of her walks, it came to her in a flash.

She would surprise him. She would travel to Geneva and find him, perhaps on his way home from work, or at his break for lunch. And they would sit and talk and gaze into each other's eyes. Already the thought of seeing him again was lifting her spirits and relieving the dull knot of tension that she had been carrying in her stomach for the past weeks. She was sure he was waiting for her and wanted to see her as much as she wanted to see him. She could feel that almost transcendentally, almost as if their spirits were connected.

Of course, Maria knew that her trip to Geneva would have to be clandestine. Her parents would not understand and would stop her going. But they had not met Paulus. If they had, then they would agree. Of that, she was sure. Maria planned her subterfuge carefully. She told her mother she was spending the weekend with Stefanie in the nearby town and simultaneously swore Stefanie to silence. Then she bought the long-distance train tickets to Geneva at the station.

The night before her train, she spent hours packing and re-packing her suitcase, trying to divine the optimal combination of skirts, blouses and scarves with matching jewellery and make up that would show her at her best. She imagined he lived with his mother perhaps in a small house with garden on the outskirts of the town, or a modest but elegant apartment in downtown Geneva. Maria felt a thrill of excitement at that she was travelling abroad to an entirely new place to see the man she could not stop dreaming about.

The overnight train journey to Geneva felt longer than she had expected. The enormity of what she was doing hit her as she crossed the border and had to show her passport, but the official barely glanced at her before stamping an empty page and returning the document. As the train approached Geneva, Maria became increasingly anxious. What if Paulus was not in Geneva? He could be away for the weekend. He might be on holiday or busy with other friends, or with another woman. But immediately Maria banished the thought. He could not have looked into her eyes in the way he had done if he already had a girlfriend or a wife.

At the train station, Maria made her way to the tourist information desk and in her halting school French asked for directions to the address Paulus had hurriedly written down for her at the barn disco. in her halting school French. The young man behind the window looked up from the paper and regarded her rather strangely.

"*Madame, vous connaissez cette adresse ?*"

As Maria struggled to respond and looked increasingly worried, the young man repeated in German.

"Do you know this place? It is not a very good place in Geneva. Do you have a friend or family there?"

"Yes, yes, my boyfriend lives there," Maria hurriedly replied, conscious of a growing queue of people behind her.

"*Vraiment, votre ami devrait vous chercher ici ! …* Your boyfriend should really meet you here and escort you!"

"I am sure I can find it. Please help me."

"As you wish." He gave her a city map and some general directions on the bus lines. She thanked him and moved away to a nearby café.

Studying the map, Maria could see that Paulus' address was not far from the station. She hailed a taxi and as they passed through the nondescript grey- and khaki-coloured blocks Maria tried to imagine Paulus' reaction when he saw her. She was convinced she would meet him. 'It's just a matter of positive thinking,' she kept repeating to herself. 'I just need to believe it strongly enough.' He would be shocked, of course, but that would allow her to hug him to give him time to recover. Or perhaps she might give a lively description of her journey while making sure she was presenting herself from the best visual angle. Or possibly, he would take her in his strong arms and kiss her deeply.

As the taxi turned into the road on which Paulus lived, she saw a small flower shop at the corner and asked the driver to stop. She decided to buy some flowers and to walk the rest of the way. For some reason, she imagined a bouquet of red roses on a bedside table or chest next to an open window in his small attic apartment Paulus must live in an attic like a student, Maria had decided, and she was determined to bring colour and vivacity to what she assumed would be a drab room.

She had not allowed herself to think too much about how and where she would spend the night. But she knew that if all went well, she hoped to spend it in his bed.

Looking at the house numbers, Maria realized she was getting close to his house number. She could already make out on the other side of the road a whitish, four-floor building with balconies. She felt her heart pumping. As she was about to cross the street the front door of the building opened, and a young man stepped out. It was Paulus. He did not see her. He was looking back toward an older man who appeared to be arguing with him. Maria was about to call out, but some instinct stopped her. As they passed by across the street, deep in conversation, Maria admired again how well-dressed Paulus was, as he had been when they had first met. For a moment, the eyes of the older man glanced over at Maria disinterestedly as both he and Paulus continued along the road.

Maria stood unsure what to do. She had not prepared for this situation. She was not sure why she had not called out. Surely, Paulus would have immediately broken off his conversation and come to her. Had she been too shy? Or had something about Paulus and his companion's interaction disturbed her? She decided to follow them as they turned a corner. Maria hurried after them and was just in time to see them step into a small Italian restaurant.

She looked at her watch. It was midday. Of course, she relaxed. He was going to lunch with a friend. Maria resolved to give them some minutes to settle at their table, while she made final adjustments to her appearance using her reflection in the window of the shop next door. Then, taking a deep breath, and weighed down by her luggage and the flowers she clumsily opened the door to the restaurant and entered.

Maria spotted them in the back and made her way between the tables. Paulus was sitting with his back to her, and his companion did not seem to notice her until she came close. Sensing someone was behind him, Paulus turned his head. Maria froze. The look on his face was one she had not prepared for. He looked terrified. Rather than the smile Maria had imagined and dreamt of so often, his features seemed locked in a grimace, almost as if he was in pain.

Maria felt a shiver pass through her body.

"Paulus … I …"

Paulus' companion, who seemed to have understood the situation, rose and pulled out a chair inviting Maria to sit. Paulus stood and rather awkwardly leaned forward to kiss her on the cheek.

"What are you doing here in Geneva?" he asked.

"Here, I brought you these" she said, handing him the flowers. It is a surprise. I mean the visit, not the flowers. Though I guess they are also a surprise."

"Thank you very much."

Maria noticed a quick, furtive glance between Paulus and his companion.

"Have you come all the way to Geneva to see me? Or were you here anyway?" Paulus asked.

"No, I was here anyway," Maria lied. "I am visiting a friend from boarding school who lives here, and I thought I would check if the address you gave me was genuine," she said with a laugh. "Aren't you going to introduce me to your friend?"

"Of course. This is Michael. Michael is ... a friend of mine."

Maria noticed but ignored the slight hesitation.

"Hello Michael. I am Maria. Nice to meet you. Are you also Swiss?"

"Yes," Michael replied, offering the briefest of handshakes.

Michael was considerably older than Paulus, hair greying at the temples, his skin sallow around the eye sockets. He was heavy set and exuded a sense of authority that intimidated Maria. She also noticed that, like Paulus, his hands were superbly manicured, and that he and Paulus were wearing the same colour and style of shirt.

Before she could say another word, Michael rose and looking at Paulus said:

"Have to leave now, I'm afraid. Nice to see you. Paulus, we'll talk later."

And with a curt nod toward Maria, he left them alone at the table.

"I hope your friend didn't leave because of me," Maria said.

Paulus leant back in his chair and shrugged.

"It's not you at all. Michael can be a little difficult at times. He is not so good when he meets new people." Then Paulus looked at her and smiled. "I must say, you look wonderful. It is such a nice surprise to see you again."

"And you," Maria replied, relieved at his warmth.

"You must be hungry."

"A little, I guess."

"Good. Me too."

Paulus ordered.

"Tell me what you have been doing since we last met."

Maria excitedly described the gossip from the island and her train journey, the disdainful tourist information clerk, and how she had followed Paulus and Michael, embellishing details to make them more entertaining.

"I was hoping you would write to me," Paulus said. "And I didn't have your address, or I would have written to you."

"You could have just written to the König department store on the island. It would have reached me."

"I didn't think of that. Sorry."

Maria picked at her plate but was too nervous to eat much.

"I imagine you live in a small attic apartment. Show me where you live."

Paulus hesitated momentarily, and then smiled.

"Of course."

When they finished their meal, Paulus paid the bill and took her case. She carried the flowers. They retraced the route back to his apartment. Maria resisted the temptation to link her arm through his.

The small, three-room apartment was not a garret, but on the top floor of the building with attractive views of the lake. Paulus immediately found a vase for her flowers and placed them prominently on the small dining room table. He removed a framed photograph that had been standing there, and quickly placed it face down in the bookcase behind the table.

"Let's celebrate," Paulus said. He went into the kitchen and came back holding a bottle of champagne and two glasses. They stepped out onto the small balcony. "I am so honoured that you made time to see me on your visit to your friend."

"Actually, I am not here to visit a friend. I only came to see you."

He smiled. "I thought so. It's even more of an honour then." He opened the champagne and poured, offering a glass to her.

Maria hesitated, took it, then, battling the sudden tightness of her throat she started speaking. "I've missed you so much."

She was standing close to Paulus, their shoulders and arms touching as they looked out over the lake.

"Did you miss me?" she asked in a quiet voice.

Paulus was quiet, turning his glass by the stem between his fingers.

"You know, I really enjoyed our time when we met," he said, reaching behind her and putting his arm around her shoulders. "It's so touching that you came all this way to see me. I don't think anyone has ever done anything like this for me."

The touch of his arm around her shoulders was so exciting.

"And the moment I saw you today, your beautiful smile again. It's like a rising sun. You give so much warmth. I have never seen anything like it before.

Maria moved closer to him, putting her arm around his waist and buried her head in his neck. She had dreamed of this moment for weeks. She wanted the moment to last forever.

After a few moments, Paulus moved to loosen her grip.

"Maria, I need to tell you something."

They went back inside and sat down on the worn red leather sofa.

"You see ... Michael is a good friend. A very good friend. He was one of my teachers my last year in school, and the only one who was kind to me. The others bullied me."

"He seems like a very nice man." Maria's stomach suddenly felt hollow.

Paulus paused to look out of the window. Then he clenched his eyes shut and shook his head.

"Michael has helped me and my mother so much. He was very kind to her, and he has supported her financially. She has no pension, you see, and since my father abandoned us, and all the money she earned was spent on my boarding school, she needed support. He also helped me get a job, and he pays for this apartment."

Maria listened intently, through what felt like a torrent of background noise. She was not sure she could understand what Paulus was saying and why it mattered.

"Michael and I are very close and have been for many years. What I am trying to tell you is that Michael and I are together. We are a couple."

Maria barely heard the last few words, as Paulus' voice trailed off. She didn't know how to react, or what to say. She felt like such a fool.

"I'm sorry to have bothered you then," she said, standing. "I'll leave."

"It's getting late. Where will you stay?"

"I don't know."

"Please stay here."

"I couldn't possibly under the circumstances."

"It's the least I can do. You've travelled so far."

Too exhausted and upset to argue, Maria agreed. Paulus made up the sofa for her.

After Paulus had gone to bed, she crept into the dining room and to the bookshelf. She found the framed photograph she had seen him place there face down. It showed Paulus and Michael, their arms around each other in ski suits posing on a wintery slope. They were both smiling. Paulus looked genuinely at ease and happy. Tears filled her eyes.

The following morning, Maria awoke to the smell of brewing coffee and fresh croissants. Paulus had laid the breakfast table. The framed photograph was up and standing next to the vase of roses.

They spoke in fits and starts. Paulus told her about his work in a travel agency and his plans to visit his mother. Maria talked a little about the boutique and her plans for Christmas. In truth she had none. Glancing toward that photo of Michael and Paulus, she even asked for Paulus' advice about skiing in Austria.

After breakfast, Paulus insisted on taking her to the train station. He stayed until the train arrived. They promised to stay in touch and hugged goodbye. But she knew she'd never see him again.

As the train rattled through the same mountains, tunnels and fields, Maria wondered if she was always going to be an outsider. An outsider on the island rejected by her school mates, an outsider at boarding school rejected by aristocrats, and now an outsider in romance, falling in love with someone who could not return her love. Was it something in her? She wanted simply to love others, and to be loved in return.

Maria returned to the island and was surprised that her mother did not question her about her time with Stefanie.

After a few days, she began to feel better. Although she still thought of Paulus, it was no longer with any sense of longing. A week later, a letter with Swiss postage stamps arrived from Geneva via the König department store. Paulus had written her a long letter explaining that she meant a lot to him as a friend, and that he hoped she would understand. He had even included in the envelope the cost of her return train journey, explaining that he hoped this would help rectify any mistake of his if he had in any way encouraged her inappropriately, or unreasonably.

Stefanie had warned Maria soon after her return that her mother had called while Maria was in Geneva and asked for her. Although she had dissembled and said Maria was at the shops, she suspected that Johanna had probably suspected something.

Maria was therefore prepared when one evening her mother confronted her.

"So, how was your visit to Geneva?"

"Geneva?"

"I assume you visited that young man you met. Is that why he wrote to you?"

"Yes. I saw Paulus. It was nice to see him again," Maria said, barely looking up from the magazine she was leafing through.

"Where did you stay the night?"

Deciding she had nothing to hide, also doubting she had the energy to lie, Maria told the truth.

"I stayed in Paulus' apartment. I slept on his sofa. It turns out he is more interested in men than women. He has a boyfriend."

Her mother pursed her lips and was silent. After a few moments, she said quietly,

"I am sorry for you. That must have been painful."

Maria said nothing, surprised and warmed by the sympathy in her mother's words.

A few days later, Johanna asked Maria to keep the coming Saturday afternoon free. She had invited some business associates of the family for coffee and cake.

"They are good people. They have a successful supermarket chain on the mainland."

On the day of the invitation, Maria noticed how well-dressed her parents were. They must want to make a good impression.

"Perhaps you want to brush your hair again," her mother said appraising Maria. "You look best when your hair is pulled back from your face."

As she combed again through her long blond hair in the upstairs bathroom, Maria heard the doorbell ring and the sounds of voices welcoming and thanking each other.

Maria came down to find a couple about the same age as her parents sitting on the sofa, with a young man about her age who was clearly their son. Maria felt herself reddening, not because she was embarrassed, but because suddenly she understood her mother's plan.

"Maria, let me introduce Mr. and Mrs. Denholz. And this is their son, Dirk."

"Nice to meet you," she said and sat on one of the sofas across from them. She told herself to remain calm and to suppress her anger and resentment. She tried to look interested as Dirk was explaining how he had just returned from an internship in another supermarket chain in the south of the country and was now looking forward to working in the Denholz family business.

"Have you ever worked abroad?" Maria interrupted him somewhat sharply, silencing the other small talk in the room.

"No … no, I have not," Dirk said. "I am sure that would be interesting. Perhaps in a few years when I have some more experience."

"I think you would benefit from the experience earlier rather than later," Maria said curtly. Dirk swallowed nervously as she looked at him. "That is if you seriously want to take your parents' business to the next level."

There was an uncomfortable silence in the room. Maria wondered if everyone noticed how loud the ticking of the grandfather clock was.

Peter finally broke the silence. "Yes, one can learn a lot from visiting other markets. We are planning to travel to America in the next few years to see how they run department stores there. I have heard great things."

The rest of the afternoon passed in a daze. Maria answered a few questions from Dirk's parents politely and enquired about their family and interests. They talked about the upcoming elections, and the latest successful campaign of the national football team.

Maria noticed that Dirk mostly stared into his plate, or into his lap. As she looked at him, his soft rounded features, she knew she could never ever feel anything for him like what she had felt for Paulus. He seemed like a child, not a man, completely inconsequential, an unpolished version of his parents. When the time came for them to leave, and pleasantries were exchanged at the door Maria noticed how Dirk was unable to look her in the eye when shaking her hand.

"You could have at least tried to be pleasant," Johanna snapped afterwards to Maria. "They are nice people, well brought up, hard-working. They have a respectable business and a good reputation. Their son is a very nice young man."

"I probably would have been pleasant if you hadn't tried to arrange my wedding behind my back," Maria retorted and stormed into her room.

As she lay in bed that night and tried to make sense of her feelings, she wondered why she had been so harsh toward Dirk. It was not like her to treat someone in that way. He was probably kinder and gentler than she had given him room to show. Perhaps she had been unnecessarily difficult and hard, but at the same time she had felt imprisoned.

She wondered whether she felt an outsider, not only from others but also from her parents. She wanted to break out and see and experience more than the life her parents were living and the life they were preparing for her to live. Although the visit to Paulus in Geneva had been unhappy, she had felt for those brief hours there that her life was real and that she was living it the way she wanted with someone who accepted her as she was. She wanted to find that feeling again.

Chapter 7

Maria had decided she must escape. She could not imagine the rest of her life on the island. Despite her success at running the boutique, the prospect of doing little more than that in the future filled her with an emptiness that terrified her. As the public face of the boutique, she knew she had obligations on the social stage of the town. The appropriate greetings to all the right people, which she had practiced *ad infinitum* as a child, were now more important than ever. For a wrong word to the butcher, a too-abrupt ending of the conversation with the pharmacist, or the insufficiently effusive greeting to the dentist could have immediate business impact.

She had lost track of the number of times she had delivered a bouquet of flowers with a note of apology to make up for an apparent slight or oversight on the street or at the weekly market when she had been too lost in her thoughts to hear the greeting.

But if the pressures of her position in the small-town were stifling, the rigid expectations of her mother were oppressive. Maria increasingly found herself making decisions dependent on how her mother would react to them. Even a new hair style or new blouse required her approval before Maria could relax and enjoy the choices she had made. And a misunderstanding with the baker simply could not be mentioned in case Johanna became enraged by the implications for the family name.

Where, as a child, Maria had learnt to avoid telling her mother about events, as an adult Maria found herself feeling every step she took was on hold pending final approval. She could not understand what had changed. But whatever the explanation, she herself was sinking under the weight of her expectations.

Increasingly, she found herself taking long walks alone along the beaches or coastal cliffs distraught at not knowing how to navigate between her own desires and her mother's expectations. The skin on her arms broke out in angry, itchy red rashes. The doctor was flummoxed, unable to recommend a treatment aside from some foul-smelling lotion that didn't help. Distressed at the devastating impact this was having on her looks Maria took the advice of a family friend to consult the island's faith-healing witch.

The old woman, who lived in a small run-down house on a dark lonely lane between two large fields, was said to have a healing gift handed down from her father. Though many islanders dismissed the woman as a fraud, some consulted her secretly when they suffered any ailments which the local doctor simply dismissed out of hand as "emotional muddles". A session with the woman required observing certain rituals. For the power of her gift to take effect, many said, one must never mention the words "Thank you" when in her house and in her presence. Payment was voluntary but expected and was left in a pot in the middle of the dining room table. Some islanders claimed to have heard that if the money paid into the pot was considered inadequate, one would hear a loud and extended creak of a door in an upper floor room. Afterwards the stingy visitor would most certainly suffer some kind of setback.

Already feeling uneasy at the prospect of meeting a witch, Maria shuddered as she approached the dilapidated house. The wind was blowing in gusts and the branches of a tree groaned as they brushed against the gable of the roof. After knocking at the low-framed door, Maria heard a shuffling gait inside and then a loud metallic clunking as a key was turned in the lock. As the door opened Maria made out in the gloomy interior a wizened face framed by long, black locks of hair. She was dressed in a long white gown that trailed on the ground. Immediately Maria was drawn to the woman's striking blue eyes. They exuded a gentleness and serenity. As she looked into the woman's eyes, she sensed understanding and a willingness to listen. It was almost as if she already knew why Maria was there.

The woman stepped back and motioned for Maria to sit at a small table below the low ceiling and exposed wooden beams. In the middle of the table was the payment pot that Maria had heard about. She felt the banknotes in her trouser pocket. Through the lace curtains, Maria could see out into the large grassy field where a lazily grazing deer raised its head to stare back at her.

"What is the unhappiness that has brought you here?" she asked.

"I have come about my skin," Maria stammered, pulling back her sleeves to show the rash on her arms.

Glancing briefly at her arms, she then looked calmly into Maria's eyes. "Something is making you unhappy—what is that?"

Maria was not uncomfortable with the woman's direct gaze and sensed that she could trust her.

"I feel I am locked in. Trapped."

"Are you trapped by yourself, or by others around you?"

Maria could not answer that question. In truth, she had never considered whether she was the source of her own discontent.

"I am locked in from all sides. My parents, my mother wants me to work here, to marry here and to die here," she burst out. "This is not what I want … I want a different life out in the world with different people and different places. I feel like I am being crushed here. I cannot be the way I want to be, but I have to be the way my mother wants me to be."

The woman listened.

"It is not the people or the island. They are nice people and I love my home, but I feel like everything I do is monitored and watched, everything I say is measured and evaluated … if I say the wrong thing I am punished, or ignored, or criticized."

Suddenly with unexpected force the old woman clasped Maria's own hand. She noticed the blotchy puckered skin on the back of the woman's hands, and how one finger seemed short and withered.

"Your life belongs to you. Only you can decide what is right for you. Only you can choose your path. But you must look inside yourself to find your way," she said. “You cannot let anyone take that responsibility from you.”

Maria was silent, terrified by the implications of her words and overcome with a fear that she had somehow been wasting her life until now by letting others determine her fate rather than deciding herself.

Still holding onto Maria's hand, the woman closed her eyes and started chanting in a low almost inaudible tone while she passed her free hand lightly over one of the red and inflamed areas on Maria's forearm. Maria could not understand what she was saying but the woman's voice was rising as she moved her head in a circle faster and faster. Her voice rose as she chanted three indistinguishable sounds or words over and over, almost at a shout, with her eyes clenched tightly shut as if she were in pain. Suddenly, her grip on Maria's arm became tighter and tighter, then without warning she released her and fell silent.

Through heavy gusts of wind Maria heard the grandfather clock in the hall ticking loudly. The woman opened her eyes and reached behind her to open a glass door in the upper half of a cabinet. Inside Maria could see boxes of vials and small brown-glass bottles. The woman hesitated momentarily, looking for something particular and then took out a small flask containing a transparent liquid and placed it in front of Maria on the table.

“This will help your skin. Apply it before you go to bed, and when you wake up in the morning. Also, stop eating any vegetables that are grown under the ground.”

Maria took the flask, deposited her payment into the pot on the table and stood up.

At the door, the old woman gripped her arm.

“You must find what is right for you. This place is not good for you.”

As she walked home along the narrow lane between the fields of yellow, shoulder-high sunflowers, the woman's words rang in her ears. ‘This place is not good for you’, ‘This place is not good for you’. She noticed the dark florets in the sunflowers and suddenly saw them as threatening. It was as if they were listening and deciphering her thoughts. Her uncle, a farmer with large plots of land on the mainland had once told her, that sunflowers turn their heads during the day to follow the sun and she was sure at that moment the sunflowers were turning and following her as she passed.

Maria knew she had to leave, to escape. Her mother would never understand. She felt a familiar tightening in her stomach and could already hear the tone of ridicule if she told her she wanted to do something different with her life. She could see the pursing of lips and the gaze into the distance that she had come to know so well during her childhood whenever she had questioned or challenged her mother's opinions. Already she could feel her determination, so strong when she had left the witch's home, beginning to waver. Where could she go? How would she live? Her parents would not support her if she abandoned the boutique and moved away.

She loved her mother and could not bear hurting her. And even more than that, she wanted her parents to be proud of her. She knew that if she announced she was leaving the island, and perhaps even the country, she knew that beneath the harsh reaction her mother would have, she would also feel sad, and disappointed that her daughter wasn't following a path that reflected the König family's success. Maria had determined long ago never to be a burden to her parents or to make them unhappy. Perhaps there really was no way out, and she should just accept her situation. Many others did. They seemed quite content to live the same lives their parents and grandparents had, and not to rock the boat. What was the home-spun proverb her father was so fond of? "Only he who does not strain at his chains is free."

Chapter 8

Maria slept fitfully for several nights following her visit to the witch, often waking up after powerful dreams she could not remember which left her feeling exhausted throughout the day. Although she could not for the life of her imagine where or how to start, she was convinced she could not ignore the witch's words. Her treatment seemed to have taken effect and her rashes were slowly fading away. She had followed the instructions and stopped eating carrots and potatoes.

One afternoon several weeks later, her mother asked Maria to join Peter and her for a dinner the following evening.

“Mr. Meier, who is head of the Puchring Association, is visiting. It would be good for you to meet him. Your father and I think you are ready to make your first wholesale purchasing trip on your own. When I was your age, I was doing the same for the department store. We buy clothes which are produced in Asia at much cheaper prices through Puchring.”

Maria knew her parents saw this as a momentous step in her development. But ever since her visit to the witch, she had spent far more time and energy wondering how to take control of her own fate, rather than to follow steps prepared by her parents, however well-intentioned, for her future.

Meier turned out to be a portly and jovial elderly man with a kind disposition. He was keen to hear about

Maria's schooling and experience, and asked how she was running the boutique, and what trends she could identify in the buying habits of both the islanders and increasing number of tourists who were now visiting the island.

"I am impressed—you have really hit on a unique model here for the department store," he beamed to Peter. "Other stores in other cities are already struggling with urban planning restrictions and car-free zones, but your focus on vacation centres is clever. More and more families want to go on holiday these days and they are coming to places like this."

"Thank you," her father said. "I believe that in life you can hit the target a thousand times and people see it, accept it, and they move on. But if you miss just once, the smallest tyke will not let you forget it."

"You are completely right," said Meier. And then, steepling his fingers and looking at Johanna and Peter, he said, "I am amazed at the speed of your expansion. Your store is ten times bigger than any other shop on the island, and you have also opened on the mainland." How did you ever find the capital to finance this growth?"

Johanna stiffened in her chair and then, before Peter could respond, leant forward to offer Meier another slice of the island's famous walnut layered cake.

"Tell us about more about purchasing from Asia. How could we take better advantage of that?"

Meier leant back in his chair. "Yes, that is definitely the way forward." Then, looking across at Maria he added, "In your generation, everything will be produced in China and Asia, and no longer in Europe. It is incredible to see the size of the factories they have there and the hours they work, and the low wages they pay. We have no idea here in Germany what kind of revolution this is going to be."

At the mention of these places she had barely heard of and knew nothing about, Maria started to listen more closely.

"I was in Hong Kong last week. An incredible city! Skyscrapers on every street corner, some of them 40 or 50 floors high. Shops selling anything and everything you can imagine. Markets open day and night. The city never shuts. They say that 24 hours a day somewhere in Hong Kong there is a shop open. Everyone is rushing around to do business and everything and everyone is flexible. Whatever service or product you want, someone will produce it for you for the right price. People are everywhere, the streets are so crowded you literally can't see the pavements sometimes there is so much bustle. There is so much activity that when I land back in Germany, I feel like everyone here is sleepwalking."

"That sounds so exciting," Maria said, now listening with bated breath. She felt he was speaking directly to her, although he was not. Every word about Hong Kong was like a nail into the coffin of Maria's life on the island. She knew immediately that this was the kind of outside world she wanted to experience. She could sense already the pulse and excitement of the city he was describing, even though she had scarcely ever heard of it. She had a thousand questions on the tip of her tongue.

"I am sure it is quite dirty and unpleasant there with all those crowds," her mother interjected. "And not very safe. I couldn't stand having so many people around me all the time. I love our beautiful nature and clean air and peaceful life here."

"Yes, this is the world's eighth continent," Peter added with a smile. "It's unique, and there is no better place."

"Yes, I can see that it is beautiful here, but the world also has many new opportunities."

"We were wondering, Mr. Meier, if you could chaperone Maria a little when she goes to the buying fair next month? It will be her first experience of wholesale buying for our boutique store and she will be there on her own for the next spring collection."

"One day she and our son Karl will inherit all of this, and we want them both to be well prepared," Maria's father chimed in, patting Maria on the head like a little girl, so that she could barely restrain herself from brushing his hand away.

"I would be delighted."

While dimly in the background she heard Meier and her parents discussing when she was to travel to the fair, and how he could meet and help her, the world he had described in Asia filled her head. She could already see herself walking through those crowded streets, experiencing the colours and smells of the markets, the cacophony of sounds and foreign languages, the excitement and energy of the place.

Perhaps the conversation had planted the seed she had been looking for?

Over the next weeks, Maria could think of little but the fair, and the meeting with Meier. In the library, she found a travel book donated by a retired schoolteacher renowned for his travel to exotic destinations. To her excitement, it was filled with photographs of Hong Kong. She pored over those pictures every night before going to bed, looking at the colourful street scenes with dozens of small shops overflowing with merchandise, neon signs inscribed with characters she couldn't decipher, the panoramic views over green, shrub-covered hills against bright blue skies, and the harbour, teeming with ocean-going liners and freighters as well as strange Chinese wooden vessels with unusually shaped hulls and ribbed dark-coloured sails.

One day, while idly flipping channels on their brand-new television with remote control, she happened across a documentary in English about Hong Kong. There on screen was image after image of the place she could not stop thinking about. She was transfixed. Her English was good enough for her to understand the commentary by the British foreign correspondent who lived there. She could almost taste and feel the warm air in the images on the screen. Perhaps there would be a tang of salt, as there was on the island when the wind blew and chased the sea spray over the coastal paths.

And one day, as Maria was towelling herself dry after a morning shower, she noticed that the red weals and rash had disappeared completely. The weeks of applying the witch's evil-smelling ointment had worked. She let out a yelp of joy and, dressing quickly, rushed down to tell her mother. Busy preparing breakfast, Johanna paused briefly from laying out thin slices of sausage on a plate, to listen to Maria's excited exclamations and, after glancing briefly over her shoulder and acknowledging that the skin had indeed healed, resumed her task without a word. Used to her mother's lack of emotion, Maria just sat down at the table.

Several weeks later, Maria was on the train to Düsseldorf, the central German city that was a Mecca for international clothing chains selling next year's fashion trends. As a buyer for one boutique alone, Maria could not expect producers to be particularly interested in her business. But her parents had given her strict guidance on one large order she could place for all the branches of the department store, now a chain based in several locations, which would attract more attention from the vendors. Meier, who met her at the fair, introduced her everywhere as the daughter of the König family. She could not help but feel pride at the respect and courteousness her family's brand triggered.

At one booth, she noticed a large crowd had gathered. As she and Meier approached, she saw a small Chinese man and a red-faced German in what looked like a heated discussion. Between them on the counter was a woman's white blouse. Although she was too far away to clearly understand what was being said, voices were raised as first one and then the other would pick up the blouse and highlight some aspect of it before dropping it down to gesticulate further. Maria noticed the Chinese man, unlike his German counterpart who stared directly at him the whole time, avoided all eye contact. He would bluster profusely, gesture with his hands as they struggled, presumably over the proposed price, but always look elsewhere, at the blouse itself, or the crowd, or into the distance of the cavernous hall. It was almost as if he was not interested in the outcome of the discussion.

"Why do you think the Chinese man is not looking at the buyer as they negotiate?" Maria asked.

"In my experience, it is their way of bargaining. I see it all the time in Hong Kong. It can be quite effective."

"I would like to learn more about doing business there."

Meier looked taken aback. "Yes, it is interesting. Why don't we get a bite to eat?"

They made their way to a red-carpeted area of the hall where waitresses in pinafores were serving guests at tables prepared with white tablecloths, silver cutlery and crystal wine glasses.

After placing their orders, Maria leant forward, her elbows on the table, and looked at Meier.

"Are there many business opportunities in Hong Kong?"

"Yes, but it very difficult if you don't know the culture there. It took me years to understand the mentality and how to work with the people."

"It would benefit our business if we could buy directly from their manufacturers. I would like to try."

"But, why? They come to the fair. No need to travel there. Besides, your parents would never allow it."

Then a knowing smile spread across Meier's face.

"Is the island not big enough for you?"

From the look in his eyes, she felt she had found someone who understood her.

"I want to see more of the world."

"It's very different in Hong Kong you know … life is different, people are different, food is different … it would be quite a big step for anyone to take and particularly someone with your very … very German background."

"I want to try."

Meier took a sip of wine. "Just supposing, I could help you find a job there, and that your parents would agree, you realize you wouldn't earn a lot of money, and you would live in a small, cramped apartment, nothing like the spacious home your parents have, and you would need to work harder than you have ever worked before including on weekends. Are you sure you are ready for something like that?"

"Completely and utterly." Maria did not hesitate for a second.

Meier smiled, clearly impressed by her resolve.

"Fine. Call me next week when you are back on the island. I may have something for you. But you must promise me that you let your parents know that this was your idea, not mine. Otherwise, I am sure they will never forgive me."

"I will."

Their orders came. "Now, let's finish our lunch. We have other booths to visit. Before the day is through."

The rest of the day at the fair passed as in a dream for Maria. She placed the large order for her parents, then selected a few pieces from the new spring trends for her boutique. But her mind was elsewhere. She barely even negotiated prices.

Back on the island, Maria could scarcely wait until the end of the week when she thought it was reasonable to phone Meier. She called from the boutique, telling the sales ladies that she was skipping lunch today and that they could all take a break together. Her heart beat quickly as she gave her name to his secretary and waited for him to pick up the phone.

"Yes, Miss König. I have made some enquiries, and there is an opening for a junior manager for one of our Asia buying offices in Hong Kong. The salary is low. However, they would give you some help with housing and pay for your flight to get there. Of course, you would be on probation for the first three months. If it doesn't work out, they would send you straight back home."

Maria could barely restrain herself from shouting with joy while he was talking. 'Junior manager' and 'Hong Kong' were the only words in her head, and they kept on resounding like two large cymbals crashing together again and again.

"The position won't stay open for long," Mr. Meier warned. "When will you let me know your decision?"

"I'll phone you back as soon as I've arranged things here. Thank you so much," she added hurriedly before hanging up.

She knew that whatever time she chose to break the news to her parents would be the wrong time. She chose the family dinner that same evening. Karl was away with friends, and it was just her and her parents.

"You remember Mr. Meier who showed me around the fair in Düsseldorf?" she began, having planned her story carefully.

"Of course." Johanna said. "I meant to tell you that you should thank him for his help when you were there."

"Yes, he called me in the boutique today and so I did. Apparently, he has a contact at one of the Puchring Hong Kong buying offices and he offered me a junior manager's position there. I accepted it."

"You did WHAT? Have you gone completely mad?" her mother screamed.

"It's a great opportunity. I need to see the world and have new experiences."

"It's outrageous. He should have spoken to us first. I will speak to him personally," her father said.

"Please don't," Maria rushed out her words. "I spoke to him to ask his advice when I was in Düsseldorf. It was completely my idea. He tried to persuade me to change my mind, but he couldn't. I want to go."

"He's absolutely right. It's not the place for a young woman," her mother said. "It's filthy and dangerous there. You don't know the language. You don't understand the mentality. Besides, what about all your responsibilities here? The boutique? The family business …"

"I don't want that. Don't you understand?"

Her mother continued as if Maria had not spoken.

"Besides, how would you even get there? Don't think for a moment that we are going to pay for your travel!"

Maria was quiet for a moment. "The offer includes travel expenses and support for a place for me to live."

"Why anyone would want to leave this beautiful island for a loud crowded foreign city is beyond me," her father added.

He stood up, releasing his dinner napkin from the silver clip he always had with him to fasten it to his tie, and made to leave the room. As he turned Maria could see that his eyes were red and that what looked like a few tears were trickling down his cheeks. Her mother retreated to a stony silence and was staring at the tablecloth. Then, she looked up and Maria could see her face was angry but also unnerved by her daughter's resoluteness.

"We can give you more responsibilities here ... perhaps we could open a second boutique for you to manage. Your father and I talked about this last week."

"Give it all to Karl. He's going to take over anyway."

"Very well, go if you must be so selfish! I won't stop you. But you're only thinking of yourself and abandoning your family and your responsibilities here, so don't expect us to help you. You'll have to survive on your own!"

She rose and left the room, slamming the door behind her, leaving Maria alone with a kaleidoscope of thoughts and emotions. Although she was on the point of tears herself, she was convinced she was making the right choice for herself and more determined than ever to go ahead with her plan.

Chapter 9

Several months passed before Maria could make the move from the island. Responsibility for the boutique was passed over to Karl who planned to integrate it into the operations of the family department store next door that he would soon be running. Stefanie and Maria found time one evening for a relaxed candle-lit dinner at a small Italian restaurant on the island.

"This is great news. It's your chance to find a new direction that suits you," Stefanie said. "Who knows? Maybe you'll find that English aristocrat in Hong Kong."

The idea of Maria marrying an English aristocrat had become a standing joke between them.

"More likely a Chinese emperor's son," Maria laughed.

But now she was sitting on her flight, breath bated and glued to the transparent plastic protective screen separating her from the thick glass window of the aircraft as it descended on a myriad of blue sea, green islands and sparkling bright light.

Her parents had driven her to the airport in almost complete silence with only occasional monosyllabic communication about bare essentials. At the security and immigration gate, first her mother, then her father had embraced her briefly.

"Make sure you stay safe and do a good job," Johanna had said with a grim smile.

"Even in times when life's storms rage, your home will always be your harbour," her father said, and Maria could see he was holding back tears. After clearing all the checks, Maria looked back over the queue behind her. She saw her, still where she had left them, standing silently next to each other and gazing rather forlornly and unhappily in her direction. She raised her hand to wave, realizing at that moment that despite everything, she would miss them. But her parents probably could not distinguish her in the crowd.

She felt the smoothness of the small white pearl earring against her fingers in her pocket. She had secretly taken the earrings from her mother's jewellery box one evening a few days before her departure. They had been a gift from her father on their 25th wedding anniversary, but she rarely wore them. She wanted to have something of her mothers with her all the time so that she wouldn't feel completely alone. As she gently rubbed the polished surface against her fingertips, she felt a glow of warmth run through her body and was happy that she had taken something with her that celebrated her parents' wedding.

The flight had seemed interminable, with two stopovers when Maria had wandered through duty-free shops staffed by yawning and bored sales assistants. As the aircraft descended on its approach to Hong Kong, Maria could make out the short green shrubbery and what looked like undergrowth on the hills interspersed by dark grey outcrops or slabs of granite, she remembered from the guidebook. Directly below the plane were white buildings, some of which seemed to be quite tall. She could see roads and cars and people, a few of whom seemed to be carrying umbrellas, presumably against the sun since it wasn't raining. It all seemed very, very close and Maria began to feel uneasy. She tried to peer ahead at an angle but could not make out a runway or an airport. If anything, it looked as if they were flying directly towards a range of steep hills.

The aircraft suddenly banked steeply to the right and for a few moments all she could see was the flat tops of buildings just below her and pieces of laundry hung out to dry. This could not be normal! Everyone around her seemed calm, but surely something was seriously wrong. The plane righted itself again and began to sink very fast. They seemed to be flying into a gap as the buildings now appeared alongside the aircraft and she could look directly into their windows. She clenched her eyes tight shut and gripped the arms of her seat preparing for a disastrous crash. She just had time to wonder whether her mother had been right all along and that this whole venture had been a folly before with a shuddering impact the aircraft's rear wheels hit the runway, the nose wheel settled and then the engines roared as the pilot sharply braked the speed. When she opened her eyes, the plane was taxiing along a runway next to the sea and all the passengers around her were completely calm. Further out on the bright blue water Maria could see one of those wooden boats with strange dark ribbed sails and beyond that, rising steeply out of the sea, the mountains of Hong Kong. She sighed deeply. She had arrived.

Someone from the buying company was waiting, holding a sign with her name. They greeted her and insisted on taking her bags. Despite the unusual pronunciation Maria was able to understand their English.

Soon she was driving through streets that teeming with people, cars, buses, small-wheeled hand trolleys piled high with stacked cardboard boxes and shop-front after shop-front selling everything imaginable: electric appliances, fresh meat, vegetables, clothes, hardware, jewellery, shoes. It was exactly as Meier had described. But it was the behaviour of the people that most intrigued Maria.

Everyone was moving urgently with a very clear sense of purpose. There was very little interaction, almost as if everyone was ignoring or even oblivious to each other. It was so different from her where simply crossing the market square was an obstacle course of social interaction and a strict examination of etiquette and hierarchy that could easily fill half an hour.

She felt the damp stifling heat as the car stood at a traffic light. She saw a pearl of sweat trickle down the back of the driver's neck and disappear under his white T-shirt as he leant forward to turn down the radio on which an announcer had been talking in a language that Maria didn't understand. Automatically she found herself trying to assess the quality and fibre of the driver's shirt, as she would have done in Germany to try and estimate the origin and price of the garment. The island she had left was so far away, but for a few moments it washed over this one she had just landed in like the wave of an incoming tide. What were her father and mother doing now? And how about Karl? She felt alone and nervous in this new and foreign place.

But this was what she had wanted. She had engineered her escape from the island, and now she needed to make what she could out of the hand she had dealt herself. She remembered a phrase of her father's: "It is not because something is unachievable that we do not strive for it, but because we do not strive for it that it becomes unachievable." That was the mindset she needed now. She would need to strive for the unachievable. And make it happen.

The car was approaching the harbour. Through the windscreen, Maria could see a ferry bound for Hong Kong Island with various vehicles already loaded on the upper deck. Their car was directed to the lower deck, however. After bouncing across a wide ramp, they drove to the front of the vessel where a flimsy rope strung between two bollards separated them from the gentle swell lapping at the bow. With some shouts and the ringing of a bell on the bridge above them, the ferry started to vibrate and shudder heavily, then slowly began to make its way into the harbour swell.

Her companion suggested they get out and stand behind the rope between the bollards so she could see the city better. As some light haze ahead of them cleared, Maria gasped. In front of her was an overwhelming panorama of skyscraper after skyscraper, all different heights, shapes, sizes and colours and seemingly packed so tightly together that she could not imagine how anyone could possibly move between them.

The setting sun was glowing just above the horizon and at that moment the rays were reflected in the glass surface of one of the tallest buildings so that it appeared to glow as if on fire. Maria was spellbound, and barely listened to her companion who was pointing out different buildings and introducing the city. She knew at that moment that her decision had been the right one. This was the world she wanted to see and experience.

Chapter 10

The first few months of Maria's new life were a breath-taking whirlwind of impressions. From her tiny apartment on the thirty-ninth floor of a narrow tall building she looked out every morning through a small window, fitted with an anti-burglar grill, on the blue sea of Hong Kong harbour. Her panorama was actually a restricted narrow view in the gap between two even taller and newer skyscrapers in front of her building. In a few early enthusiastic letters and post-cards to her parents she had effusively the large ships competing for space with colourful bobbing boats on the choppy waves and wakes of the narrow waterway between Hong Kong Island and Kowloon, which in Chinese meant nine dragons, she had learnt, on the mainland peninsula.

She was even more fascinated by the daily morning routines she could witness through the windows of the flats in the skyscrapers across from hers. In one an elderly Chinese gentleman seemed to complete a slow-motion ritual of movements with his arms, body and legs that seemed to represent some form of exercise. In another an enraged mother appeared to be shouting at her young recalcitrant son to complete his homework every morning before school.

Soon after her arrival, she experienced a typhoon, a raging tempest of a storm, the imminent arrival of which miraculously cleared the normally crowded and busy streets of people and cars so that she imagined all the buildings around her suddenly teeming from within like overcrowded anthills. For one entire night the wind and rain had howled and whistled around her and, however tightly she had tried to close the windows, water still seeped through the hinges and jambs, as well as from the air conditioning unit embedded in the wall in the upper corner of her small bedroom. As she lay in her bed, unable to sleep for the fury of nature around her, she was sure she could feel the building swaying on its foundations.

One part of her was terrified, but another was exhilarated by the sheer, unadulterated, primordial force she was experiencing. It reminded her of times on the island as a child when sudden squalls had skidded across the sea to the beaches or cliffs of the coast, and she had wanted to stand in their way and scream in a kind of ecstasy at the sheer natural power around her.

Despite her frequent letters and postcards, some of which she had sent while on one or two business trips she had already been asked to make to nearby Seoul and Taipei, she had only received one stiffly formal reply from her mother.

Dear Maria,
Thank you for your letters. Father and I hope you are well, and that you are doing your best at work. We wish you much good fortune and enjoyment and, above all, good health.
Your loving Mother.

As she read and then re-read the short note that had accompanied a pair of heavy woollen bed-socks her mother must have believed appropriate to the climate, she tried to sense her mother's feelings beyond those few words on the page.

As the weeks, then months, passed, Maria found her former life on the island receding more and more into the background of her memories. Her days were so busy, demanding, and long. The willingness of her colleagues to work late hours at tiny desk cubicles they could barely move in and out of was so different from the indifferent apathy of the sales ladies in the boutique.

She knew, because of her blondness and her height, that she attracted attention from the Chinese around her. On the busy streets she sensed how groups of young women were looking at her and even discussing her but when she turned to look at them and smile and perhaps even establish some eye contact, they always instantly looked away, sometimes hiding their giggles behind raised cupped hands.

As Maria had originally noticed many months ago at the fair with Meier, eye contact was not favoured here. While Maria had learnt to use eye contact as a way of exploring someone's inner self, here an unwavering stare into another person's eyes was an aggressive statement of disrespect. The normal practice was to cast one's eyes down and remain wordless when travelling in the same elevator or during gaps in a conversation. Initially, Maria felt uneasy, unable to decipher whether people were ignoring her, afraid of her, or merely disdainful.

On her first solo trip to Seoul, she met the owner of one of the largest textile production plants in South Korea in the lobby café of the hotel where she was staying. The rather overweight, grey and prematurely balding man, a good head shorter than her, smiled genially as Maria arrived exactly on time. She introduced herself, but he offered no greeting in return. Taken aback, Maria sat and waited for him to speak. But he said nothing, and indeed, barely seemed to register her presence. He looked round the café, and when the waitress came, ordered himself a coffee speaking excellent English, but nothing for Maria. She had to order her own.

After what felt like an eternity, Maria leant forward and asked: "Excuse me, but are we waiting for someone to join us?

"I would like to wait for your manager to come," the man replied quite politely.

"He is in Hong Kong. He is not coming. He has sent me to meet you."

For a moment the man froze as if in genuine anguish. Then he leant forward in his chair, gave her a broad beaming smile and asked, "Miss König, how can I help you?"

Harald Schwarz, the office leader in Hong Kong who had been born in the city to German parents, had laughed when she told him the story a few days later.

"He is indebted to you eternally now, for having made you lose face so badly. I think we'll send you there on all trips from now on. He'll always give us the best prices whenever he sees you, out of sheer embarrassment."

Sometimes, Maria found herself in situations where she simply did not know what people around her were thinking. Was the deep theatrical groan and exclamation an indication that someone was outraged or close to compromise? Was the long pregnant silence a sign of resolute resistance or of final willingness to agree? For several months, Maria was nonplussed. But gradually certain manners, gestures, facial expressions, tones of voice, shakes of the head began to repeat themselves, and Maria started occasionally to feel she could decipher this kind of communication. At times she could even see its benefits Rather than the immediate resort to open and direct communication whenever there was a misunderstanding, this cautious tiptoeing around delicate moments of human interaction, although more time consuming and complicated, somehow seemed more fitting to the true complexity of people than the confrontational, black or white battles she was used to at home.

Most of all, Maria loved to visit the bustling night markets. She would allow herself to be swept along with the throngs of people in the narrow alleys, between brightly lit stalls selling cheaper versions of the merchandise available in regular shops during the day. She marvelled at the vitality and industriousness of it all. Once, when she had stayed on a little later, she saw how an elderly couple, from whom she had earlier the same evening bargained mercilessly for a handbag that had caught her fancy, stoically pack up their wares into large baskets. Then, each suspending a basket on either ends of a bamboo pole which they placed over one shoulder, they both rose cautiously to take the heavy weight and sway slowly off into the night's darkness.

Maria knew that in Germany this scene would have triggered all kinds of righteous dismay at the unacceptable hardship the old couple was enduring. As she watched them disappear into the darkness a Chinese expression her boss had mentioned to her during an office dinner came to her mind. "When the Chinese face great hardship they say they are 'eating bitterness' and simply endure it."

It was part of a mindset of Hong Kong. It did not matter what your background was, whether you were young or old, well-connected or newly arrived, rich or poor, you were only as good as the value you could create. Maria felt free in a way she never had before. She felt she could allow her fantasy and imagination run wild and whether solving a particularly difficult request for one of the office's clients or hiring a couple of people off the street to help transport a large new table she had bought up the stairwell of her building, it all depended on her. There were no conventions or limitations set by those around her on what was or was not possible. No one was put in a box because of the success of their parents, or their lack of a noble lineage.

After six months had passed her parents suggested they might come to visit her. Peter was always one for new experiences and he wrote to her how he wanted to get a sense for the new textile production techniques in Asia that Meier had extolled. She was excited. So much had happened, there was so much she looked forward to telling them about and secretly she hoped that really their reason for coming was that they missed her.

She picked them up on their arrival and, bubbling with enthusiasm, didn't stop talking during the whole trip in the car from the airport to the five-star hotel where they had insisted on staying. She was surprised at how happy her mother had been to see her, much more than she had anticipated. It really did seem that in the 12 months that they hadn't seen each other Johanna had realized how much she had missed her. In the arrival hall, her mother held her close for much longer than in the past. Over the next few days, her mother frequently would put her arm around her at the breakfast table in the hotel, where Maria joined them every morning or during taxi rides around the city.

Maria had planned a busy morning to evening programme for the days they were staying and, for the times she couldn't avoid going into the office, arranged for a German-speaking friend to show them some parts of the city.

Peter ordered ten suits from one of the famed Hong Kong tailors who could measure out and complete a suit in just three days. He immediately connected with the industrious entrepreneurship of Hong Kong and would stand in wonder at the large department stores and shopping malls, amazed at the frenzy of buying and selling swirling around him.

On their last evening, Maria took her parents to one of her favourite places, an open-air restaurant a short ferry-ride from the central business district. Maria loved the plain, shiny formica tabletops, the rickety stools on the stone floor often littered with some of the meal remains from previous guests. The menu was a grimy, hand-written plastic card with descriptions of the dishes in Chinese characters and English script. The tables were close together, and the loud cacophony of raised inebriated voices made normal conversation difficult. At the large tanks at the front of the restaurant, guests could select the fish that they wanted for dinner. Although some of the bigger fish barely had room to move or swim freely, she always thought they looked strangely content as they moved lazily from one end of the aquarium to the other, even though at any moment the whim of a guest and a trawling net could make it their last one. For Maria, the tank felt like a microcosm of Hong Kong. It reminded her of the way Harald Schwarz had described the city soon after her arrival.

"Foreigners like Hong Kong because here they can be a large fish in a small pond," he told her. "The problem with large fish, however, is they are usually the first to get caught. It is a sink or swim kind of place. You make it, or you disappear."

Maria knew what he meant. Here she was given responsibilities she would never be entrusted with back in Germany. But that was because everyone was given a chance to prove what they could do. If they succeeded, they would be given more. If they failed, they would be forgotten. "I feel like I am not being judged here," Maria tried to explain to her mother.

"What do you mean you are not being judged?" Johanna asked.

"The only test is whether you can meet the challenge. No one cares about my background, or where I come from. They are only interested in what I can do and whether it has value. It is so different from home, where everyone judges you before they even know you. There, I have to be so careful what I say, who I say it to, and how I say it. I feel free here."

"That's not true," her mother said. "People in Germany want to know more about you to know whether they can trust you. You have to build your reputation and your status and get people to accept you over years and years. Look at how hard we had to work to build our family's name. When you come home, you …"

Maria could feel her pulse rising. She knew she was happy and unencumbered and independent here, perhaps happier than she had ever been. "I don't care about that," she burst out. "I am happy here, and I want to stay here. I am happier here than at home!"

"Don't be ridiculous. You belong in Germany. It is your home. You don't belong here in this crazy place with strange customs and strange people and strange food, and a language you can't speak. Just look around you," Johanna continued in a voice loud enough for some of the guests at other tables to turn and look at them. "This is below you. This is not what we sent you to boarding school for. You should be with people who have more style and class."

Maria felt an emptiness in her stomach. She looked away, hoping to conceal her tears of guilt and anger.

Was she wrong to be so proud of her new life and of what she had achieved in six months on her own? She had arrived in Hong Kong knowing no one and nothing and had managed to find her own feet. Surely it was not too much to hope her parents would be proud of her. Before her parents had arrived to visit, she had imagined her father raising his glass to toast and congratulate her with Johanna looking on approvingly and nodding in agreement. Instead, she now felt the return of that all too familiar feeling that she had done something wrong and had disappointed her parents.

Johanna and Peter left the next day. At breakfast before going to the airport, Maria sat stiffly, disappointed that her mother didn't understand her new life. Johanna seemed to notice and tried to revive the closeness of the earlier breakfasts, but Maria resisted, participating only formally in the conversation.

At the airport her father, after checking in their bags kissed her cheek and said:

"I am proud of you. You are doing a great job here. All this experience will really help you when you decide to come back to the island."

But Maria barely heard him. The disappointment over her mother's words was too great and had cut too deep. She brushed her mother's cheek with hers in a quick parting kiss and avoided a hug.

"Have a safe trip back," Maria said. "Say hello to Karl."

Then she turned and walked out of the terminal building rather than wait until they had disappeared behind the security barriers.

Chapter 11

She threw herself at once back into her work. By the end of her first year she had been promoted from junior manager to senior manager, which entitled her to a private office, rather than a partitioned desk. In recognition of her hard work, Harald Schwarz had even ceremoniously presented her with an expensive ladies' watch at the traditional annual Chinese New Year dinner. Maria had never felt so proud.

But something was wrong. Maria was no longer as happy as she had been.

"How is everything going?" Harald Schwarz asked her as he found her still working late one Friday evening.

"Oh, ... very well, thank you," Maria replied. "The orders are all on track, and I will be sending out the telex to Vietnam before I leave."

"I'm sure that's all fine. I know I can rely on you. Do you have any plans for the weekend? From what I can see you are doing nothing but work."

"I've got a few more documents to finalise," Maria had replied quickly, convinced she must show commitment and no weakness. "It's easier to do when everybody's gone. I'll think about my weekend tomorrow."

"You need some time to yourself. Are you making friends in Hong Kong?"

His words had touched a nerve. She was worried that the aching loneliness she had started feeling every evening when she went back to her apartment or the dull pain in the pit of her stomach she woke up with every morning was becoming noticeable.

The long evenings in the office were a cover for her having no friends to meet or parties to attend. She had been to the cinema a few times on her own but had soon given that up. It made her feel even more lonely as she looked around at the happy couples, or the groups of friends chattering and sharing popcorn all around her. She had started visiting a German-style beer bar, an evening haunt for tired, mostly German businessmen. On one occasion, she noticed a man eyeing her from across the bar. However, when he came over to buy her a drink and start a conversation, she couldn't get the image of that surf in Hamburg out of her mind and after one round she made an excuse and hurriedly left.

"I'm trying but with my schedule ..."

"Hong Kong can do that to you. I really think you should try and explore more than just this office."

Maria just smiled weakly.

Increasingly, she had taken to buying a bottle of wine on the way home from work and drinking it all alone in front of the television with some take away dinner, only to wake up the next morning feeling guilty and sometimes hung over. Was this really the exciting, exotic life she had dreamed of?

As she looked around at the crowds on the street, she felt more isolated than ever. Her mother's words echoed in her head. Nobody seemed to care about getting to know her as they did back home. No eye contact meant no chance at connection. Perhaps they did all lack etiquette and were without class or style. Even her favourite restaurant had lost all its previous idiosyncratic charm as she sat there alone almost deafened by the cacophony of noise. More and more she found herself frequenting the bars at five-star hotels where foreigners congregated but found little comfort in their superficial conversations or obvious pick-up lines.

She preferred to linger in the open-air Chinese vegetable market out on the steep streets just below her apartment where one very old woman selling from a small stall always kept back some fruits for her. The woman would see her coming from afar and always beckon her over in that unique Chinese style with her hand held high, palm facing down and the cupped, closed fingers gesturing in sharp downward movements for her to come. The woman's face was so well-meaning and warm. Once she had said to her, gesturing at the bottle of wine already in her hand for the evening:

"No good missee, no good missee!"

But at the end of every day, she went back to her little apartment, which at first had seemed cosy and comfortable, but now seemed cramped and isolated.

One day, Harald asked her if she was free to join him on an evening the following week at the birthday party of an old school friend of his.

"My girlfriend is busy that day, and so I would be honoured if you would join me."

Maria was reluctant. She had lost all interest in meeting new people and preferred to be left at home on her own in the evenings. But as it was her boss inviting her, she felt she couldn't refuse.

Harald took her to a part of Hong Kong she had never seen before. Here some of the buildings were less tall than most of the other skyscrapers she had seen in the streets in the business district. They also seemed considerably older and more run down.

This was clearly a less exclusive residential area in the city. They entered a narrow doorway at street level, and Harald pushed a bell button on a directory of names. A remote buzzer opened the grilled gate. Instead of a lobby, they passed along a narrow corridor to a steep, stone staircase. There was no lift. Maria was thoroughly out of breath after they had climbed for at least five floor and reached the top. This had clearly been a mistake and she would have done better to stay in her apartment. She could hear Johanna ridiculing the location and the kind of people who were likely to live here. Ahead of them was a large dark brown wooden door. She could hear the loud music and voices of the party inside. Harald had already rung the bell. After a minute or so, the door opened.

A tall figure filled the doorway. Maria felt herself take a step back. The man at the door was completely different from her expectations. Wearing a loose Indian-style linen shirt and a colourful piece of material like a skirt around his waist, he extended his hand in greeting.

"Mischa Freeman, it's nice to meet you."

"I'm Maria König."

As she shook his outstretched hand, Maria was immediately struck by his deep blue eyes that seemed to glow like the Sri Lankan blue sapphires that she had seen recently on an expensive necklace at a jewellery shop. He stared directly into her eyes. She hadn't experienced that since her arrival in Hong Kong.

"Come, the party is upstairs on the roof."

Their host led them up another narrow staircase that led to the rooftop terrace. Loud music was blaring out of a large cassette player and amplifier and all around the terrace groups of people were standing, chatting and drinking. As Maria looked up, she gasped in amazement. The rooftop they were on was dwarfed by taller buildings surrounding them, each of which seemed to have hundreds of windows like the bright eyes of a hydra, peering down at them.

Harald arranged a glass of wine for her and was soon chatting to an old friend he had spotted in a huddle of guests in one corner near some potted plants. with large arching green ferns. Maria wandered over to one side of the rooftop and looked down.

"It's a long way down."

Maria knew from the deep voice before she turned who was behind her.

"Yes, I was surprised—it feels dangerous up here," Maria said turning around to face Harald's friend. "Your name is Mischa, isn't it?"

"Yes, that's right."

"That is an unusual name … where is it from … is it Chinese?"

Maria wanted to bite her tongue, but it was too late. She knew immediately the name could not be Chinese and realized she had only said that because she recalled from Harald that Mischa had grown up in Hong Kong.

He smiled gently. "It's Russian. My parents are English, but they seem to have liked Russian names since they gave them to all their children. To this day I don't really know why."

Maria liked his voice. His relaxed tone made her feel at ease. She had looked directly into his eyes a few times as they spoke and sensed there something she hadn't seen when they arrived—it felt like a deep vulnerability hidden behind a façade of politeness. The few times their eyes had fleetingly connected she had felt an unexpected quiver of excitement.

"Perhaps they had family there?"

"Yes, that would have been a nice story," he smiled again, his face suddenly alive like a radiant sun. "I have always thought I should make up a story of White Russian ancestors who escaped the Red Bolsheviks in the civil war and came through Shanghai to Hong Kong."

"I guess my parents just liked the way the names sounded. They even took us all on the Trans-Siberian railway when I was a child. We went from Nakhodka on the coast opposite Japan through all of Siberia to Moscow in nine days. It really was quite an experience."

Maria was fascinated. Images of Russia from *Anna Karenina*, one of the few books she had read in class at boarding school, flooded in. The long train of imperial Tsarist carriages steaming through the frozen snow-covered landscape. The thick dark forests.

"That sounds amazing. What do you consider to be your home?" she asked suddenly. "Harald told me you grew up here?"

"I don't think I really know the answer to that question. I've lived here the longest and feel comfortable here, but I know I don't really belong here. But then, I also don't belong in Europe either."

"Why is that?"

"I am different from the people there, and they are different from me." He looked away. "We don't have the same life expectations and goals."

"Perhaps India is your home," Maria said with a little laugh, pointing at his colourful sarong.

Mischa smiled. "This is from Burma, actually … do you like it? I bought quite a few back from my visit last year. It's very comfortable in hot and humid weather."

Maria felt foolish. Was there any place in the world he hadn't already been to? She had felt so important and unique for her big leap into the unknown when she had left the island to come here, but it seemed in comparison to him she had seen nothing of the world. She was not sure she knew where Burma was, and she knew absolutely nothing about it.

"We travelled by boat down the Irrawaddy River from Mandalay to Pagan to see the plain of four thousand temples. It was incredible to climb a few of the temples and see the sun set over the horizon. It was almost like being in another world."

"I don't think I could ever wear something like that, I would be far too embarrassed."

He laughed. "Oh, I know it looks a bit strange, but I really don't care what people think. I feel comfortable and it reminds me of my wonderful time there." He sipped his drink. "But enough about me. "You've been asking all the questions. Where are you from?"

"A small island you won't have heard of off the coast of Germany."

"And what brought you to Hong Kong?"

"I moved to Hong Kong about a year ago to work in textiles. It's interesting because I travel around Asia a lot and visit lots of cities. In my office I have a small team of people who help me plan the designs and production. Harald is my boss."

"Are you happy here?" he asked. Suddenly, he looked straight into her eyes. Maria had to look away.

"It's a wonderful city. And there's so much to do."

"Yes, it is, but some people end up working too hard here and don't get to enjoy it and wind up quite lonely and unhappy."

Maria hesitated. His calm and understanding voice made her feel comfortable and she had to resist the urge to confide in him that she was one of those people. She couldn't. She barely knew him. Although something told her he would understand and would make no judgement.

"I like the Chinese markets and watching the people there."

"Yes, they are almost all that's left of old Hong Kong now. Let me show you something." He crossed to the other side of the rooftop and pointed at a gap she hadn't noticed between two of the surrounding buildings.

"Do you see that flashing red light on the top of that dark mountain?" he said, standing close behind her, his arm stretched out over her shoulder for her eyes to follow his hand. She could barely concentrate on where he was pointing, so strongly did she feel how close he was to her.

"I see it, yes."

"When I was a child, our family used to climb that mountain every New Year's Eve. We would listen to all the ship fog horns at midnight. I always thought they sounded more melancholy than happy about the New Year."

Maria thought how different her New Year's Eves had always been with her parents. Everyone formally dressed, a wide group of friends and a stiff, sit-down dinner at which her father invariably gave one of his impromptu speeches, and then the fireworks in the garden. The idea of climbing a mountain to listen to ship fog horns sounded so exotic and so free of convention.

"Well, I can see you have got to know each other," Harald said jovially as he joined them. "Isn't this a great place?" he said to Maria

"Yes. It is," Maria said, disappointed that she and Mischa couldn't continue their conversation.

"This is the Hong Kong we grew up with ... low-rise buildings without lifts, potted plants everywhere and very few of the huge modern air-conditioned towers, right Mischa?"

"Yes, I do miss those times."

Even in her short time in Hong Kong Maria had sensed what Harald was talking about. She'd noticed how quickly old constructions were replaced by new ones. On one street, on her way to and from work, there had been an older looking building with balustrades and interior verandas and some worn stucco carvings. Although discoloured into a grubby, dark khaki colour the building's architecture reminded Maria of some of the houses in streets in Hamburg. Sometimes on her way back in the evening she spied an elderly Chinese man sitting serenely on a first-floor veranda wearing what looked like a long wide-sleeved jacket buttoned tightly up to his chin and matching wide-bottomed trousers. On his chin he had a large brown mole from which protruded several long strands of grey hair and occasionally she had seen him straightening them attentively with a small comb. On some days he would rest a two-stringed instrument upright in his lap and play strange music on the strings with a long bow. Above him, hanging from a rusty hook embedded in the stone ceiling hung a small cage with a bright yellow bird that fluttered and sometimes chirped loudly.

However, one day, rounding the corner into the street again, she stifled a gasp. The building was surrounded by a lattice of bamboo scaffolding and a plastic tarpaulin and from within she could hear the heavy, dull thuds of destructive blows and the constant shower of small debris cascading down interspersed by the shouts and commands of workers as the building was demolished. Only a few days later the scaffolding and tarpaulin were gone and all that remained was a gaping bright crevasse of freshly exposed inner walls between the two neighbouring buildings. She had wondered where the old man and his bird had gone.

She was shocked at the pace and ease at which local tradition and life could be erased. But life continued unabated in and around where the building had stood and the streams of people that passed by every day seemed completely oblivious to what had changed so that very quickly it felt as if the building had never existed.

Once, a few weeks later, Maria believed she saw from a distance the same elderly musician sitting on a bench amongst mothers and their children in a tiny community playground serenely surveying his surroundings and cradling his birdcage on his lap, but she couldn't be sure and, as she was late for work that day, had to hurry on. It was almost as if the past with its set ways of doing things and expectations of how things should be had no hold on the future and that everyone had to find their own way of adjusting and staying afloat in a constantly changing environment where anything was possible.

She and Mischa couldn't continue their conversation, as Harald and other guests enveloped them. So she let herself out of the apartment and down the narrow, dark and somewhat dingy staircase into the road.

Chapter 12

One day Maria received an unexpected invitation to a weekend boat outing. In the hot months of the year in Hong Kong all-day outings on pleasure boats to the beaches of the outlying islands were a relief. Maria, however, barely knew the person inviting her—Johnson Wang, a young local textile designer whom she had met at a dinner several months earlier together with Harald. She was planning to turn the invitation down as trips on the open sea frightened her, when Harald appeared in her office.

"Are you going on Johnson Wang's boat party? You met him at the dinner we hosted at that noisy restaurant with local designers a couple of months ago. Should be fun. I heard that Mischa's coming too."

"Yes, I remember Johnson Wang," she answered casually.

"By the way, I never asked you whether you enjoyed Mischa's birthday party?"

"Yes. It was interesting to meet a different group of people," Maria said non-committally. But what she had really enjoyed was meeting Mischa. She hadn't forgotten how he'd stood close behind her pointing out that flashing red light on the distant hill.

The boat outing was planned for the coming weekend. Maria had a two-day trip outside Hong Kong during the week, to a demanding new garment producer in Taiwan, that kept her mind fully occupied. But in occasional empty moments she sensed a small tremor of excitement that she couldn't suppress, however hard she tried to convince herself that nothing would happen if she saw Mischa again. When she returned from her trip, the bright late summer sky seemed bluer to her than before and she noticed for the first time the bright and contented morning cawing of two black crows who seemed to have decided that the small shelf outside her window was their ideal nesting spot.

On the morning of the outing, she woke early with butterflies in her stomach. She stood in front of her wardrobe and in the space of an hour put on, took off and put on again countless combinations of blouses, pants and matching necklaces to find the perfect combination. Finally, a glance at the watch convinced her she must decide and wearing what she hoped would give her the greatest sense of confidence she gave herself one final check in the mirror before rushing into the elevator to catch a taxi to the marina.

When she arrived, Maria saw the rows of sleek, white-hulled pleasure craft moored not far from dark, oil-streaked and heavily patched fishing junks. The guests, many of them already in shorts and some of the women in revealing bikini tops, were waiting on a weather-worn jetty. As she joined them, she saw how in small groups they were stepping down into *sampans*, which looked like flat, elongated wooden dinghies, that would transport them to their host's large motor vessel.

At the rear of the *sampan* an elderly Chinese woman, dressed all in black and wearing a wide, round- brimmed hat with a short curtain-like piece of cloth hanging down from the brim as a sunshade, stood on a small platform and navigated the boat with a long, single oar fastened to the rear transom like a rudder. Maria sat next to her and watched in fascination the woman's practiced movements and the ease with which she balanced, her calloused flat feet gripping the planks as the unsteady boat pitched and wallowed in the wakes of heavier craft passing through the harbour.

"She is probably one of the original boat people," a young Eurasian woman seated next to her said. She was wearing torn-off jean shorts and a bright, fluorescent bikini top accentuating the deep olive tan of her skin. "Most likely grew up on one of the fishing boats moored here and has almost certainly never lived on land."

"I wouldn't have guessed that if you hadn't told me."

"Aren't you hot in all those clothes?"

Maria suddenly felt self-conscious of her long-sleeved blouse and silk pants more appropriate for an evening engagement not a boat trip.

"Not really."

The woman shrugged. "Look, it's Harald and Mischa," she said waving at the two men arriving on another *sampan* behind them. Maria felt a knot of nervousness in the pit of her stomach.

Soon they were aboard the motor yacht and nosing out from behind the harbour's storm breakwaters into the open sea. While the bulk of guests had quickly changed into swimwear and boisterously made their way to the rooftop sundeck of the boat, Maria stayed on the lower main rear deck where she could sit comfortably in the shade and admire the surrounding scenery of rugged shrub-covered islands and passing boats as well as huge sea-going container ships. She could see Mischa standing at the bow of the boat, where some guests had congregated, and hoped he might come to the rear deck later. Meanwhile she engaged in desultory conversation with a few who had like her chosen to remain under cover from the powerful sun.

After about an hour the captain steered into a sheltered and secluded bay and anchored not far from an empty beach, a bright and unblemished streak of white-yellow paint against the backdrop of deep blue water and green hillsides. Maria marvelled that such a place of peace and serenity existed so close to the bustle and urgency of the city. Most of the guests leapt or dived from the boat into the water almost immediately and made for the shore.

Maria noticed that Mischa didn't join those swimming to the beach but instead settled himself down with a book on the front-deck.

"Hello, you must be very intellectual," she said, surprised at her own forwardness, as she stood in front of Mischa. who was reclining against a windscreen pane on the front deck of the boat.

"Oh hi," he said, tipping his dark sunglasses briefly. "Why do you think that?"

"Because you're reading a book instead of swimming on the beach … and it's so thick."

"Yes, it is a bit long … I'm finding it's starting to get a bit boring, really. Too long-winded in some passages. Sometimes I prefer the calm and quiet of reading to a crowd of people."

Maria nodded. "Me too."

"Are you Jewish?" she asked completely out of the blue.

"That's an intriguing question. As a matter of fact, I am, ... or my mother is, to be exact. How did you know?"

"Your book. Exodus. It's about Israel, right?" Maria said with a big smile.

But Mischa laughed out loud. "So, it is. Nobody has ever asked me that so directly. Please join me," he said making room next to him.

"Thank you. I enjoyed your party the other night, by the way. Which birthday were you celebrating?"

"Oh, I had just turned nineteen."

Maria momentarily looked confused.

"I'm joking. I'm now thirty. Nothing special. Does that seem old to you? It does to me."

And there it was again, the warm radiant smile that Maria had seen on the rooftop.

"I don't think it's old ... May I ask you a favour?"

"Maybe ..."

"Would you mind taking off your sunglasses. I find it difficult to talk to people if I can't see their eyes. I find I understand people more from their eyes."

"Maybe that's a reason for me to keep my glasses on," Mischa said with a smile, but then removed his sunglasses and squinted in the bright light.

"You never told me where you felt most at home," he continued.

"I used to think it was where I grew up. But I don't fit in there anymore. If I ever did."

Maria could see in the way he listened attentively without any judgement that he understood completely.

"When I am here, I feel freer, much more accepted for who I am."

"Yes, Hong Kong is unique in that way. You aren't judged here for who you are, only for what you have to offer."

The sound of the other guests who were shouting and swimming back to the boat filled the air.

Seeing that her time with Mischa might be interrupted, on impulse, she picked-up his book, opened it to the back cover and, using the pen she always kept in her pocket, wrote her name and telephone number.

"When you finish the book, you can call me … if you like," Maria said with a smile and stood up.

"If I finish the book," Mischa responded with a small laugh. "Of course, I could just flip to the end and skip the reading."

As Maria walked to the rear of the boat, she felt proud of herself for taking the initiative.

Chapter 13

Mischa called her a few days later and left a message. She let him wait two days before she returned his call. They met in a restaurant of her choice, and for the first few moments when she saw him, she had been disappointed. His trousers were a bit worn and a few centimetres too short, his shoes scuffed. But very soon they were talking animatedly. He enthralled her with stories of treks through undergrowth up mountains, recovery of bullets and other remnants from hillsides where ferocious battles had been fought during the Second World War … fresh food markets with exotic animals and reptiles … a metaphorically named Walled City near the airport where crime ruled and law enforcement dared not enter, the etiquette of the Chinese that she realized now she had never understood. The list was endless.

Mischa listened closely to everything she said as well. He asked a stream of relevant and penetrating questions from which she could see he was simply interested without any judgement. Maria found herself completely at ease. Relaxed, she was able to tell him everything of her childhood, the bullying at the island school, running the aristocratic gauntlet in boarding school, her failed relationship with Paulus, how she had arranged her job in Hong Kong.

They began seeing each other regularly. Mischa showed her parts of Hong Kong she did not know existed. One Sunday, she followed him to the mysterious Walled City. A grimy collection of densely packed and run-down 13-storey buildings, separated by dark, shoulder-wide alleys, filled with poorly illuminated shop fronts and cheap dental clinics. Mischa explained that it was reputedly still under the sovereignty of mainland China, although Maria could not understand how this was possible since it was in the middle of Hong Kong. She felt uncomfortable and scared and hoped the outing would be a short one. To her relief, Mischa did not lead her into the narrow gaps between the buildings, but instead brought her to a cement stairwell at the foot of one of them on the perimeter.

"I'm afraid it's 260 steps, but it's worth it." he said, smiling and started confidently up the stairs.

As they ascended, Maria saw huge machines behind grilled gates on several floors, some of them idle, others ear-shatteringly loud, vibrating so violently they seemed to shake the building to its foundations as they produced what looked like thousands of red plastic flowers.

She felt beads of sweat beginning to build on her back and just as she thought she must ask Mischa to pause, he came to a halt before an iron door with a sliding bolt. He slid it open and stepped out into a blast of sunlight and fresh air on the roof-top of the building. All around her she could see a jungle of television aerials and with a start she noticed there was no guardrail at the edge of the building. She hung back away from the ledge. Ahead of her she saw an unblocked view of the airport and the runway she had landed on when she first arrived in Hong Kong. Aircraft were taxiing slowly like toys around the apron.

"This is why I brought you here," Mischa said, standing behind her and pointing to the sky.

Heading directly towards them was a huge passenger aircraft, landing lights shining brightly and the wheels of the undercarriage extended. The enormous plane seemed barely higher than the rooftop they were standing on. Maria gasped and felt the urge to drop to the ground or run, but Mischa held her shoulders tight.

"Watch!"

Maria could see the pilot and co-pilot through the front windscreen. She was about to scream in terror and closed her eyes tightly as the aircraft came close. Then she felt the wind as it suddenly banked sharply. She heard the roar of the engines receding into the distance. When she opened her eyes, the plane was descending fast towards the runway. A few seconds later, with a puff of smoke its wheels hit the ground and the nose settled.

She was exhilarated. It reminded her of the squally thunderstorms on her island when she had screamed with excitement at the racing clouds, the rain and rolls of thunder, the mighty power of nature, before her parents dragged her inside, warning of the dangers.

"The next one is coming," Mischa shouted.

This time, Maria kept her eyes open. And as the plane again banked at the last minute, she raised her arms and shouted in delight.

Mischa was watching her.

“I thought you might like this.”

“It's incredible. I've never seen anything like this before.”

They watched a few more landings before Mischa suggested returning down into the Walled City.

“There is something else I want to show you.

She followed him back down the long staircase, and then into the narrow walkways between the buildings that stood so closely together daylight barely penetrated between them. Electric cables were suspended in messy bundles from building to building. The ground squelched and oozed unpleasantly beneath their feet. Sewage gutters ran openly into the pathways. Liquids, of one sort or another, splattered down from above. Disinterested faces looked out at them from windows or dark doorways. Bare chested men with heavily tattooed upper torsos squeezed by them.

What could Mischa possibly want to show her in this filthy place? She had soon lost all sense of direction and knew that on her own she would never have found her way out again.

At last, after a few more corners, Mischa stopped in front of a solid corrugated metal door. Emblazoned on the door in thick white paint were some Chinese characters and underneath them the English words *St. Stephen's Society* next to an image of a crucifix. Near the bottom of the door someone had written more neatly and in black: *Goodbye to Chasing the Dragon*.

“What is this? … Are we safe here?” Maria whispered to Mischa.

"Absolutely," he said and pulled open the door.

Inside the room, illuminated by bright white neon lights, Maria saw a circle of chairs with Chinese men of different ages sitting on them. Some were bent over almost double. Others had their eyes closed and were clasping their hands together in prayer, intoning quietly to themselves. On one chair Maria noticed a middle aged, well dressed Western woman who was singing quietly with her eyes closed and, as Maria listened more closely, she recognised the harmony of a hymn she had once sang with her parents and the congregation in the church on the island.

Mischa motioned her to sit down next to him on two free chairs against the wall at the back of the room.

Maria noticed how emaciated most of the men looked. They all seemed to have an unhealthy almost yellow pallor and deep eye sockets. After a while the woman stopped singing and the men's chanting subsided. A silence spread over the room. Suddenly with a guttural scream a younger man in short trousers and a grimy short-sleeved sports shirt jumped to his feet and stretched his arms upright above his head to the ceiling. His arms were covered with prick marks as well as blue and brown bruises in the pits of both of his arms.

He began singing in a high-pitched voice. She couldn't understand the words but was sure they weren't Chinese. His singing got louder, more crazed, almost hypnotic. He began to move in a jerky, disjointed way as he sang. His voice was rising to a crescendo. First the woman and then the others on the chairs rose to form a circle with eyes closed and arms raised around the now wildly gesticulating and gyrating young man, humming loudly and creating what looked like a protective shield around him.

As suddenly as he had started, the young man in the centre stopped moving and became silent and then started to sway. As he fell, he was caught by those around him and gradually and carefully laid out on a rattan mat on the ground between the chairs. Almost as if a spell had been broken, the rest of the group sat and started chatting easily amongst themselves. After a few minutes the Western woman knelt down over the young man and held a small, chipped cup with tea or water to his lips. He took a few sips, then gradually rose and took his seat again on one of the chairs.

Misha caught the Western lady's eye and waved briefly, motioning as he slid some large denomination Hong Kong dollar bills into a donation box near the door. She nodded her thanks.

"We should leave now," he said quietly to Maria.

They walked again through the grimy alleys. Passing one doorway, Maria looked in and saw a skeletal figure, she couldn't tell if man or woman, lying on its side on a bed holding a solid round pipe of bamboo at its mouth and enveloped in a cloud of smoke.

Mischa remained quiet until they had left the Walled City behind them. He led her to a simple Chinese restaurant, similar to her favourite where she'd taken her parents. Mischa ordered their meal from the waiter in Chinese.

"So, what did you think?"

"The rooftop was amazing. I felt so free. It was almost as if I was flying myself." She looked into his eyes. "I had a similar experience as a child back on the island when there were big thunderstorms. There it was the power of nature and here it was the power of those huge machines as they fly through the sky towards you, and you feel they are going to hit you until they turn at the last minute."

"What about St. Stephen's Society … the room we were in?"

"I didn't understand what was happening. I … it was disturbing."

"The people in the room were all members of triads, illegal criminal gangs, but they are also all heavy drug addicts, probably on heroin. The woman is called Helen. She is an English missionary who came here as a 25-year-old and started teaching at a school in the Walled City. She's devoted her life to helping the addicts beat their addiction. Some of them have come off it with her help. All of them are killers, but they trust her completely and would never harm her. She's saved their lives and many others as well."

"How did you come to know her?"

"My parents know her well. I've met her several times over the years. She is quite controversial. For many years she was the only outsider allowed into the Walled City by the gangs. Not everyone in the church agrees with her approach of praying in tongues, but she has achieved great things."

"Praying in tongues?"

"It's a mystical language that people speak when they're said to be possessed by the spirit."

"Is that what that man was singing?"

"Yes."

Maria was fascinated. A scene that she had found unsettling and, if she was honest, almost repulsive was suddenly coming to life for her.

"And what is chasing the dragon?" Maria asked, remembering the script on the door.

"It means inhaling the smoke you get from boiling a solution of opium and heroin and other drugs through a pipe."

"I was afraid, to be honest," confessed Maria.

"That is what I love about you," Mischa replied.

"What is that?"

"You are so close to your emotions. You say what you feel. I wish I could do that, but I can't. Sometimes I don't even know what I am feeling, or even if I am feeling anything at all. I think I can only understand things logically. I am probably missing so much. Life must be much easier if you not only know you are feeling something, but also what it is that you are feeling."

"I'm not sure that's true."

That evening, as they took the short but wonderfully panoramic cross-harbour ferry back to Hong Kong Island, Mischa slid his arm around her waist. Later, as he embraced her before she got into the taxi home, she felt she was melting into his arms and had to tear herself away.

Chapter 14

"Hello ..." Her mother's voice sounded sleepy, and with a start Maria remembered that her mother always took a post-lunch nap. Had she woken her? She had not thought about the time difference.

"Sorry, did I wake you? It's me."

"Yes, actually I was sleeping. I always sleep at this time. You know that. It doesn't matter. Why are you calling? Is everything okay with you?"

"I'm fine. More than fine. Great. I have met someone, and I like him very much," Maria said to her mother on the phone, barely able to contain her excitement.

"Well, tell me about him ... what does he do?"

Maria could hear the judgement in her mother's voice. And as she noticed this, she felt her enthusiasm and energy fading away.

"I ... I don't really know. I just know he's nice. His name is Mischa. I'll tell you soon, I'll write it all in a letter. It will be easier."

"Isn't that a Russian name? Is he Russian?"

"No, he's English."

"Sounds strange. Remember what happened last time you met someone nice. You need to know more about him."

Changing the subject, Maria asked how her father and Karl were, then ended the conversation saying she would write soon. She sat staring at the wall in her small apartment for several minutes. Even in that brief call all the memories of the world she had left behind her came flooding back. Her mother's reluctance to accept her new life. How could these worlds ever fit together?

She couldn't even begin to imagine how her parents would react to someone like Mischa or what they would think of him. And equally she dared not think of what Mischa would think of her parents and the provincialism of the island. The more she reflected, the more nervous and worried she could feel herself becoming. for the inevitable moment when these two worlds would finally meet.

Mischa had not yet asked her to marry him, but she was convinced he would very soon. They were spending the nights at each other's apartments regularly now and she had never felt so at ease, not even with Paulus, as she did with Mischa.

The first time together had been both beautiful and nerve-wracking. They had spent the day, hand in hand, hiking on one of Hong Kong's outlying islands free of the noise and congestion of the city centre. The warm sunshine late in the year with lower humidity was now much more pleasant. The gentle undulating paths across open hillsides offered unrestricted views of the blue water of the South China Sea as well as peaceful images of simple villages, farmland, rice paddies near a temple and occasional haphazardly dispersed graves built in the traditional Chinese semi-circular form to leverage the optimal view of water with the backing of a big hill behind it. The graves were laid according to the old belief in *feng shui*, a unique mix of "superstition and pragmatism", Mischa had called it.

At the end of the day, they returned to the city centre on one of the open-deck passenger ferries. With the balmy wind blowing through her long blond hair and caressing her face, Maria luxuriated in a feeling she believed must be close to the complete serenity she had heard a saffron-robed Buddhist monk describe recently at a talk Harald had invited her to attend. She recognised this was something that she'd never experienced before.

Mischa invited her to come back to his place for dinner and prepared what he confidently described as his personal *gazpacho* recipe. Afterwards they had eaten on the same roof-top terrace where they had first met. Maria could feel the intensity in the air.

Unexpectedly, Mischa stood and asked her to follow him to the spot where between the two buildings they could see the flashing red light he had pointed out to her before on the distant hill. Again, he stood behind her, but instead of directing her view to the light he turned her around to face him and then slowly lowered his head to kiss her lips. Maria felt powerless to resist and returned his kiss, holding his face gently between her hands.

"Would you like to stay the night?" Mischa had finally asked in what sounded to Maria like a strained, taut voice.

"I would like to very much."

Mischa offered her his hand.

"We can sleep under the stars," he said leading her to a corner of the roof-top she had not noticed before that was covered by a trellis structure with vines and foliage. Underneath there was what looked like a soft divan, but without sides where Maria could see Mischa had prepared sheets and covers to make a bed.

"I often sleep out here. I ignore the buildings and enjoy seeing the sky and stars."

She looked at him with eyes that she knew could not conceal her fear and began to cry.

"I'm sorry, I am really sorry," she said between sobs.

Mischa enveloped her in his arms. She felt the comfort of his body touching her back and arms, and felt herself immediately relaxing.

"I'm sorry. I thought you ..."

"I do, but it's just that ..."

She was terrified Mischa would misunderstand, or worse that his feelings would change, but she knew she couldn't avoid telling him about the surfer's assault in Hamburg.

When she'd finished Mischa said nothing for a few moments. Then

"Thank you for telling me."

"So you understand?"

"Of course, but it doesn't change how I feel about you."

She drew him to her and kissed him deeply. She felt him reach for the zip at the back of her dress and then the balmy air on her naked back. Her hands reached for his belt but found he had already opened it. Suddenly they were lying down, legs and arms entwined. Mischa was over her and her legs were spread wide, and she could hear his heavy breathing. But then she closed her eyes as an intensity of emotions she'd never felt before overwhelmed her. She felt her body tense and her back arched and then with a cry she fell back to the mattress.

Now Mischa and she spent all their free time together. She was happy and proud when he introduced her to his friends as his girlfriend. On the few times she still walked home from the office alone, up the steep streets and through the vegetable market, she no longer carried a bottle of alcohol with her. The old woman who always kept back fruit for her seemed to have noticed.

"Missee look good."

Maria had never felt happier. Whether she was at work or with Mischa on one of the outlying islands near Hong Kong, where they often spent the whole day hiking along hillside trails with dazzling ocean panoramas, or simply spending time together, Maria wished for nothing to change. But an inner voice told her this time was limited and would not last for ever.

One evening over dinner on Mischa's roof-top he was unusually silent. Maria was worried she had offended him in some way. Suddenly he reached across the table with a very serious look on his face and clasped one of her hands in his.

"I would like to marry you. I mean, I would like you to marry me," he had said, a bit flustered.

"I want to marry you, too," she said without hesitation.

In her mind she had played out all kinds of romantic scenarios. Perhaps on a secluded beach on one of the outlying islands with a candle-lit dinner, or as part of a mystery trip to a surprise destination in the region, or even on top of the Walled City buildings with aircraft roaring overhead. But she could see that Mischa had proposed to her authentically in a way that was very emotional for him.

The next morning the full force of his proposal suddenly hit her. She was going to marry a tall Englishman—perhaps not an aristocrat, but apart from that Stefanie's forecast had been accurate. She called her mother again—taking care to work out the time difference accurately to catch her at a more opportune moment.

"Mischa has asked me to marry him," Maria said proudly and barely able to get the words out to her mother on the telephone.

Her mother was quiet. "Who? The Russian?"

Maria's stomach tightened at the seemingly disparaging tone.

"Yes … no. He's English and works for a small German company here."

"But we've never met him. You can't agree to marry him without our knowing anything more about him."

"He's got a business trip to the headquarters of his firm in Hamburg in a few weeks or so. I'll come before then and we'll all get together."

"Can you wait until we meet him before you decide?"

"Oh … I've already agreed. I want to marry him."

There was silence on the other end. Maria wondered whether her mother was looking into the distance in the way she knew so well or was going to explode in anger.

"I see. So, what you're really telling me is that you're already engaged," she finally said in a matter-of-fact voice.

"Yes, … I suppose that is correct, that is what I am saying."

"Have you thought about a date?"

"We want to marry in three months," Maria continued, fearing that this suddenness would additionally displease her mother. But she was wrong. Her mother seemed to have changed tack and welcomed the idea.

"That doesn't give me much time. Of course, you'll get married here on the island in the church," she said with a tone of finality. Maria realized she and Mischa had not yet even considered that question. They had toyed with the idea of marrying in Hong Kong, since that was where they'd met, and restricting the wedding to family and close friends.

"We'll have to check if the church is available … and the pastor. We'll need to book Weissenberg for the reception and dinner. They're the only hotel on the island with a ballroom big enough and their kitchen is probably good enough too if we push them hard. A lot of people will come out on the streets just to watch the event. This will be the wedding of the year! I'll speak to one of our suppliers about the dress and …"

Maria wanted to say that she and Mischa needed to discuss all of these plans first, but something held her back. Perhaps she did not want to risk derailing her mother's positive enthusiasm. If her mother was preoccupied with the arrangements, then maybe she would accept Mischa when she met him and not challenge Maria's choice of husband. In any case, if she was honest, she wasn't sure she'd want or even be able to organize a wedding on her own.

As her mother continued talking on the phone with an unstoppable stream of organizational details and complexities, Maria found her eyes wandering to the narrow sliver of the blue harbour that she could see from her bedroom window. She was happy and proud that she was going to be a married woman, and she could sense her mother's satisfaction, even though Johanna knew nothing about her future husband. But she could not ignore a dull feeling of foreboding in the pit of her stomach.

When she saw Mischa later that evening for dinner, she was short-tempered and curt.

"What's wrong? You seem so annoyed and angry."

"I spoke to my mother today and she is helping organize our wedding on the island. She'll check with the church and reserve the location for the reception."

"Shouldn't we be discussing this first before your mother makes the decisions?"

"A wedding doesn't happen by itself, you know. It's fine for you to say you want to get married, but I don't see you doing much for all the arrangements. We're lucky my mother is doing it all for us."

"I am happy to help, but it seems like your mother has taken over."

She could sense he was angry from his harder voice and how the softness of his features and eyes disappeared and were replaced by an unnatural firmness that made him much less approachable. She also knew he was right, but she was desperate not to lose her mother's support. The last thing she wanted now was a difficult conversation with her mother.

"I don't think you realize how important this wedding is. It's going to be a major social event on the island. Some of the people attending are really important for my family."

Maria had raised her voice and was almost shouting. It was the first time they had disagreed with each other.

"Is that you speaking or is it your mother?"

Maria remained silent. If she was honest, she wasn't sure.

"Well, it's going to make you anxious, maybe we shouldn't get married like this."

"What do you mean?"

Mischa stood up from the table on the rooftop and walked wordlessly to the staircase down to his apartment. Maria felt an intense physical pain enveloping her whole being. She was terrified by the sudden distance between them. But even worse was the fear that she had ruined everything.

As she looked at the hydra eye windows staring down from all around and above her, she imagined behind every eye an observer watching and breathing to themselves 'How could you do that? How could you be so foolish?'

Maria made her way downstairs. She found him sitting on the couch aimlessly leafing through the day's newspaper.

"What did you mean when you said we shouldn't get married like this?"

"I meant that if the wedding is more of a social event for your family than something we've chosen for ourselves, maybe we should think of a different kind of wedding."

Maria breathed an inward sigh of relief.

She sat down and hugged him, her cheek resting alongside his.

"Then you still want to marry me?"

"Of course."

"I'm sorry. I'm just so nervous about it all and about my mother. As long as we're happy nothing else matters."

"I'm very happy."

Chapter 15

Several weeks later Maria stood on the platform of the island railway station, excited that Mischa was arriving shortly, but anxious at the prospect of presenting him to her parents and the island society.

In the few days since her return many had stopped her in the street or in the weekly market in the town square and were eager to hear about her life in Far East. They seemed to know so much about her travels and the upcoming wedding that Maria realised she had underestimated how much her mother must have replaced her misgivings about a son-in-law she knew little about with pride at the impending social highlight.

As the train pulled in nosily, Maria scanned the carriage windows hoping to catch a glimpse of Mischa, perhaps already standing ready to leap off and envelop her in his arms. But she couldn't see him anywhere. She felt her heart beating furiously and became increasingly nervous that something must have happened. Perhaps he had changed his mind? Then, she saw his tall figure as he stepped down from the last carriage at the far end of the platform. Immediately all her fears disappeared and, restraining the urge to run, she walked towards him. Secretly she hoped he would rush towards her, unveiling a bouquet of roses from behind his back, to sweep her off her feet and swing her round like she had seen in movies.

Instead, Mischa came towards her at a steady, unchanging pace. However, once they had embraced wordlessly for several minutes on the platform Maria's doubts disappeared, and she walked proudly arm in arm to the car, past a few local people staring at them.

As they entered her parents' home, Johanna came out from the living room to greet them.

"It is a pleasure to meet you, Mrs. König," Mischa said in his excellent German.

"Why don't we just go straight to first names?" her mother said, extending her hand to Mischa. "I'm Johanna and this is Peter, my husband."

Mischa smiled and shook her father's hand.

"Shall we?" her mother said, ushering them into the living room.

Once they were sitting in her parent's expansive living room, Maria could see at once that Mischa was nervous. Beneath the superficial politeness and social conversation, she knew he sensed her parents assessing him. His usually sonorous voice seemed a little higher pitched and tight as he answered their many questions, hoping to make a good impression.

Over lunch Johanna revelled in her role as future mother-in-law, insisting on second and third helpings of the *Königsberger Klopse* meat balls, and cajoling a reluctant Mischa to try the turnips that had come directly from her own garden.

When her father, who had chosen one of his favourite ties for the occasion, enthusiastically and boisterously described their trip to Hong Kong to visit Maria and the miraculous 24-hour tailoring of shirts and suits, Maria felt he was indirectly commenting on Mischa's less than fashionable clothes. But Mischa either didn't notice or didn't care.

Eventually, Johanna raised the topic Maria had half hoped they could avoid, at least for their first meeting.

"Have you finalized your guest list yet?" her mother asked looking not at Maria but at Mischa. Maria could see that Mischa was taken aback by her directness.

"Actually, we were thinking perhaps it would be a good idea to have a smaller wedding just for close friends here on the island and then another celebration in Hong Kong for all our friends there," Mischa said.

In the silence that followed Maria could see the disaster looming even before she looked at her mother's face.

"We gave that idea up long ago," she said quickly looking at him and willing him to understand.

"I'm afraid that is impossible," Johanna said firmly, reaching for the empty plates to take them out to the kitchen. "This is the wedding of the König daughter … do you know what that means?"

"Mother …"

"Of course, I understand," Mischa said. "It was just an idea we had."

"I hope so," her mother said curtly, as she went into the kitchen.

"When life's storms rage, direct your gaze towards the heavens," her father interceded to fill the sudden silence.

When her mother returned, she began to lay out all the plans and arrangements she had prepared for the wedding celebrations. Mischa said little except to occasionally acknowledge some detail. After dessert, Maria suggested she and Mischa should leave to explore the island.

"Excellent idea," her father said. "It's the eighth continent, you know."

Mischa looked confused by that comment but didn't say anything.

As they walked back into the town, Mischa silent beside her, all her childhood worries about disappointing her parents, fears she had almost forgotten in her life away from the island, welled up inside her. But now she had an additional anxiety. Would Mischa continue to accept and love her after he had met her parents?

"Your mother is quite formidable," Mischa said.

"Yes."

"Your father's comment about the storms was quite apt. Although I didn't quite understand his remark about the island ..."

Maria squeezed his hand. "As far as I can remember he has always made up these proverb-like phrases. He really loves this island. It's the centre of his world."

Mischa stayed a few days before returning to Hong Kong. He would only be away for two weeks before returning for the wedding. Maria had reached agreement with Harald to take a longer break.

Chapter 16

During the week before the wedding, when Mischa had returned, Johanna became increasingly tense as she tried to control all the final logistics. In traditional style, the wedding was planned to extend over three days. Guests were already arriving on the island and the first pre-nuptial celebrations had already started with a string of dinners and parties across the town. The local newspaper had sent a journalist to her parents' home. He had interviewed both Mischa and her and taken a photo for an article gushing in island pride at an event that was attracting so many international visitors.

When the article appeared on an inside page of the paper, her mother was furious. "Should have been on the front page. Don't they realise who pays most of their advertising?"

For several days, Maria had felt she was in a trance with things happening over which she had no real control or influence. Relatives appeared at her parents' front door and shook her and Mischa's hands and exchanged pleasantries. Gifts, measured by how much they must have cost, were delivered in an unending stream at the front door. Johanna made sure to keep a close record of who had sent what. The seating plans for the afternoon coffee immediately following the church ceremony and then for the evening wedding reception and dinner had been reviewed almost hourly, it seemed to Maria. Her mother had personally beautifully and touchingly decorated the pews in the church with white tulips, which she knew was her daughter's favourite flower. Maria knew she could never have mastered all these arrangements and details on her own.

Mischa's parents arrived a few days ahead of the wedding. Gertude invited them to lunch. While Maria had worried about the gap between Mischa and her parents, she knew the gulf between the two sets of parents would be almost unbridgeable. Maria had met Mischa's parents frequently at their family home in Hong Kong. His father was an academic and his mother a former stage actress. They lived in a rambling, messy, almost tatty, book-filled house that was so different from the expensively polished home of Maria's parents. Maria had very quickly sensed in Mischa's father a serenity that Mischa for all his quiet calm did not possess. And when his father had looked across the dinner table at her, she had been surprised how his eyes seemed even more capable of deciphering her inner world than hers could his.

When the two sets of parents met, they all tried valiantly to make the occasion both enjoyable and meaningful. Her parents were keen to highlight their business and material achievements, while his parents, who both spoke German well, wanted to explore what was beneath the surface.

"We built the department stores out of nothing really—just a small corner shop when we started," her father explained proudly. "And now we have a chain of locations across the resort towns of the northern region."

"And how do you feel about all these new stores. Don't you miss the atmosphere of the old corner shop where you started?" Mischa's mother asked.

"In the modern world, progress marches on," her father replied.

"How did the people on the island recover from the turmoil after the War," Mischa's father intervened, trying to give the conversation new direction.

"That's all in the past and everyone has forgotten it," her mother interjected. "Now we all just focus on building new businesses and seizing opportunities for the future."

"Exactly!" Peter chimed in. "Standing still is moving backwards, so we always make sure we are in top gear and moving faster than the rest!"

"I see," Mischa's father said quietly.

Maria and Mischa had both remained completely silent during the lunch and avoided looking at each other. She was sure he felt as uncomfortable as she did. As it ended with mutual expressions of friendship and joy at the celebrations of the coming days, she had stolen a glance at Mischa and been rewarded with a complicit grimace that she knew reflected what they were both feeling.

She noticed how Mischa became increasingly withdrawn in the days before the wedding as the momentous scale of the event built up. Perhaps he was disturbed by how powerless he was feeling as he realized he was just a passive participant. Living in her parent's home, in the separate rooms her parents insisted on, they seemed unable to recreate the simple and relaxed intimacy they had found in Hong Kong. Mischa had met both Peter and Johanna a number of times, and they seemed to have found a reasonably natural informality. But Maria could not help noticing that Mischa was quieter and more passive than his usual self whenever he was with her parents. It was almost as if he was never engaging fully in the conversation or committing to the relationship with his future parents-in-law.

"He seems very quiet, not very energetic, almost passive," her mother had said to her one morning in the kitchen as they were clearing away the breakfast dishes together. Maria said nothing to that and managed to largely ignore it. After Mischa had joined her father on one of his regular evening strolls through the fallow wheat fields to the small fishing harbour and back, her father took her aside.

"He's very nice, but he's never going to make a businessman," he said definitively.

Maria felt her heart sink. She knew how much her parents respected and admired self-employed, stand-alone entrepreneurs. Mischa would never reach this pinnacle of respect in his eyes.

That evening, when she and Mischa were alone in the living room, "How was your walk with my father?" she asked.

"He certainly loves this island and the impact he has had on it. He talks of nothing but business."

"Yes, he's proud of his success. Would you ever be interested in starting your own business?"

"That's what your father asked me. I told him I am happy with what I do. He seemed a bit surprised at my answer. What did he tell you about our walk?"

"He said he likes you a lot, but he just doesn't think you are an entrepreneur … You're too cautious."

In truth, she had made the last bit up. Peter had not said anything about caution. But if she compared her father's expansive, beaming gregariousness bestowing munificence on all around him with the withdrawn quietness of Mischa, it did feel as if he didn't fit the mould. She could imagine people on the island saying: 'Very pleasant new son-in-law the Königs have got themselves there. But nothing like the father, of course.'

She felt his disappointment. 'Why can't I keep my mouth shut?', she thought to herself as silence again fell between them. In Hong Kong, they'd never found it difficult to talk. Usually, she was describing her latest experiences in colourful wonder and amazement and Mischa would then analyse in a way that would fascinate her until she lost his train of thought and then simply bathed in his soothing and deep tone of voice. But here more and more they sat in silence. It felt almost as if he was exhausted and lacked the enthusiasm that used to fill his eyes and which she had found so energizing when she first met him. She'd be happy when it was all over and they could return to Hong Kong.

On the morning of the ceremony, Karl drove her to the church. He had married the year before and so fell naturally into the role of the experienced veteran.

"Feeling tense?" he asked. She settled into the back seat of his Mercedes almost completely enveloped by her voluminous dress.

"More exhausted, I guess."

"I know. I was nervous. But it all goes away once you are sitting in front of the altar."

Peter helped her out of the car when they arrived. They entered through the heavy oak doors of the town church that Maria knew so well from her childhood. She felt her throat constrict so tightly she feared she might have difficulty breathing.

Every seat in the church was filled and Maria felt as if she was entering a dark cavern consisting of nothing but staring faces. She kept her gaze firmly focussed on the twelfth century grey stone blocks and engraved tombstones on the floor.

Perhaps she was making a huge mistake, she thought. Mischa had seemed so different over the last few days here on the island compared with when they had spent time together in Hong Kong. Were her parents right? Were the differences too great? Would it have been better to marry a local businessman instead?

The emotions, questions and doubts seemed to be coming from all corners of her mind faster than she could bat them away with logic and reason.

When they reached the nave and front pews and Peter stood back, she raised her head to see Mischa, looking elegant in the coat and tails that he had initially resisted and then consented to rent for the occasion.

She looked at her parents in the front aisle. Peter' eyes were alive, and she could see he was already enjoying the occasion. Her mother's face, however, was ashen and stony. And as their eyes connected briefly, she felt a cold shudder pass through her body. Despite all the work she had put into the preparations, she seemed resigned and disappointed. Her eyes appeared flat, almost hard, and preoccupied. Maria quickly looked away and tried to focus on the black-robed priest standing in front of the altar.

But try as she might to listen to the words of the kindly cleric, she couldn't focus on what he was saying. The image of her mother's face and gaze would not leave her, and it was as much as she could do not to rise from the chair and rush from the church. Even as she imagined herself tearing down the aisle, the long white train of her dress catching and ripping on the corners of pews, it was her mother's furious voice, accusing her of humiliating the family, that kept her firmly rooted to her seat.

With the sermon and ritual ceremonies finally ended, they stood and, facing each other, exchanged vows and wedding rings. The priest invited Mischa to kiss the bride. As he leant forward, Maria involuntarily took a half-step back, and Mischa, unnerved, looked at her with a half-questioning expression and then took her hand and turned towards the congregation to begin down the aisle. She felt her face turn bright red as they started to walk towards the doors.

Despite the applause that now spontaneously sprang up, she could not look to her left or right to thank the guests with a smile and concentrated instead on the bright sunshine that she could see through the open entrance and the escape it afforded.

On the receiving line outside, the seemingly unending stream of friends, family and other guests offering congratulations helped her bury some of the doubts she'd felt during the ceremony. She was too preoccupied with the enormity of the step she had just taken with Mischa, to feel that she was completely present. She saw the faces around her and heard the excited voices, including her own, as she responded and smiled, but at the same time she felt as if she was observing herself from outside her own body, completely separated from actual events.

Johanna had ensured that the ballroom of the island's largest hotel had been transformed into a mesmerizing candle-lit dream-world of bright, shining silver cutlery and candelabra. Sparkling reflections of light from the wide selection of crystal glasses dazzled, while live music sounded from a small orchestra on the improvised stage. As they were waiting outside the ballroom to greet the guests, Maria gave her mother's hand a squeeze and whispered her thanks. But Johanna seemed too preoccupied with the arrangements and welcoming the guests to notice.

Her father gave a witty, homily-filled opening speech with metaphors of ships going to sea but returning to safe harbours when they needed to. Maria hadn't listened closely but could see his words had been well-received by the hundreds of guests as they all clapped loudly. He sat down heavily in his chair further down the head table and looked across at her and smiled with a mixture of hopefulness and melancholy. Maria felt her tears brimming and composed the best look of warm gratitude she could muster.

Mischa's father now started to address the room and initially Maria paid little attention to his words. But suddenly she sensed a change in the room's atmosphere, almost a collective intake of breath.

Gradually Maria began to pick up the train of his words and her stomach began to tighten. He seemed to have mentioned the War and, if she had understood correctly, something about the shifting sands of history, which to her seemed inappropriately academic and intellectual for this kind of event and audience.

"Is it not remarkable that we can stand here today," he continued in a firm clear voice, "both Jew and German, to celebrate a wedding where only a few years ago our parents were opposing, persecuting and liquidating each other?"

Without moving her head, Maria looked out of the corner of her eyes to her parents who were sitting further down on the one side of the head-table that faced all the guests. Johanna was sitting bolt upright and staring unblinkingly ahead. Peter was looking into his lap.

"From the very island where the architect of extermination originated, it is only fitting that a wedding that represents the triumph over this evil should be celebrated."

Maria's thoughts flashed immediately to the thatched villa on the southern beach of the island where the tired lady had served her hot chocolate and cake ahead of the other dark-eyed children. But even without looking around the ballroom, she knew the topic that no one on the island talked about, but everyone knew about, was now at the centre of everyone's minds.

She recalled her flippant conversation with Mischa about his religion when they had first met on the boat. It played no part in their lives. If anything, it was simply another thread in the rich tapestry of his life. Now, as she heard the unnatural quiet in the ballroom, she realised she had never mentioned Mischa's religion to her parents.

Mischa seemed as surprised by his father's words as she was. Was the whole wedding on which her mother had worked so meticulously to create the perfect and most memorable social event of the year, if not in the island's living memory—was it now ruined? Would she be blamed for disappointing her family?

Mischa's father had ended his speech rather well with some self-deprecating jokes that had relieved the tension and now the usual healthy bubble of lively conversation mixed with the clink of cutlery and glassware against the backdrop of live music filled the high-ceilinged room. She tried to enjoy the rest of the evening but could not. The ceremonial first waltz in a circle surrounded by all the guests, the tossing of the bride's flower bouquet, and late in the evening a quiet moment when Mischa had looked deeply into her eyes, perhaps trying to repair the damage of the missed first kiss in the church ceremony, all had passed Maria by as if she was in a daze, as she wrestled with the question what her parents would say when it was all over.

Mischa and Maria had already agreed, rather unromantically, to spend their wedding night at her parent's home because leaving for their honeymoon the following day. He collapsed onto the bed, exhausted from the celebration, and fell fast asleep, but Maria didn't sleep at all.

The next morning, as she entered the kitchen, her mother confronted her.

"You never told me he was Jewish."

"I'm sorry. Why does it matter? For Mischa it's irrelevant. It's only because his mother was Jewish that he is. It doesn't mean anything to us."

"We should have known. The priest should have been told. We should have let our friends know. It is all terribly embarrassing for our family. This is the only thing everyone will be talking about today, not to mention his father's speech."

"I'm sure that's not true. It was such a wonderful day. The church was beautifully decorated, and the dinner was a dream. You did such a fantastic job."

She knew her words rang hollow with her mother and could already hear the chatter on the market square or among the staff of the department store. There would be no other topic of discussion. Mischa's father had broken all conventions and practices on the island. The normal, unencumbered, fixed format and flow for social events on the island had been disrupted.

"What would my father have thought if he'd still been alive?" Johanna muttered under her breath.

Her mother rarely mentioned her father, who had died several years before Maria had entered boarding school. It indicated how upset her mother was, staring out of the window into the gloomy dark winter morning, completely lost in her thoughts. Maria quietly let herself out of the kitchen, not knowing what else to say.

Chapter 17

As planned, immediately after the last wedding guest had left the island, Maria and Mischa also departed. Maria had left all the honeymoon arrangements to Mischa and was not entirely sure exactly where they would spend the next two weeks. It turned out to be on an exotic island somewhere in Southeast Asia at a secluded luxurious resort. Almost as soon as they landed, she was relieved to see how quickly Mischa returned to his usual self. His energy and enthusiasm resurfaced, as did his previous boyish encouragement to explore the small coastal villages near the hotel, to visit an underwater grotto with dolphins, to climb an extinct volcano. His rejuvenated intensity and fervour to enjoy life became infectious. This was the Mischa whose deep voice and sensitive gaze she could never stop luxuriating in, the man who had fascinated her and accepted her without judgement, the man with whom she had fallen in love. With him, she felt freer than she had every believed possible.

Back in Hong Kong, they began their new life together. They found a new home. Mischa's friends became her friends as well. Maria discovered a self-confidence she had not known before, fully engaged in conversations, asking questions and sharing her opinion on a wide range of topics.

Having missed their first they decided to celebrate their second wedding anniversary with a formal dinner party. Maria spent hours setting and decorating a beautiful table, not dissimilar from the style her mother would have approved of.

"We seem to be dining with royalty now," Harald had said with a half laugh, as he stood in awe of the white tablecloth, crystal glass and brightly polished silver.

"Always thought that that was where I belonged," Mischa had responded with a smile.

As Marie surveyed her efforts, her friend Stefanie's prophecy she would marry an English aristocrat came into her mind. Perhaps she had not been so far off the mark, after all. She certainly felt her life was now privileged.

"Hong Kong has worked out well for you well. Sink or swim, I told you when you got here and now you are swimming magnificently," Harald said, lifting his glass to her.

Maria felt a surge of pride. Her courage to leave the island and come to Hong Kong really had liberated her into a world free of judgement where she could develop and grow in whatever direction she wished. For a moment she felt almost light-headed as if floating on her own in the room above the table of animated guests with the sounds of conversation and cutlery on dishes and the soothing music. Within her she felt a strength, a power to choose as she wished. No obligations, demands, or expectations from others. No one whom she must please or avoid upsetting. Her life was her own to explore a future full of promise and exciting options.

“Thank you. Yes, I'm happy here,” Maria responded, shaking herself free of her thoughts.

“And your new apartment is wonderful, just right for you and Mischa. But you don't have much room here for children.”

Harald reminded Maria of something she had sub-consciously been trying to forget. She and Mischa had first talked about having children on a hike they had taken one day through villages and bright green rice paddy fields away from the bustle of urban Hong Kong before they were married. Mischa had told her how he had spent months in hospital as a child with an obscure tropical disease and nearly died. The side effects of the treatment meant he could almost certainly not father children.

Not wanting anything to disturb her happiness, Maria had brushed the issue aside and tried to put it out of her mind.

“We'll cross that bridge when we get to it,” Maria said to Harald.

In truth Mischa's revelation on the hike had disturbed her and she had made an appointment with a specialist for tropical diseases in Hong Kong soon after.

“Do you know the name of the disease?” the Chinese doctor had asked with a scathing and dismissive look, as she faced him across his desk in the small room barely large enough for the two of them. Maria was distracted by a nurse hovering at the side in front of a glass-fronted medicine cabinet full of different coloured and sized bottles of capsules and tablets.

"I don't know the name, but I do know my fiancé was sick for a long time as a child and was told the disease would prevent him from fathering children."

"I can't really tell you if I can't see the patient or know what disease he suffered. There are many such diseases." Ask your boyfriend to make an appointment," the doctor had said firmly and then continued under his breath in Chinese to the nurse who had smiled superciliously and avoided Maria's eyes.

"My fiancée does not know I am here."

"Well, I can't help you without more information. Some tropical viruses can have that effect on some individuals."

"Could he get sick again?"

"If he hasn't had any symptoms after all these years, it is unlikely it will reoccur."

"I see. Thank you."

Frustrated at her own failure to gather more information, she had left.

Maria had only mentioned this to her parents on the phone about a year after the wedding.

"It's been over a year now, Maria. Where are our grandchildren?"

"I'm not sure we'll have children."

Her mother was silent for a minute. "What do you mean? That's the reason why people get married."

"Mischa was very sick as a child with a rare tropical disease, which may have left him unable to father children."

"And you still agreed to marry him?" her mother said.

"My choice of husband did not depend on whether we can have children."

"Any children you have will inherit a lot of wealth and property once you have inherited it from us. So, if you are not going to have children, we need to know that."

Maria hated discussing death, wills and inheritances, especially since it meant having her marriage reduced to some legal and financial transaction. She felt her eyes smarting, and a tear start to trickle down her cheek. She was unable to continue. She could hear her parents talking in the background.

"This is quite a sacrifice you are making," her father said, having taken the receiver.

"I don't see it that way."

"Well, who knows. Maybe we'll be surprised. Remember, whoever is happy can make others happy. Whoever makes others happy changes his own fortune."

"Maybe we will be."

She hung up and they had never spoken about it again.

The few times Maria and Mischa had talked about children, he had always seemed very clear that he wanted them and nonchalant about where they would come from.

After the guests had left Maria took Mischa's hand and moved to the small balcony where they often enjoyed the balmy panoramic view across the bright glowing lights. They never tired of watching the busy slow-motion exertions of the myriad boats and ships and other vessels in the narrow strip of harbour water between the island and the mainland. From this perspective the panorama always seemed to her alive with the constant hum of the city, like a bubbling cauldron, an unstoppable force that never ceased even at night.

"They should organize things better so that the city switches off some of the time," Maria said. "It's crazy to have lights and people and boats on and active all the time."

"It's what I like about the city," Mischa replied. "Always exciting, stimulating. I thought that was exactly what you liked about it."

"People never get any rest here. It can be exhausting."

"Only if you let it get to you."

"You're just used to it because you grew up here."

"You mean you would like it to be as quiet as your provincial little island."

"At least you can find peace and quiet there."

"I really don't know why you're being so difficult tonight. Didn't you enjoy the evening?"

"It's not about the evening."

"Well, what is it about then?"

Maria took a deep breath.

"Maybe it's about us … or about our children, or the possibility of us having children. It's fine to celebrate our anniversary but everyone is wondering why we don't have children. You don't see to want to talk about that."

"I have told you I am fine with having children."

"Yes, but how? It doesn't look like I'll be getting pregnant anytime soon."

“We could begin IVF any time you want or explore adoption. There are so many options …”

“What if neither is possible. You always assume there's a solution. Suppose there isn't for us.”

She had never spoken to Mischa like this before, challenging him on something so fundamental in their lives. She could tell that he was shocked and unnerved.

“Where is all this coming from?”

“It's always been there, but you aren't doing anything about it. You're just letting the question pass by. It's not just about us. It's about the future. We need to take it seriously not just avoid the issue forever.”

“Maria, just because we haven't spoken about it lately, doesn't mean I'm avoiding the issue. Maybe if you'd brought it up …”

“How dare you blame me!” she exclaimed. “I'm not the one with …”

Fearing she might say something hurtful she got down from the bar stool and walked into their bedroom. She dumped his duvet cover and pillow outside the bedroom door and then closed and locked it. She had never fought with Mischa before, and it was upsetting.

She slept fitfully. In the morning her anger had died and one part of her wanted to crawl into the bed she assumed Mischa had made on the couch, but something held her back. After she had washed and dressed and opened the door, she found Mischa outside drinking a cup of coffee at the dining room table.

“Coffee's in the pot,” he said, not looking at her.

She could hear the distance in his voice.

"Thank you."

For several days a strange formality seemed to guide their behaviour, almost as if they were both taking extra care not to provoke the other. They lived like two room-mates, respecting each other's space and time and avoiding anything that could be interpreted as unfair or impolite. Maria was terrified that she had triggered some irreversible change in their relationship, but she felt powerless to change it. What she had said seemed so distant now, and she wasn't even sure she knew exactly what she'd hoped to achieve.

One morning, when she got up, she found a note from Mischa on the table, asking her to meet him that evening at a bar they'd often gone to when they first met. She didn't know what to expect. All day in the office, she couldn't help imagining countless relationship-ending scenarios.

She arrived at the bar first and waited anxiously.

At last Mischa arrived and kissed her on the cheek. Something had changed.

"You were right, we need to do something about starting a family. I wasn't doing anything to help. So, now I have."

"What do you mean?"

"I've been to see a few IVF clinics and found one that has a very high success rate. I can make an appointment for us if you like."

Maria was flabbergasted. She'd been expecting and prepared for a demand for an apology, or some kind of explanation, or even a reprimand.

"But what about …"

"At the clinic, I discussed it with the doctors there. Given my history, we would need to involve donors. I hope that's okay with you?"

She leant over the table, took his face in her hands and kissed him on the lips.

"Thank you. I love you." she whispered. Then said it again, "Thank you."

Mischa smiled and then reached for the menu.

Chapter 18

Maria stared again at the small card calendar, with its different pictures of infants and children for every month, which she'd hung next to the mirror in their bathroom. Mischa had given her the calendar when she started the first IVF treatment, saying the images might inspire her but increasingly the calendar seemed to have become a cruel reminder to her of how many times she had failed to become pregnant. But still she felt a flicker of hope. She was three days overdue for her period, three and a half to be precise. Maybe this time, she thought.

Her parents had been overjoyed she told them that she and Mischa were trying to conceive with IVF. They supported her throughout the process and called frequently to check on her status. After each of the past disappointments, her mother had always encouraged Maria not to lose hope and to make another attempt.

A July conception would mean an April birth. Try as she might, she couldn't restrain her galloping imagination. She'd been to the familiar white room in the clinic exactly four weeks ago. The procedure had become almost routine, and she no longer asked Mischa to join her as she had done for the first couple of attempts. The overweight, grey-haired doctor with the soft voice and melancholy, drooping eyes had been kindly and positive as always.

“Everything looks perfect. The timing is just right. The chances are really quite good, we just need a bit of luck," he had said to Maria as she lay resting after the insertion and laid his hand lightly on her arm.

"Rest as much as possible. No exertions or sudden movements. The best would be if you stayed in bed for the next few days. That way we have the best chance of not dislodging the egg," the doctor told her.

Her visits to the IVF clinic and doctor seemed to have taken over their lives. Every second month, with a three-month pause after three treatment rounds to recover from the heavy hormones that Maria was injected with, they had lived a cycle of heady optimism and hope followed by crushing disappointment when, usually coming out from the bathroom, she'd given a brief shake of her head signalling another failure. On the first few occasions Maria had burst into tears. Mischa looked crushed but had tried to console her that it wasn't her fault.

But increasingly she felt it was. She was the one who had to perform, and she was failing. She knew she had disappointed her parents in so many ways and here was the opportunity to make up for all of that. When she pictured herself telling her mother the treatment had worked and she was pregnant now, she imagined Johanna's stern face creasing into the warmest of smiles as she enveloped Maria in a tight embrace. It would feel like when her father took her in his arms, natural, easy and above all unconditional. Maria sometimes missed her father's positivity, his energizing conviction that things would work out fine in the end, that believing in success put you in a mindset better suited to achieving it. Mischa, for all his love and support, was more likely to see the challenges before the opportunities.

Although she had truly never felt closer to anyone in her life than Mischa, she nevertheless sometimes felt very alone. Sometimes she longed for him simply to hold her as she cried after another unsuccessful attempt instead of analysing and explaining why it would be wrong to give up and how they could optimize their chances on the next attempt. She wasn't sure whether she was more upset because he was hiding his real feelings behind a wall of logical, rational structure, or because he didn't feel her whirlpool of melancholy and sentiment. that was leaving her exhausted and unable to think clearly. Occasionally she wondered whether Mischa felt any of the same feelings that she did, such was his apparent indifference compared with her daily roller coaster of emotions.

The strain was impacting their lives. They both seemed to welcome the flimsiest of excuses to avoid meeting friends with children and, even worse, their jocular accounts of unplanned pregnancies. At night now they would only sleep next to each other lightly holding the other's hand as anything more than that reminded them both too much of what they were trying to achieve.

As she stared into the mirror, she felt the trickle on the inside of her right leg. She looked down and saw red spots on the white bathroom mat.

"No!" she screamed, then began sobbing desperately. She had to hold onto the sides of the wash basin to stop herself from collapsing to the floor. Her shoulders were heaving, and tears ran down her cheeks in a torrent. Slowly she let herself sink to the floor and curl up into a foetal position as her body shook uncontrollably.

She had no idea how long she lay there. Her tears had dried. She stood up, cleaned herself, put on a bath robe and made her way to the balcony. She looked out at the activity below her on the streets and in the harbour. It all seemed so inconsequential and yet also so brutally impartial, as if everyone out there was saying "Stop making a fuss, just get on with life."

She must have fallen asleep in the warm sun on one of the balcony chairs. It was several hours later that Mischa woke her gently touching her shoulder.

"What happened? Didn't you go to work today," he asked and, suddenly understanding, his face fell. "It didn't ..."

Maria nodded and tears rolled down her cheeks. "I'm sorry."

"Don't worry. We'll keep trying," he said with a tone of forced optimism.

"No, I have tried enough. I can't take any more of this."

"Are you sure ... the doctor said the chances are good. Maybe next time ..."

"No ... I CAN'T ANYMORE," Maria screamed. She bent forward, her face was on her knees, and she covered her head with her arms. "I can't do this anymore ... why don't you understand?"

Mischa had never seen her so distraught. He tried to stroke her shoulder, but she shrugged his hand off.

He sat down on the other balcony chair, looking out at the late afternoon sun setting blood red behind a hill covered in green vegetation.

“Maybe you're right,” he said gently. “It's all too much.”

Maria immediately felt an enormous sense of relief, as if a weight had been lifted from her shoulders. Anything not to have to face that roller coaster of fragile hopes followed by feelings of desolation and inadequacy anymore. But as Mischa spoke, she detected disappointment and wistful regret in his voice.

Chapter 19

Several months had passed and almost by silent agreement, they no longer talked about the IVF treatments. It was as if they had simply closed that chapter in their lives. Maria felt relieved. They took long hikes in the hills of Hong Kong where it was possible to walk all day without meeting another person.

But Mischa seemed distant. He had retreated into a place of solitude where he was not willing to let anyone enter. Although with others he managed to maintain an air of polite friendliness, Maria found it increasingly hard to talk to him as they had before. It was as if he had raised a barrier, or more than that, almost gone into a separate room, and when they spoke it felt more like a meeting at the threshold of a half-open door. Maria tried to recreate the closeness they had felt when they had first met, but he seemed out of reach.

Although he would participate in the nature walks, or late-night cinema shows, or social meetings with friends, and would laugh and look as if he was enjoying himself, Maria knew he was only partially there. He could just about pull himself together to behave close to normally when with others, but the moment they were alone, he retreated into himself, shutting her out.

Once she had tried to surprise him with a midnight picnic on one of the beaches. She had prepared a cold meal of salads and red wine and, equipped with folding beach chairs and table, had led him down to the remote beach from the road where they had parked the car. Mischa had seemed excited at the mystery and the change of routine, but as soon as they had finished eating, their conversation became desultory. Finally, they had simply sat silently next to each other listening to the lapping of the waves against the shore.

On another day, she suggested they visit the Walled City again to experience the exhilarating final approach of the aircraft landing at the airport.

"I am too tired today. Anyway, it's so dirty there ... maybe another time," he said, turning back to the magazine he was leafing through.

More and more Maria found herself wondering whether this was what the collapse of a marriage felt like. She had no clue what was going on inside him. She wasn't sure whether Mischa blamed her for the failure of the IVF treatments, or for not persevering enough to meet the challenge head-on in the way he approached everything in his life. Did he find living with her but without children a second best? She couldn't bring herself to discuss it with him.

A couple of weeks after they decided to abandon the treatments, Maria had called her parents to tell them. They had said little, but been understanding. Peter had tried to lift her spirits with one of his favourite sayings.

"With the right attitude no peak is too steep."

But this time Maria had found it annoying rather than endearing.

One evening, about six months later, Mischa returned from his office and Maria sensed immediately something had changed. The energy and pace of his step as he entered their apartment, the expression on his face as he came towards her on the balcony and the excitement in his eyes were all things she hadn't seen in him for months.

"I've been offered a new assignment in Bombay, well Mumbai as it is known officially. We'd need to move there in a couple of months."

"Wonderful … exciting!" She spoke before she was conscious of the decision she'd taken. Then she realized this was the opportunity for them to make a fresh start.

"Congratulations. I'm ready to move."

"It's a fascinating country. You'll love it there."

She felt sure this development was no coincidence. For several weeks she'd been secretly visiting a small Chinese temple nestled into the side of a road near their apartment. On a day she felt particularly forlorn, she'd stepped over the ankle-high threshold, a guard against evil spirits, to enter the building.

Initially she wasn't sure whether she liked the interior of garishly coloured dragon and tiger sculptures. They surrounded what looked like a raised centrepiece of large and fearsome figures, clad in long, wide-sleeved robes, that she presumed were various deities. Above her, from the old wooden-beamed ceiling she could smell the acrid smoke of large coils of burning incense.

A young Chinese woman, dressed in formal business attire, was kneeling in front of the deities with closed eyes. She whispered a few words, then began shaking a painted cylindrical bamboo container vigorously with both her hands. The bamboo was filled with a large bunch of flat, brown bamboo sticks tipped in red at the top. Eventually one of the sticks fell out to the floor. The woman immediately paused and, picking up the stick, read a Chinese character painted on the red-tipped end. She stood, bowed to the figures behind the altar and then quietly left.

Now Maria began visiting the temple more often, attracted by the calm it offered. Although she didn't understand the Chinese characters on the pillars and walls, she found the atmosphere comforting. The more she studied the faces of the gods, the more she felt she detected some empathy or understanding for her situation. On her visit the day before Mischa had returned home with his news of the opportunity in India, an elderly bald man in a traditional black silk full-length Chinese gown, knelt down beside her.

"I have seen you come often to our temple," he said in perfect English.

"I find it very peaceful here."

"Yes, we come here to find help when life appears confusing to us, and the way forward is unclear." He smiled. "You must trust the wisdom of our gods and spirits. We understand our lives better if we listen to them. They can help us make the right choices."

"Why do people shake the bamboo sticks?" Maria asked.

"We use the sticks to give us guidance when we face a challenge or are unsure what decision to take. Are you facing a difficult challenge?"

"I am … that is, we, my husband and I, are," Maria said, feeling an impulsive trust in the man. "We would like to have children but cannot."

The man looked at her. "This is the right place for you."

They stood and he grasped her wrist with a grip unusually firm for someone of his age and led her to the long narrow table at the centre of the temple facing the deities. From the numerous cylindrical bamboo containers, he selected one and motioned to her to hold it with both hands while he guided her back several paces until she was standing in open space. He knelt on his knees again and, as he was still holding her wrist, pulled her down with him.

"You must reflect carefully what question you wish to ask for guidance on from the gods. Formulate your question very clearly in your mind. The gods will not be able to help if the question is too long, or too complicated. When you are ready, tilt the container forward and shake it while speaking the question."

The man paused and looked at her expectantly. She closed her eyes and tried to focus her mind. What was the question she wanted to ask? She suddenly found it difficult to encapsulate all the turmoil and emotions and thoughts of the last year into one simple question. Was it, why they couldn't have a child? Or was it, why she had failed to give them a child? Or should she be asking the bigger question of whether they should have children at all? Maybe the real question was how to achieve happiness and serenity in life despite all its challenges and disappointments? And as she followed this train of thought, Maria felt her mind begin to calm. This was not the first time she had been unhappy as she recalled her life on the island.

“Take as long as you need. I will be waiting when you are ready,” the elderly man whispered to her before quietly standing and disappearing through a small doorway.

As she closed her eyes, kneeling before the imposing figures in front of her, she suddenly had a moment of clarity. She and Mischa needed a change, they needed a new direction. They were stuck in a routine of melancholy they wouldn't be able to extricate themselves from on their own. She took a deep breath then whispered: What new direction should we take in our lives?

Then she grasped the bamboo container firmly between her hands, closed her eyes and, whispering the question to herself again and again, shook her arms vigorously both vertically and horizontally. She heard the sound of the bamboo sticks in the tube and, just as she thought she might have to alter the angle of the container, she heard one of the sticks bouncing on the grey pavestone floor. She opened her eyes and picked up the stick and looked at the red Chinese character painted on it.

Through the doorway the elderly man was sitting on a wooden stool in a small dark room behind the altar of the temple's gods. On three walls in the room, illuminated by dim bulbs at the top of each wall, Maria saw dozens of small rectangular sheets inscribed with Chinese characters hanging in neat rows and columns from hooks in the walls. She handed him the stick that had fallen out. He glanced at the character on it and then, turning to the wall, leafed through a number of sheets until he found the one he was looking for.

"Before I can interpret this for you, we must first check if the answer is genuine with the *jiao bei*."

He placed two smooth wooden blocks into Maria's hands. One side of each block was flat, the other curved.

"Drop the blocks on this table here. If one block lands on its *yin* side and the other on its *yang* side, then the answer is genuine. If both blocks fall on their flat side or both on their round sides then the gods are angry or laughing at you and you must ask a different question."

She let the blocks fall from her hand. They fell on different sides.

The man smiled broadly at her.

"The gods have accepted your question, and given you an answer," he said, gesturing at a sheet in his hand.

"Here is your answer, from an ancient Chinese source: 'The dove flies through the dark sky and seeks ever new and bright skies in the spring. The eagle swoops from above but loses sight of the dove as it flies in an unexpected direction and passes by. The dove finds new nests to settle in and pass the summer in peace.'"

She looked at him blankly. "I don't understand."

"Let me interpret for you," he said, pulling out a well-thumbed, thick old book from the drawer of a small table near his seat. He asked Maria for her date, day and time of birth and then leafed through the pages until he found what he was looking for.

"This oracle is describing a situation of change and opportunity and good fortune. The dove is a bird of peace and is looking for new opportunities. The eagle represents the risk, but the unexpected change of direction by the dove allows it to avoid the eagle and complete the change successfully. So you should have the courage to make changes and be open to new experiences. Beware of the risks, but do not be deterred by them because you can invent new ways to deal with them. When you reach your destination, you will find peace."

Maria found the interpretation inspiring. It seemed to confirm that looking for change was the right thing to do, for both her and Mischa. She didn't know what change or where it would come from, but she left the temple feeling calmer and happier. She and Mischa were on a journey and clearly it was time to take their next step.

Lying in bed that evening after they'd discussed the move to India, she felt a sense of deep contentment. She saw now that her visit to the temple had prepared her for Mischa's news. So it hadn't been a coincidence? Those fierce-looking gods had played a part in it?

The preparations for the move to a country she knew nothing about injected energy into her life. And Mischa had rediscovered all the energy and enthusiasm he had when they first met.

The four months they were given to prepare for the move disappeared in a whirlwind of vaccinations, farewell parties, and packing. Harald was understanding when Maria told him she was leaving. When she called her parents and told them the news, they seemed happy for her.

“It will be good for both of you to start in a new place,” Johanna said. “What language do they speak there?”

“Many people speak English. It will be easy for me.”

They would be moving to a building, quaintly called Cedar Grove, in an exclusive part of the city. Although Maria did feel a little trepidation at the step they were taking, she was infected by Mischa's enthusiasm for a country he'd often visited and travelled through. He assured her she would love it.

Chapter 20

In the first week after they arrived in Bombay, she hadn't stepped outside the hotel for fear of contracting an incurable disease from the swarms of excitable, dark-skinned people she could see in the streets from the hotel room window. Even crossing the immaculate, white marble hotel lobby, required her to run an intimidating gauntlet of seemingly countless and ever-attentive staff. 'Can I help you, ma'am? Are you enjoying your stay, ma'am? How was your breakfast, ma'am?'

When she finally did venture out onto the streets of Bombay, she was immediately enveloped in a crowd of jostling adults and children, trying to sell her taxi rides, postcards, cheap plastic jewellery, or simply tugging at the dangling ends of her expensive silk scarves begging for money.

She hated that. It was so different from the vision of the luxurious and exotic life she'd imagined she'd be leading there. The grimy faces of the children, tired, hollow-eyed young women—young girls really—with screaming sick infants in their arms gesturing plaintively to their empty stomachs and open mouths while her car waited at the traffic lights were the hardest to bear. Wherever she looked, they appeared at every window. Eventually, she would screw her eyes shut and wait for the car to move, not caring how ridiculous she must look to them.

"*He … chale jao*", she heard the driver shout a few times when, stuck in a traffic jam, he would make to open his door as if to give chase to the vagrants. But it was like swatting flies.

"Don't give them money, whatever you do," some well-meaning, dowdy expatriate wife, who had spent 20 years in India and considered herself an expert, said at the exclusive Breach Candy Club, where Maria and Mischa were new members. "When I first arrived, I made that mistake, and we had hundreds of them around our car in a matter of minutes. We couldn't move" she had continued in a breathless nasal tone, that Maria had found rather unpleasant. "We had to get the police to come and rescue us in the end."

But it wasn't just the poor on the streets. India was turning out to be very different from what she had imagined. Maria found the superficial jollity of social acquaintances equally off-putting—the countless consular receptions, evening functions and cultural events that the small social circle of the well-appointed in Mumbai attended.

"Hello, I am Maneesh," one stylishly tailored young man had introduced himself to her at her first chamber of commerce event in an ornate five-star hotel, his hair slicked back, his skin unblemished and his white shirt and dark trousers spotless and perfectly creased. Maria wondered whether he might be a film star in the country's famous and massive Bollywood film industry, so self-assured did he seem. In a way, coupled with what looked like immaculate manners, it made him quite attractive, and she wondered idly whether he thought the same of her.

"Hello, I'm Maria."

"Where are you from?"

"Germany … I just arrived two months ago with my husband after a couple of years in Hong Kong … It's my first time in India."

"Welcome to India!"

"Thank you. It's a wonderful country—from what I have seen so far," she added quickly.

"We are many countries combined into one by the British." He smiled. "I would love to show you round," Maneesh continued. "Show you things I'm sure you've never seen before."

She wasn't sure how to react. But she was already imagining remote temples in exotic rural landscapes that no foreigner had yet seen or even heard of. She could see Maneesh acting as a friendly guide and interpreter of local customs and becoming a good local friend.

"Where do you stay?"

"Cedar Grove, near Breach Candy." She still found it difficult to suppress a smile at the incongruity of the building's name that bore no relation to cedars, or trees, or any kind of vegetation at all, but was rather a discoloured construction that allegedly had once belonged to a maharaja's family.

"A lovely place. Your husband, is he a diplomat?"

"No, he works at a small German trading company. The company has just started business here in India."

Almost imperceptibly, Maneesh took a small step back. His smile didn't change, nor his tone of voice.

"Please enjoy our country. It's a pleasure to meet you." Then he turned to a nearby group of Indians and entered into their midst with a loud and cheery greeting.

For a moment Maria was speechless, unsure whether the conversation had come to a natural end or whether she was being shunned for having said something inappropriate.

While Mischa was clearly enjoying the new challenge, for several months Maria felt she neither liked nor would grow to like India. She felt almost disconnected from the vast country she was now living in and for the first time homesick for the simplicity and familiarity of life on the island or alternatively for the intensity of Hong Kong.

"You have to become hard to survive in India," Susan Wader, a wife of a foreign bank managing director, advised her. "It's so extreme. Rich and poor, beautiful and disgusting, rewarding and frustrating, superficial and deep," she said, as they walked between green and tee at the Willingdon Golf Club.

But Maria was not so sure she wanted to become 'hard'. If anything, when she saw how the throngs of helpless beggars or the filthy roadside children accepted their hopelessness, she felt deep sympathy. As she looked into the eyes of the destitute sitting vacantly at the side of the streets and saw how they smiled back, she sensed their years, even centuries of stoic suffering, and uncomplaining willingness to accept their fate. She wondered if they felt that to complain would not only be futile, but also remove the last rags of self-respect they still possessed.

However, as the months went by she noticed how in India the way she had liked to look deep into people's eyes as a child was for the first time reciprocated without reservation. Everywhere she went, people were searching as much as she for the eye contact in which whole life stories were exchanged in split seconds. She found her smiles, frowns, laughter, every expression immediately accepted. Often words weren't necessary. A glance and a gesture, all pregnant with a profound depth of meaning and tolerant understanding, were more than sufficient.

The fears and resistance she'd felt when she first arrived began to evaporate. Now, when she walked on the streets and was quickly surrounded by beggars hoping to benefit from a foreigner's squeamishness and guilty generosity, she looked deeply and warmly into each of their eyes, and the tired gazes around her were rejuvenated to smiles and jaunty repartees without her giving any money. Even the wailing babies, often crying from the deliberate pinches they'd received moments earlier to enhance the chances of getting alms, stopped whining and giggled back.

Chapter 21

After almost two years in Bombay Maria was surprised how comfortable she was living in India. She had explored many parts of Bombay and was equally interested in the colourful markets and the historical sites. She had also travelled to the holiest Hindu city of Varanasi, once with Mischa and then subsequently many times on her own. Although she didn't like the unhygienic filthy streets of the old town on the banks of the Ganges, she was increasingly fascinated after every visit by the hundreds of river-side cremations. She had built up an unusual friendship with Kamal, one of Varanasi's leading suppliers of funeral pyre wood, and now would call him in advance to arrange a hotel room ahead of her visits.

However, in Bombay there were still some poor and crowded parts of the city where she felt uneasy. One of these was a mosque located offshore on a small island connected to the mainland by a narrow causeway. The mosque had looked overrun with people every time she had passed by with their driver in the car. But she was intrigued, remembering how the visit to the Chinese temple in Hong Kong had helped her.

One morning, she summoned up the courage to visit. When she arrived, she saw the narrow walkway leading to the mosque was only a few feet above the surface of an already choppy monsoon sea. At the crowded entrance to the causeway, she pushed through the mothers with outstretched palms, crying infants perched on their hips and past a handful of mendicant tradespeople selling everything from desiccated vegetables and fruits to spiritual trinkets on simple cloths spread out on the caking hot ground.

Part of the way along the causeway she suddenly noticed two small infants lying on a soiled cloth on the hard stone. Behind the two babies, whimpering in the heat and bright light, she saw a woman down on her haunches, her head covered with a fold of her sari against the burning sun. The woman raised her head and met her eyes. Maria felt her breath catch in her throat and a chill pass through her body. She felt she was looking into a fathomless pool of indescribable and endless desolation and pain.

The woman's gaze flickered briefly as they focused on Maria and then retreated to a look of infinite emptiness, gazing into the far distance beyond the horizon.

Maria felt fear and anger rising in her voice: "It is too hot for them. Give them water," she shouted, her voice climbing to a high crescendo. She ripped her wide-brimmed sunhat from her head and attempted to provide the infants with some shade.

The woman simply looked down at the babies helplessly and then vacantly back at Maria.

Maria's raised voice attracted attention. Passers-by and other tradespeople began to gather around chattering to each other and observing.

Before she could say anything else, a tall, bearded man in a dirty *lungi* appeared alongside the woman.

"Our children, Madam," the man said. "No water. No money. No food. You like to buy?" He pointed to the infants.

"Buy … buy your … children?"

Maria felt her head spinning. Suddenly she felt weak and staggered back. Around her, the crowd of people, who had closed in tight behind her, parted to give her room. Immediately, she heard the clamour of voices rise.

"This man no food, Madam, no money."

"You buy Madam, good price Madam."

"Help babies, Madam."

She stumbled away, tears welling into her eyes. Not knowing what else to do, she somehow managed to make her way through the crowds along the causeway to the mosque. The image of the two infants lying side by side on the hot ground and their desolate parents burned into her mind. Girding herself for the return journey, she passed the same spot on the causeway, which was now almost awash in the evening tide, but the couple and the babies had gone.

That night she kept waking, shivering, sweating. Images of the woman's blank eyes kept appearing in her mind. When she did doze off at last, she dreamt she was the woman and Mischa the bearded father. The infants' faces were turned towards her, scowling in reproach. As she tossed and turned, she saw her father waiting as she came out of the gynaecologist's practice her mother had taken her to after that incident with the Hamburg surf instructor and then stalking off angrily and wordlessly. And then suddenly there was her mother, standing furiously where she had stood on the causeway. “I told you this would happen. I told you!”

The next morning Maria woke with a high fever and quickly slipped into delirium. Mischa was worried and called a doctor. After checking her blood pressure and lungs, the doctor diagnosed a local virus and prescribed some pills as well as several days in bed with plenty of liquids. She slept for two days solid and gradually the vivid visions and images in her head subsided.

As the fever eased, she wondered whether this was the challenge of the swooping eagle that the Chinese priest had interpreted in the Hong Kong temple. She had made a successful fresh start in India and escaped the sadness of their failure to have children in Hong Kong only to face a cruel, almost vindictive, twist of the knife in the wound.

Several weeks later, Mischa surprised her with a trip to a boutique resort hotel in northern India to celebrate their second year in India and also to help her recover from her collapse after the mosque visit. The hotel in the Himalayan foothills had been renovated from the ruins of a small palace that once belonged to a colonial viceroy.

Maria gasped as she looked out at the inspiring panorama of massive mountains of deep grey stone capped in white snow. She stood in awe at the scale and majesty of the soaring chain of peaks. The mountains seemed to form an impenetrable wall as far as the eye could see from one side of the horizon to the other. The bright midday sun accentuated the clear white and grey of the mountains against the crystal blue cloudless sky. She had never seen such natural beauty before.

"All mountains over 8,000 metres, Madam," the butler said as he opened the doors to the terrace after serving breakfast.

Mischa had decided to take a day-long hike with a guide through the foothills, which had required a crack-of-dawn departure. But she had preferred a less strenuous option, later making her way alone on foot from the hotel down a narrow trail through Alpine-like fir trees to the small town below. As she followed the path, she wondered at the seemingly limitless diversity of India. From the crowded streets and sapping humidity, burning heat and cacophony of Bombay, to the deserted foothills of the Himalayas where the climate was temperate, comfortable, almost refreshing.

She soon reached the small town and started to wander through fresh fruit and vegetable market stalls and vendors selling varieties of rice and other grains. Mischa and she always looked for the markets on their trips around the country. She knew that he enjoyed the colours and smells and the vibrancy of real-life far more than architectural or historically significant sites. But it was the people's faces she found most fascinating. Their expressions. How quickly they could switch from a flat, neutral indifference to bright smiles and laughter the moment they noticed she was observing them.

The children, in particular. Once they had seen her, they tended to follow her around, mesmerized by her bright blond hair, height and her striking blue eyes. They would stare at her wide-eyed as she walked through the streets, breaking out into shrieks of embarrassed laughter if she started talking directly to one or the other. Sometimes she would pause in front of a stall selling sweets or chocolates, turn to the gaggle of children following her and signal that they should choose one item each which she would then buy for them.

On this occasion, one young girl in a bright red full-length *kurti* covering the tight dark-green leggings she was wearing beneath, caught Maria's eye. Her dark eyes shone like two pieces of onyx out of a perfectly shaped and proportioned face. Her delicate olive skin was distinct from the other darker children. But it was the air of forlorn melancholy in the girl that most caught her attention. She stood to one side away from the other smiling and boisterously laughing children.

Noticing Maria's interest in the girl, the other children started to shout and goad her, as if they were angry with the girl for distracting their benefactress. One of the children tried to push the girl away, but she stood her ground expressionlessly. Another boy ran toward her with a stick raised in his hand, as if about to strike her. The girl flinched, anticipating the blow to the face. But before it fell, Maria shouted and the boy turned, hesitated and then ran. She approached the girl and knelt in front of her, so that their eyes were at the same height. The other children, suddenly quiet and intrigued, gathered around them in a tight circle.

"What's your name?" Maria asked.

The girl was silent. But the other children seized on the question.

"Was 'er lame? Was 'er lame?" they cried out, laughing.

Maria offered the girl her open palm. After staring unblinkingly at her and then at her hand, the girl slowly placed her own small hand in hers. Maria led her to a stall she had already noticed selling sweets. She pointed to the small bars of chocolate behind the grimy plastic glass.

"Take any one you like."

The girl licked her lips nervously and looked furtively over her shoulder. After hesitating for a few moments, she slowly raised her hand and pointed at one bar. Maria signalled to the stall owner to give the girl two bars of her choice. Just as she was about to pay, a loud male voice shouted and all the children suddenly ran off. Terrified, the girl dropped the two bars of chocolate to the ground.

A man with a bushy black beard strode up to them and grabbed the girl so tightly on her upper arm, she cried out in pain. He shook her so hard her head jerked wildly, as he shouted at her furiously. She began to wail, big tears welling out of the corners of her eyes. With an angry glance in Maria's direction and still gripping the girl tightly the man marched her away and around the corner.

Maria felt her pulse racing. The appearance of the man had been so sudden and so violent that she felt as if she had been attacked herself. But before she had even had a chance to say, or shout, anything, they had both disappeared. The stall owner looked out sheepishly at Maria as if to apologise for his countryman's behaviour. She stooped to pick up the bars of chocolate and placed them on the counter.

"Please give this chocolate to her when she comes back," she urged him, giving him the money.

"Madam, you good woman," the stall owner replied. "Bad man. Bad father."

That evening, in the comfort of their hotel, over dinner near the hearth with an open fire in the hotel's oak-panelled and deeply carpeted restaurant, she described the scene to Mischa.

"How can a parent treat his child so cruelly?"

"It's not just here … I am sure it happens everywhere," Mischa replied.

"It's ironic really," she continued. "We would probably be wonderful parents, but we can't have any children and those parents who can have children treat them horribly."

Mischa was silent, his eyes lowered to the floor, and for a few moments she was unsure why. Then suddenly she realized what she had said.

"Oh, I'm sorry. I did not mean to discuss that … I just meant … it was sad to see that scene today … it's nothing to do with us," she said carefully, hoping she hadn't unlocked a topic that they'd taken care to keep hidden for over a year now.

"No, you're right. It is a shame. We would make good parents."

He was looking into her eyes.

"Whenever you see children your face lights up and you find time for them," he continued. "And they like you … their eyes shine the moment they see you looking at them."

She knew he was right. She was drawn to children whenever she encountered them on the street. She loved their innocent expressions of emotion, free of adult judgement. And she had seen herself in the melancholic unhappiness of the ostracized girl in the red *kurti* in the market.

And she knew what Mischa was going to say before he said it.

"Perhaps we should consider adopting a child. Perhaps that would make us happy?"

Perhaps it was that simple? She couldn't really visualize what adoption meant or would feel like, but somehow it now seemed right.

"Do you really think we could do it?"

"I don't see why not. When we get back, we can look into it."

Chapter 22

Within only a couple of weeks of their return to Bombay, Mischa had identified an orphanage in the outskirts of the city where abandoned babies and children were fostered. The home, funded and run by a Catholic order of nuns and perennially struggling financially was willing to offer their children for adoption for an appropriate donation and the assurance that the child would be issued a foreign passport and eventually be taken to live out of the country. That allowed the orphanage to bypass local legislation on preference for adoption to Indian families.

Maria let Mischa manage the countless forms and documentation that needed to be completed and submitted. The whole idea still felt very surreal to her. Now that there was a clear path to having a child, she found she could not really visualize what would happen if she had an infant to care for. Would she be able to bathe it, put it to bed, hug it, even kiss it?

Maria decided not to tell her parents at all about their decision to adopt and would wait until they had actually brought the baby home.

Mischa was happier than she had seen him for a long time. They grew closer as they made plans for their future as parents. She felt a tremor of excitement when he put his arm around her waist or entwined his fingers in hers as she had when they first met.

However, before they could adopt a child, a social worker would need to interview them in their home to assess their suitability as parents. Maria felt a pang of trepidation that they might not pass the test. The day before the meeting, she told their two house staff to make sure the apartment was spotless, and the silver ornaments dispersed around the room highly polished. She chose a simple but elegant dress for the occasion and arranged for assorted snacks to serve.

When the doorbell rang, Maria opened the door herself. An elderly bespectacled lady stood there in a green and red sari. Over her shoulder she carried a black satchel.

"I am Mrs. Singh, from the municipal social welfare agency."

"Please come in," Maria said, smiling.

As Mrs. Singh entered the large and high-ceilinged living room with its crystal chandelier, her eyes widened.

"Your home is very beautiful," she said quietly.

Mischa appeared and, introducing himself, led her to one of the large sofas in the living room. One of the house servants brought three glasses on a silver tray.

"Fresh lime soda, Madam," she said, leaving it on a small ornate table, then bowing slightly, left the room.

They chatted about the weather for a few minutes, then the woman took out a black notebook and a pen from her satchel.

"Let's begin."

She asked them general questions about how long they had been in India, what their professions were and other routine personal facts.

"Why do you both want to adopt a child?"

Maria was taken aback and suddenly unsure of herself. She let Mischa explain their history of trying to conceive on their own, including the IVF treatments. The woman listened with interest, jotting down a few notes.

What would she say if the woman asked her directly? Maria was unsure how she would answer. Suddenly it seemed she was asking herself the question for the first time. And she realized she didn't know the answer.

Then the lady turned to her.

"What about you, Mrs. Freeman? Why do you want to be a mother?"

All the pat phrases she had practiced with Mischa in the previous days, about how much she loved children, loved playing with the children of their friends and feeling life was empty and meaningless without children, had suddenly gone out of her head.

"I … I … think it would be … good … I mean, nice to have a child, or children."

"Yes, children can be nice, but they can also be a lot of work and sometimes not nice at all. It is a great responsibility. Children need a mother, not a beautiful home and servants who do the parenting instead."

"I'm sorry. I'm feeling … I don't know why."

"Maria would make a wonderful mother," Mischa offered, "She is so caring and good. Children love her."

"Thank you, Mr. Freeman. But I would like to hear from your wife."

Maria looked at the lady and into her eyes, she sensed a warmth and understanding that she had not noticed initially. She seemed to want to connect with Maria.

"Please take your time and tell me about your life as a child."

"I grew up on a small island in Germany," Maria managed to complete the sentence, but feeling as if there was a tight noose around her throat constricting her vocal cords.

"I have a younger brother and my parents own a department store. I went to school on the island, but then … things … happened … or changed … and I was sent to a boarding school, where I was happier," she continued haltingly.

"I started working on the island, but then I wanted to leave … escape actually … and I decided to move from Germany to Hong Kong where I met my husband."

She stopped talking. She didn't know what more to say and lost her train of thought.

"Were you a happy child?" the lady said gently.

Maria felt tears stinging her eyes. Suddenly words started flowing like a torrent. "No! Not really. My parents were very, very strict and I had to conform to their rules," she said. "I want my child to be happy, to have friends, to be free to be themselves." Then she added, "And, and they have to be loved by … to feel they're loved by their … by me," She covered her face in her hands, sobbing quietly. "I'm sorry. This means so much to me … to us."

"I understand. Thank you very much. This has been very helpful."

Maria was dimly aware of Mischa accompanying the lady to the door. After a few muffled words between them, he returned to Maria who was still sitting on the sofa. He sat next to her and put his arm around her as she leaned against his shoulder.

"I'm sorry. I hope I didn't ruin it."

"Don't worry. I think she liked your honesty."

"I hope you're right."

A week later, an official letter arrived confirming that they had received permission to adopt an Indian child.

"She was persuaded by your vulnerability," Mischa said admiringly. "You told her exactly what you felt."

A few weeks later they were on the slow trip through the gridlock of traffic, potholes and unexpectedly blocked roads on their way to the orphanage. At almost every traffic light, rag-clad children of all ages glued their faces to the car windows clasping the fingertips of their right eating hand together, imitating in practiced routine the movement of putting food into their mouths.

Suddenly, the memory of those two crying infants on the causeway outside the mosque came to her mind. She wondered whether any of the children on the other side of the glass had also been offered for sale by their parents and found it quite impossible to imagine adopting one of them. Was what they were planning so different?

Mischa had visited the orphanage several times before, but it was the first time for her. She was surprised to see it was a decaying old colonial mansion behind the walls of a compound with rusted steel gates at the entrance.

As they drove slowly up the drive to the entrance portico of the house, she saw dozens of children of all ages running and playing on the ground which was mostly bare earth except for a few areas of dry browning grass. She noticed a rather unstable-looking seesaw with a handful of children on either end. On a merry go round nearby, two older boys were standing in stable-wide stances, slapping the arms to spin it faster while a young boy hung on in squealing terror. They all seemed to be wearing a mixed bag of clothes. Very few had shoes. Attracted by the arrival of the car the children gathered round and peered in. They looked well-fed and substantially cleaner and happier than the forlorn beggars and waifs in the city streets.

An Indian nun in a grey habit met them as they stepped out of the car. She introduced herself as Sister Anne. With a sharp and sudden movement of her arm, she motioned to the clamouring children, some already tugging at Maria's sleeves, to silence and then led them in a practiced choral welcome.

"Welcome Auntie, welcome Uncle," dozens of young voices rang out in ragged unison. Then the nun shooed them back to the playground and motioned Maria and Mischa to follow her up the entrance staircase and through a large doorway into an entrance hall. Maria was barely listening as the nun explained the history of the orphanage while taking them on a tour of the building. In some rooms older girls were making clothes with decrepit manual sewing machines. In others teenage boys were working at carpenter's benches building simple furniture. She showed them the dormitories—two cavernous rooms, one for boys and the other for girls, filled with three-storey bunk beds with iron rungs set into the sides of the frames.

"The children need to sleep in pairs in each bed … toe to head," Sister Anne explained. "We have too many children."

Maria tried to imagine the room full of sleeping children, some perhaps restless with nightmares, others tossing in the heat and humidity. She felt beads of sweat starting to trickle down her back beneath her white blouse.

"Where are the children from?" she asked.

"Most of them have been abandoned by their mothers. We hang a basket out from the front gate every evening and two to three times a week we find an infant there the next morning."

"How awful," Maria gasped.

"For most children, growing up here with us is a better fate than staying with their parents in the slums. Many of the older girls here are escaping rape and abuse. With us at least they receive a basic education and the skills to earn money and become self-sufficient. Some of the children are also handicapped or deformed and they would simply be a burden on their families and probably be disposed of by their parents."

"Which children do you make available for adoption?" asked Mischa.

"Any child you wish. Most couples like you want to adopt infants or young babies. But occasionally some people want to take an older child."

Maria felt a sudden ache in the pit of her stomach.

Things were moving so quickly from a comforting idea that had given them both solace, to something that was becoming a very present reality. She hadn't imagined choosing between different children, like products in a market. Something felt wrong.

"Mischa, I'm not sure this is the right place," she whispered, hoping the nun wouldn't hear.

"Let's just see what is possible now that we're here," said Mischa, looking at Sister Anne. "Where are the infants that are available for adoption?"

"Our nursery is this way," Sister Anne said, pointing to the end of the corridor.

Maria's heart was thumping as they entered a dimly lit room. In the gloom she saw dozens of babies, some infants, some toddlers, squeezed together in rows of cots. Some were fast asleep, and others were sitting or standing holding onto wooden side panels or slats. She noticed an almost eerie silence. None of the babies were crying. As the infants noticed their entry more and more of them began to stare. She thought she could see a plaintive look and plea in their eyes. Were they saying: 'Take me please … I am the one … You can make me happy …'? Maria clenched her eyes shut to drive out the images. How could she select her child in this way? It took all her strength not to turn and walk out of the room.

"There's a very beautiful three-month old girl in the bed over there," Sister Anne offered.

She led them to a cot at the far end of the room, beneath the only window. As Maria looked down in the light streaming through, she gasped. Lying on the mattress was a baby with a disproportionally large head. One eye was in the normal position, the second was in the middle of the forehead and much larger than the left eye. The space where the eye should have been, was filled with an empty depression, not even a socket.

"I'm sorry, but I cannot ..."

Seeing Maria's reaction, Sister Anne said, "Not this girl. I meant the other one."

Sister Anne leant over the side of the cot. From beneath the soiled old sheet that had been hiding her from view, she lifted a smaller baby that had been sleeping in the opposite direction and was now waking at the commotion and yawning in Sister Anne's arms. As Maria looked at the little girl, she turned her head and looked back at her. For a moment they gazed at each other and then the baby's face broke into a broad happy smile, and it reached out a tiny hand towards her.

"She likes you. Do you want to hold her?"

"I ... I don't know ... I can't ..."

But Sister Anne had already passed the little girl into Maria's arms.

She was terrified. She didn't know what to do, or even how to hold the child.

"Just cradle in your arms, one hand under her head," Sister Anne instructed.

"Like this?" Maria said, trembling.

Sister Anne nodded.

Maria looked down and the girl gazed back at her with large round dark eyes, chortled, then smiled again and closed her eyes to sleep.

"I'll give you both a moment with her. I'll be in my office down the hall. "I can see she is in good hands." Sister Anne left.

"She's so beautiful," Maria said.

"Yes, she is."

Maria was proud that the baby felt so comfortable with her. Mischa went to Sister Anne's office and when they returned, she had lain the baby back down and was leaning over the cot, the girl's minute fingers wrapped around her thumb. Neither wanted to let go.

"You can come back as often as you like to continue to get acquainted with her." Sister Anne said. "It will take a month or so before we get all the final approvals. I know you'll all be happy."

On the way back in the car, both Maria and Mischa were silent. There was no need for words. Both knew they'd crossed a line. That little girl was their child, their daughter, waiting to be picked up and brought home.

Chapter 23

Maria awoke early to the tweeting of the green parakeet that nested in the tree outside their bedroom window. As she lay in the early morning peace before the cacophony of the streets began, her mind was filled with images of the baby girl. The warm glow she had felt when holding the tiny body, looking into her defenceless and trusting eyes. There were no expectations, no rules. It was simply unadulterated, unfiltered, genuine emotion. She reached for Mischa's hand next to her and felt him stir. This child had given them new purpose. Perhaps the threat of the swooping eagle had now been met and their dove was now safely in its new habitat, Maria thought, remembering the Chinese temple priest. She snuggled closer to him.

"When will you tell your parents?" Mischa said later over breakfast.

"Maybe we should tell your parents first to see how they react."

"I know they'll be pleased. But we should probably wait until we bring her home."

"Good idea," she said, relieved to avoid the discussion with her own parents that she knew would be difficult. "I'll simply tell them we've decided," she said, with a burst of bravado.

Mischa agreed. He had completed all the necessary application forms, enquired at the embassy on questions concerning nationality and a passport and even helped Maria investigate where in the city they might find infant's clothes. His enthusiasm was infectious.

After several weeks the orphanage confirmed Mischa and Maria could adopt the girl once all bureaucratic steps were complete. All they needed from them was the baby's official name. They had decided to give their daughter a new set of names to appear on a re-issued birth certificate. When Sister Anne offered to tell them the girl's birthname Maria said she had no wish to hear it. For her, the arrival of their daughter was ordained in fate or by other spiritual forces.

"We will name her Kanisha Frederika," she said proudly.

"What a lovely name." Sister Anne said. "Kanisha means beautiful eyes in Hindi. I'm sure you know that."

"Yes, we do. It was the first thing I noticed when we met her. Frederika was my maternal grandmother's name." Maria hoped her mother would be pleased with her choice.

She enjoyed her frequent visits to the orphanage to familiarize herself with caring for Kanisha. The children all surrounded her when she arrived each time, calling out "Auntie, Auntie." She always brought snacks and small gifts for them.

On one visit a young girl, perhaps only four or five years old, wearing a bright green frock that was a size too big for her and with two long braids put her little palm into hers and, tugging her down to her level whispered: "My name is Adya. Please take me also to your home, Auntie."

Maria looked into her plaintive eyes, seeing at once all the distress and loneliness the child was feeling. All she could do was to smile back at her. She knew adopting two children would be beyond her.

On subsequent visits, she noticed the girl following her around. When Maria bounced Kanisha on her knees or fed her from a bottle, she saw Adya watching her silently from the doorway. Maria invited her to come in and play with Kanisha. She made the baby smile.

With each visit, Maria felt her confidence growing. Every time she arrived at her bedside, Kanisha's innocent and trusting eyes would focus on her, and a large happy smile would fill her little face. Seeing that smile, she felt waves of emotion course through her body. It was as if a valve had been opened to a completely new pool of feelings coming from somewhere deep inside her. In those smiles and the bright and lively eyes she felt a complete and utter trust and acceptance in a way she never had before. Kanisha had no doubts, no criticisms, no questions, no comments, no expectations—she simply accepted Maria exactly as she was.

Among the documents required to complete the adoption were copies of the birth certificates of both Maria's and Mischa's parents. Mischa's parents were overjoyed at the news and sent copies right away.

There was no getting around it now. Maria had to call her parents and tell them about the adoption. Mischa offered to join her on the call, but she was certain it would be a difficult discussion, and better if she made the call on her own.

She decided to call on a Sunday when she knew her parents would be back after church and preparing for lunch.

"Hello," Johanna answered in her usual firm voice.

"Mother, it's Maria."

"What a surprise! It's been ages, let me get your father on the line."

She heard her call out to her father. Maria listened to her mother and then her father telling her the latest news and gossip about the store, the town, her brother, and the neighbours.

"I'm glad everything is okay at home," Maria finally said, hoping to get to her important information.

"Have you had any unexpected luck getting pregnant?" her mother finally asked.

"Actually, that's one of the reasons I'm calling. I need you to send me copies of your and father's birth certificates."

"Whatever for?"

This was it. "We need them because we are going to adopt an Indian child."

The phone went silent. She felt she could see the shocked, frozen and stricken expressions of her parents on the other end of the line.

As the silence dragged on, she tried to fill the gap in a desperate attempt to win over her parents. She explained how Mischa and she had come to their decision when high up in the Himalayan foothills. In as lively and hopeful a tone as she could muster, she described the Catholic orphanage with its horde of happy and playful children, Sister Anne and the wonderful feeling of holding the tiny infant girl in her arms for the first time. But the ongoing silence on the phone began to unnerve her, and gradually her voice trailed off.

"An Indian child? In our family?" her mother said. "You can't be serious."

Maria could visualize the firm line of her mother's mouth, the blazing eyes filled with judgment and criticism that she knew so well from her childhood. She steeled herself for the barrage that she knew was coming.

"You know nothing about the child, its background, its parents. It could have some mental deficiency you know nothing about and you'll only discover later. Do you have any idea what risks you're letting yourself in for? It won't look like you. It will spend its whole life knowing it is in the wrong culture and doesn't belong there. And then there'll be the prejudice of other children who'll shun it at school. And that's before it even grows up when the exclusions will be even harsher ..."

Maria was tempted to hang up the phone just to put an end to the tidal wave of negativity that was washing over her, suffocating the happiness and serenity she'd found with Kanisha.

"First of all, the baby is not an 'it,' but a 'she.' And her name is Kanisha Frederika."

For a moment her mother was quiet, then said, "What kind of first name is that? It's not even Christian."

"It means 'beautiful eyes' in Hindi. I thought you'd be pleased we chose grandmother's name too. She is beautiful and healthy. We're very happy."

It was as if she hadn't spoken. Her mother barrelled on.

"It's not only about your happiness. You can't be that selfish. What about our family? Our legacy? What will people think?"

"I don't care what anyone else thinks. This is *our* family!"

She was amazed at her new firmness and conviction.

"You're just upset because you haven't been able to get pregnant. Maybe you both just need some more time to try some more and think things over."

She heard her mother's rigid tone soften. For a moment, she thought perhaps she had understood.

"No. We've made up our mind. We need your help with the documents so we can complete the process and bring Kanisha home."

Again, there was silence. And then, she thought she heard a stifled sob from the other end. Finally, after another long gap, there was her mother's voice again, steely in its firmness and control.

"You are making a mistake, and we can't just ignore that. Peter, please say something."

"Your mother is right. Perhaps waiting a bit might be prudent. There are legal issues to consider for the future as well and …"

"What about my future, my happiness, our …"

"Maria," her mother said, cutting her off. "We will not help you in anyway with this foolishness. I want you …"

Maria slowly lowered the receiver ending the call and broke out in tears.

She could feel the energy and conviction that had carried her so strongly since discovering Kanisha seeping out of her. Perhaps her mother was right? They had no way of knowing whether the child was truly healthy. Perhaps seeing the deformed child had been a warning flag they shouldn't ignore? And a child from a different culture would probably face challenges in gaining social acceptance throughout its life.

But even as she struggled to sort out her thoughts in this maelstrom of views and arguments what hurt her most was her mother's indifference to what she was feeling, her refusal to trust her judgement. She knew that, as far as Johanna was concerned, she was simply on the verge of adding another item to the long list of disappointments that she had given her throughout her life.

Mischa heard her crying from the other room and rushed in.

"What did they say?"

Maria just looked at him through her tears.

"They ... are ... set against it. They will not help in any way."

"How dare they interfere," he said angrily.

"They're my parents. They mean well. But they just don't understand."

"If they meant well, they'd respect what's important for you, for both of us."

"What can we do if they won't help?"

"I don't know. There must be some way round it. I'll check with the municipal department tomorrow."

In the evening Maria asked him to cancel her scheduled visit to the orphanage for the following day, saying she didn't want to risk disturbing Kanisha with the way she was feeling now.

"Do you think that's a good idea? Spending time with Kanisha always makes you both so happy."

"Maybe you're right," Maria said, wiping her tears. "She needs me, and I need her."

"Yes, you need each other. Once you see her, I'm sure you'll feel better."

"I hope you're right."

Chapter 24

The next morning Mischa left before she got up. Worried and anxious, she put her faith in his ability to solve problems and got ready to visit Kanisha. She tried to act as if the call had never happened.

At the orphanage, she was met with the now-familiar chorus of 'Welcome Auntie' from the children in the playground. Adya had made a water colour painting of a family with twin girls and shyly presented it to Maria as she stepped out of the car. Maria had to choke down her tears at the poor girl's desperate desire to be part of her family.

By the time she was holding a chortling Kanisha in her hands, bouncing her lightly on her knees and nuzzling her, she had managed to bury the call with her angry mother deep enough so that it was no longer disturbing her.

In the evening, Mischa told her that he had somehow found a way around the requirement for copies of her parents' birth certificates. With the path now clear, they focused on the preparations for bringing Kanisha home.

The brother of one of their housemaids was a painter, and they hired him to paint the baby's room in the light celestial blue that Maria had chosen. They bought a wide range of the finest babywear they could find.

"Our daughter will be the most fashionable baby in all of India!" Mischa exclaimed.

Formula, baby food and medications, diapers, baby bath, a play pen, travel cradle, even a crib that converted into a larger bed for when she was older—all were delivered by a constant stream of delivery men.

But Maria couldn't put her mother's disapproval completely out of her mind. As the days passed, it hung over her happiness like a dark cloud. As distracted as she was with all the preparations, she knew that her mother was angry with her, perhaps more than she had ever been. This time her mother not only felt Maria had failed, but that she had challenged a value that was fundamental for her: the family's legacy. Maria worried that the consequences would be irreversible.

"Perhaps they will disinherit you," Nadine Blumenthal, a German friend of hers, said with a grim laugh, as they sat under an awning at the Breach Candy swimming club while a monsoon rain squall passed.

"Really? Why do you think that?"

"My parents once threatened me with that. I was quite young and fell in love with a penniless artist from Morocco while I was in Paris for an exchange semester at university. I was sure I wanted to marry him and spend the rest of my life with him."

"What happened … what did you do?"

"My father drove all the way from Berlin to Paris one day and surprised me. He picked me up from the tiny apartment I was sharing with my Arab lover and sat me down in a nearby street café. I had never seen him so angry. He said: 'Choose right now! Either you marry him, and we'll disinherit you, or you leave him, and we won't!'"

"And … so … what did you do?" Maria asked.

"I was so upset and confused. It really shocked me. I spent the rest of the day and whole night just walking around the streets of Paris in a daze. When I got back the next morning my lover had left. My father had seen him and must have told him how he'd threatened me. I found a note when I got back to the apartment in the morning saying he didn't want to put me in an impossible position of choosing between my parents and him. I never saw him again."

"Had you decided … I mean … had you made your choice?"

"I was devastated because … I had actually," Maria was not sure if she had imagined or heard Nadine Blumenthal's voice catch. "I'd decided I wanted to marry him despite what my father had said. I didn't speak with my parents for several years after that, but eventually I got over it and met and married Hans ten years ago."

"So, you didn't give in to the pressure from your parents. I hope I'll have your strength."

Sister Anne called to let them know that all forms had been submitted, and all approvals received. They were free to pick up their daughter the following day. Mischa was beaming. He looked happier than Maria had ever seen him. That evening he opened a bottle of champagne he'd been saving for this occasion. Filling two glasses, he proposed a toast.

"To Kanisha Frederika. Our daughter!"

Maria tried to summon up the same excitement. But she was barely able to swallow the champagne.

She felt as if the mask she realised she had been wearing for Mischa's sake since the call with her parents was slipping. As soon as she felt she could, she explained that she was very tired and went to bed.

As she turned fitfully beneath the bedcovers struggling to find sleep, the image of an eagle kept appearing in her mind. Was the dove still in danger? Would it be able to escape its clutches? She heard Mischa come to bed later and, however much she wished to confide in him and let out all her fears and confusion, she held back.

The next morning when Maria awoke, it was late. Mischa wasn't there. Suddenly she realized where he must be. Today was the day they were to pick up Kanisha from the orphanage. He'd woken her earlier, but she'd told him she wasn't feeling well, so he'd let her sleep and gone on his own to collect their baby girl.

Suddenly she felt a surge of panic and, throwing the bed clothes aside, jumped out of bed. Somehow this all had to be stopped. She couldn't let Mischa go ahead with the adoption. She couldn't be responsible for ruining the work and devotion her parents had invested in building their family and respectability on the island.

A sudden horrific image came to her mind from nowhere—her parents walking through the market square in front of the town hall, cowering anxiously under the whistles and angry shouts and boos from furious faces on all sides. She clenched her eyes tight shut, willing the image to disappear. Her parents would be right to disinherit her. She didn't deserve to inherit anything if she caused her parents such hurt. She rushed out of the bedroom into the dining-room. The breakfast was still laid. Next to her plate was a note from Mischa.

> *Hope you feel better. I know you are anxious. Don't worry. Everything will be fine. I am bringing our daughter home to live with us. Love you. Mischa*

It was too late. Maria sat down heavily. She realised she couldn't stop it. Once Mischa arrived with Kanisha, her fate would be sealed. If she told Mischa that she had changed her mind, he would be devastated. She could hardly bare to imagine the crushed expression on his face and in his eyes and the slump in his gait if she asked him to return Kanisha to the orphanage.

And then the broad, chortling smile with the deep dimples of Kanisha's little face and the big trusting eyes appeared. Maria put her head in her hands, her elbows on the table edge and felt the tears streaming down her face. How could she disappoint the man she loved and the innocent little baby that already depended on her?

She knew she had to leave. It was the only way out. She was disappointing too many people and causing too much pain. It would be best for everyone if she simply removed herself from the situation so that she couldn't inflict any more damage.

She seized Mischa's note and turned it over. The pen he'd used was still lying on the table.

Dear Mischa,
I cannot do this. I don't know what to do, but I know I cannot do this. I need to leave. I don't know for how long. I don't know where to. It might be better if I don't come back. It is all my fault. Please forgive me if you can and please ask Kanisha to forgive me as well.
M.

In the kitchen Maria found the two housemaids starting to prepare lunch. She told them to stop and, giving them some money, sent them both on an errand to the fruit and vegetable market that would keep them busy for the next two hours. Once she was alone in the apartment, she quickly showered and packed a small suitcase. In the bedroom she opened the safe and took most of the banknotes as well as her passport. She saw the white teardrop pearl earrings she'd secretly taken from her mother's dressing table and took them as well before closing the safe.

She let herself out of the apartment and travelled in the elevator down to the ground floor. Affecting as nonchalant an air as she could, she walked past the building's watchman. The moment he saw her he jumped to attention and saluted before rushing ahead to open the compound gate.

"Taxi, Madam?"

"No, thank you."

He looked surprised to see Madam leaving the compound on foot with a suitcase and not in the family car but lowered his eyes respectfully and saluted again.

Maria nodded and walked away down the street.

Chapter 25

Her days were simple and deliberately monotonous as she could only tolerate basic unchanging routines. It took all her determination and strength to force herself out of bed at the crack of dawn when the sun's rays broke over the ridge to the east of her bedroom window in the simple wooden house on the eastern edge of the town. She could hear the cawing of the flocks of black crows interspersed with the shrill morning calls of roosters and then, once the sun had risen further, the sudden insistent hum of cicadas, like a massive orchestra struggling to get in tune for their daily concert.

Before she started preparing the simplest of tasteless breakfasts, she would kneel at the small garlanded *ganesha* that she had adopted as her house god and pray for some kind, any kind, of release. She knew little about the many Hindu gods and religious rituals, but some of her Indian friends in Bombay had explained the tradition of worshipping a house god for good luck.

As she bowed her head in front of the small wooden statue, its incense sticks glowing to recreate the sense of a purifying fire, the same images would come to her that circled in her mind every night as she struggled to sleep. It was a nightmare that had often terrified her as a young child and now had suddenly reappeared. She was walking along aisles between tall wooden shelves, like the ones her parents had originally had in the corner shop before it grew to become a department store. The shelves stretched from floor to ceiling and were filled with cardboard shoe boxes. The faster she moved down one aisle and turned round the end to move in the opposite direction down the next, the narrower the space between the shelves seemed to become until she was only able to squeeze her body sideways because the space was too tight and then, at what felt like exactly the same point in the dream, she would look up and see the shoe boxes tipping out of their shelves and tumbling towards her and, however much she tried to avoid them, she knew she was completely exposed.

She had left the apartment in Bombay with no idea where she wanted to go or what she wanted to do. She knew only that she must flee a situation she could not face. As she wandered along the pavement of the busy road, a few street-dwellers observed her. Something about her downcast eyes and lost expression must have dissuaded them from following her. She walked aimlessly across several road crossings and past a railway station, where she paused and considered boarding a train to the furthest point she could find in India. Finally, she placed her suitcase on the cracked grimy pavement and looked round at a loss. On the kerb a taxi driver, polishing the bonnet of his small yellow-roofed and black-bodied Padmini, paused and looked at her with a friendly, inquiring eye. He was clad in an unusually clean khaki brown uniform and wearing the traditional Indian *chapal* open sandals.

But more than his clothes it was his large bushy white moustache that made him sympathetic to her and calmed her turbulent emotions a little.

"You say where, we go there. No problem, Madam," he said with a charming and mischievous smile.

Maria picked up her suitcase and moved closer. The driver came around the car, dropping his cleaning cloth through the open front window on the passenger side, and, taking the case out of her hands, swung it expertly onto the luggage rack on the roof of the car. Once they had settled inside, he leaned over from the front seat to gaze at Maria in the back.

"Where we go, Madam?"

Maria wondered what to say. She noticed the taxi's plush purple velvet ceiling and the garland of fresh jasmine flowers draped round the rear-view mirror. Perched on the ledge before the windscreen and above the ignition key in the centre of the dashboard, was a small *Shiva* statue with a thin saffron ribbon entwined in its various protruding arms. Facing Maria, the canvas cloth covering the rear of the front bench from one side of the car to the other, was hand-painted with a Gaugin-like South Sea Island scene of dark-haired women on a beach.

"I take you anywhere Madam. To the sea, to the mountains," he said with a smile, seeing her eyes on the beach scene. "I can take you to *ashram* also," he added gesturing at the Shiva statue.

Suddenly Maria knew where she wanted to go. Once Mischa and she had spent some days in Matheran, a hill station about four hours' drive from Bombay, in the Western Ghat mountains that bisected the state of Maharashtra from north to south. Matheran would be relatively empty at this time of year, as the monsoon had already broken, and everyone would have returned to the cities.

"I want to go to Matheran. Can you take me there?"

"Ooohhh Madam ... Matheran very far, not possible," the driver said with a glint in his eye.

She had no energy to haggle and named a sum equivalent to his likely earnings for several months, and almost immediately they were on their way.

She loved the simplicity of Matheran with its clay earth that raised a choking haze of red dust in the dry months and turned to bright red mud during the monsoon. It was a small town perched in the trees at the top of a range of steep hills, with stony and slippery mountain trails accessible only on foot or horseback. Some of the paths ran close to terrifyingly steep precipices with no guardrails or safety measures of any kind.

After her simple breakfast she would usually doze and try to catch up on lost sleep. She had never felt so completely fatigued and without any energy. The simplest of tasks such as washing or getting dressed felt like almost insurmountable challenges and she found herself beset by indecisiveness and anxiety for the very few decisions she had to make on her daily visit to the small fresh fruit and vegetable market and the tiny and sparsely stocked provisions store on the dusty main street. At times she would simply stop dead and sigh deeply, hoping to shake off the heavy cloak of negativity enveloping her. But try as she could, it seemed inescapable.

She felt trapped in a maze from which there was no exit. Whatever choice she made she was bound to disappoint either her parents or Mischa and the unarticulated feelings of a child she barely knew. She understood now that she'd left because she couldn't bear to inflict as painful a childhood as she had experienced on any child of her own. But now she had already caused the innocent girl in the orphanage—she felt she no longer had the right to call *Kanisha* her daughter—so much suffering.

Every time she recalled that phone call with her parents it only seemed more painful. She felt as if she'd been thrown out of the front door of their house. She'd expected the conversation to be difficult and her parents to be shocked, but she'd hoped they would respect, or at least understand, her and Mischa's decision. By now she was sure they'd decided to disinherit her. She knew her mother well enough. When she was determined nothing could stop her.

But why had they taken this step? Was it because she hadn't been sensitive and respectful enough to the social situation of her parents? Because she'd ignored their desire only for natural grandchildren? Selfishly put her own wishes ahead of the needs of the family? And like a gaping wound through this jumble of speculation, how could her mother, any mother, inflict this on her own child? Surely there must be some misunderstanding or some confusion that had led her—and she was sure her mother and not her father had triggered this—to take this harsh step. Or was her mother not the person she'd always assumed she was, not capable of the love she had longed for her whole life?

She wondered how Mischa must be. He would have read her note, of course. And been angry at first, angry at what he'd have seen as her unpredictability, her emotional overreaction. And he'd have been bitterly disappointed on what should have been the happiest day of their lives. He would have found a way to organize care for Kanisha. The calm, measured, structured way he would have reacted to this situation was the way he responded to everything, she thought wistfully. Despite the closeness she had felt for Mischa since they'd first met, she couldn't deny that over the years she'd begun to realise how different they were in personality. Where he was calm and rational, she was emotional and effusive. Where he was structured and organized, she was chaotic but spontaneous. And it seemed as if the last months in Hong Kong and now here in India had accentuated their differences.

Although she'd always pictured herself married with children, the longer they'd struggled to have one the more she'd begun to realize she'd let a child happen to her without ever asking herself why she wanted one. At times she even wondered whether the difficulties were the punishment her father had foretold for the abortion of her own child. Perhaps it was wrong of her to even consider children. She'd allowed Mischa to use his organization and discipline to drive the process and opposed it, perhaps to avoid the emotional trauma of a confrontation. But he'd never thought to ask the question either, just assuming she shared his desire.

Without her noticing it, days turned to weeks and then to months. Gradually she began to forget why she was in Matheran. The start of every day was simply a step towards the end of the day and increasingly she would find herself staring out at the carpet of tree-covered hills and mountains in the distance from the window of the small two-room apartment, which she had rented for a pittance from the owner of the town's provisions store. Existence seemed if not meaningless, inconsequential. She couldn't think of anything worth exerting herself for and, strangely, with this state of mind she occasionally detected what felt like a consoling peace, almost a kind of serenity.

Then one day, she was shaken from her semi-wakeful state on the simple bed where she'd been lying through the steamy humid afternoon by a loud knock at the door. She opened cautiously and was stunned to see Mischa standing outside. They both remained wordless. She could see from his eyes that he was shocked by her appearance.

"How ... how are you?" Mischa asked as he entered the room. He seemed flustered, almost embarrassed by her appearance. Perhaps unsure how to react. "You look ... you seem ...," his voice trailed off.

"How did you find me?"

"It was quite easy really. The watchman at Cedar Grove saw you leaving and followed you and noted down the number of the taxi. We found the driver and he told us."

Mischa hesitated, but she could see he wanted to continue. He'd probably long prepared what he had to say but wanted to choose his words carefully.

"I wanted to give you some space and some time, so I left you alone. I thought I shouldn't disturb you. I understand how you feel. I really do. It's challenging, but I'd really like you to come back. Please."

She could see in his face and eyes how much he was genuinely missing her. She felt guilty for causing his suffering.

"I'm sure your parents will change their minds. Perhaps they just need time. And I guess becoming a mother is also a big change. Kanisha is at home now." He added, "She's so sweet."

Maria felt a pang of remorse at the sound of Kanisha's name. But she knew immediately he hadn't understood.

"It is not about my parents, and it is not about becoming a mother," she said quietly. "I need to find my own direction and my own answers. I don't know how, and I don't know where, and I don't know how long it will take. But I know I have to do this. And I need to do it on my own. I can't tell you when, or if I will come back."

Mischa looked at her wordlessly. After a moment he lowered his gaze and shook his head slowly.

"Do you need anything?"

"No, thank you."

He turned and walked slowly and heavily down the stairs. She raised her hand to call out to stop him, but then let her hand drop as she watched him walk away.

Several weeks passed and she soon forgot when exactly Mischa had come to see her. Such was the unchanging monotony of her daily routine. One day, during some aimless wandering along the narrow paths through the trees on the outskirts of Matheran, she stumbled across a small Hindu temple. It was hewn deeply into the side of a small cliff face. A boisterous waterfall, which would reduce to a trickle after the monsoon season, splashed noisily close by.

As she stepped over the raised threshold of the temple, she saw that the entrance to an inner chamber, was only wide enough for one person to pass through at a time. Intrigued by the possibility of finding tranquillity as she had in the Chinese temple in Hong Kong, she squeezed through. Once there, the daylight illumination from a small narrow shaft cut through the ceiling to the hillside above allowed her to see more clearly. Inside the space widened for worshippers to sit two-deep around a large golden statue. Maria recognised the goddess *Parvati* adorned with fresh jasmine flower garlands. The statue was surrounded by offerings of food on large banana leaves, also some coins and a few notes in a tin plate. She found the peaceful atmosphere at the centre of the temple gave her relief. She began to come every day, drawn not only by the respite at the foot of the goddess, but also by the feeling that her brightly coloured eyes seemed to be looking directly at her.

On one visit, she found an elderly bare-chested man with three wide stripes of white ash and a red vertical mark on his forehead. She recognised he must be a Hindu holy man, a *sadhu*. He was performing what looked like a *puja* ritual prayer ceremony at one side of the *Parvati* statue. Maria took care not to disturb him and knelt down in her usual position at the front. After a few minutes, Maria felt the *sadhu* looking in her direction. When she looked up, he spoke to her in surprisingly fluent English.

"Why are you here?"

"I enjoy the peace and calm," she said quietly.

"Finding inner harmony and serenity is part of the *vanaprastha* stage of life." Seeing Maria's expression of incomprehension, he continued.

"You are familiar with the Hindu stages of life, madam?"

Maria shook her head.

The *sadhu* stood and moved closer to her. It was only then that Maria saw in the dim light of the temple that he was covered in a dark oil, but otherwise completely naked. He knelt next to her.

"*Brahmacharya* is the first stage when we are students preparing ourselves for the rest of our lives with education and training. The next stage is *grihastha*, the period of family and homemaking when we have and educate our children and prepare them for life. Then we move to *vanaprastha* and withdraw from our family life and obligations and start to focus on our spiritual development. If we are fortunate, we are able to reach the final stage of *sannyasa* in which we renounce all material aspects of life and live very simply using our time as a spiritual preparation for liberation from the karma cycle of rebirth."

The *sadhu* paused, observing her closely.

"Which stage are you, madam?"

As the *sadhu* spoke to her, for the first time she could remember since arriving in Matheran she found herself able to concentrate and think clearly about a different topic from the one that otherwise constantly occupied her thoughts. The *sadhu*'s simple explanation seemed so clear and appropriate to her.

She thought for a moment.

"I think … I was in the second stage, but it was very short and unsuccessful and unhappy. I have been here in Matheran for several months and am probably in the third stage."

"Do you have family, madam?"

"Yes … No … I don't … I don't know," Maria stumbled over the words.

"Do you have children, madam?"

"No, … No, … not any more," Maria said and felt a stab of unhappiness in the pit of her stomach as she spoke the words.

"Then maybe you are ready for the final stage, madam. Perhaps you are ready to become a *sannyasini* and to free yourself from the bad *karma* in your life in preparation for the next? I have been a *sannyasi* for many years and now I am ready. I am on my way to Varanasi for my *mahasmadhi*, to pass into my next life."

She remained silent and after a few moments the sadhu started to chant in a low monotone in a language she couldn't understand. After continuing uninterrupted for several minutes, he stopped. As if splashing his face with imaginary water, he cupped his hands in the white smoke of some incense sticks glowing nearby and bathed his face. He gestured to Maria to copy him. Maria closed her eyes and holding her breath leant forward and tried to imagine water splashing on to her face as she followed his movements.

When she opened her eyes again and looked to her right the *sadhu* was gone.

She left the temple a little later and walked on the narrow trail between the trees and thick undergrowth. She heard, as if for the first time, the chatter and squeals of the packs of monkeys that roamed freely around the town. Wild mangos, large and overripe now, hung on some of the trees alongside the path. Strange that she'd never seen them before. She sensed her steps were firmer and more purposeful now. She felt a new clarity in her mind and then like a blinding flash it came to her. She must also go to Varanasi, like the *sadhu*. She had visited the holiest Hindu city many times already since arriving in India and she could recognise now the right next step. Her release, her only release, was to complete the fourth stage of her life in Varanasi and pass to the next.

Chapter 26

The indecisiveness that had defined her life for these last months was dropping away like old clothes being cast aside. She knew she had to leave Matheran and travel to Varanasi. The ancient city, nestling on the banks of the Ganges and the centre of Hindu spiritualism, was about to become the path to her final liberation.

The owner of the small wooden house she'd been renting had a cousin with a car. Within a few days she was on the back of an underfed and skeletal horse cautiously negotiating the steep and slippery path down the side of the mountain to meet the driver who would take her on the three-day journey to Varanasi. She'd managed to phone Kamal, her funeral pyre wood supplier contact there, and tell him she needed a cheap and simple hotel. Kamal had naturally been surprised, expecting her to stay in her usual choice, a former British East India Company residence and then later maharaja's small palace. He'd been even more surprised by the proposal she'd then put to him. For a moment she'd thought the line had been cut, so silent had he remained, but then she heard him sigh deeply and agree to see her when she arrived.

As the car drove across rural India Maria looked out at the life that had barely changed its never-ending and repetitive rhythm for centuries. The farmers' laborious ploughing of fields behind their impassive, white and black-skinned oxen. The back-breaking planting of seeds and then the harvest of wheat, maize and rice—it was a never-ending cycle of survival from which there was no escape. Along the side of the road, women, balancing heavy loads on their heads, strode in single file as cars and trucks sped by.

Both men and women seemed to have an expression of numb stoicism. Only the children displayed an unencumbered joyful energy for life, running and chasing each other aimlessly with boisterous chatter and laughter between the simple open bed *charpoys* under trees on the roadside and the basic mud-walled homes near the cultivated fields.

What was it that transformed the innocent and unencumbered liveliness of youth into the tired, laden and imprisoned gaze of adulthood? How did that simple spontaneity, free of any weight of expectation, give way to the restricting demands, burdens and unrealised desires as they became older?

While she hadn't suffered their poverty and hard labour, she knew she was no different. She could list her own disappointed dreams immediately. Her desire for acceptance, her desire for children, and perhaps most of all her need for her mother's love and recognition—all had plagued her, depriving her of the freedom she now knew she needed. There had to be a resolution. Because life was otherwise too full of suffering for her. As the car bumped and swerved its way towards one of the world's oldest cities, Maria felt she was approaching the end of her own journey.

It took longer than expected. The road had been blocked for six hours one day by a heavily overloaded lorry that had toppled over on a tight bend. Then her driver had insisted on stopping at the onset of darkness and staying in a simple inn because the risk of travelling on unlit rural roads at night was too great. It was dusk when at last they arrived at the hotel in Varanasi.

She was just in time to walk down the crowded streets to the banks of the Ganges to watch, as she always did, the line of chanting priests perform the *aarti* ritual of worship and dance as the holy river was put to sleep. Afterwards she took off her shoes and wandered along the *ghats* feeling the warmth off the paving stones that had absorbed the sun's heat all day. At the Jain Bachraj Ghat, emboldened by her new singleness of purpose she ventured down the long stone steps to cool her feet in the gently lapping water. On her past visits she had never dared to touch the unhygienic water, but now she felt she should assimilate as much as possible into the city that was going to be the place of her salvation. A Jain couple observed her and encouraged her to take another step deeper into the water, saying the river had the power to cleanse itself. A little later she passed one of the piers where boats could be rented. As on most of her visits, she wanted to arrange a rowing boat and guide for early the following morning so that she could witness the sunrise and observe the cremation fires from the water. A young man with an appealing smile offered to arrange everything for a reasonable price and agreed to meet her at the pier just before dawn the following morning.

"My name Samir. Just ask my name tomorrow. Everyone know me. I give you good tour, Madam."

When she returned to the hotel, she recognised that Kamal had reserved a more expensive place for her than she needed. He could probably not have imagined her staying in anything cheaper. However, for her plans that was probably appropriate. As she lay in bed, thoughts of Mischa came to her mind, but she pushed them away. She felt a singleness of purpose now. Exhausted but calm, she fell asleep easily for the first time in many months.

Chapter 27

She awoke an hour before dawn to the quiet purr of the bedside phone and the receptionist's voice with the wake-up call she had requested. As always, she was looking forward to seeing the river come to life at sunrise, but this time she also had a particular reason for seeing the funeral pyres.

When she returned to the hotel later in the morning after her trip she was excited. Her visit to Kamal, the merchant of funeral pyre wood, had been successful and he had agreed to her proposal.

"You have visiting the fire *puja* at the river this morning, ma'am?" the young receptionist cheerily asked Maria when she entered.

"Actually, I saw the *puja* last night and this morning. But later today I am going to Bhavana Guruji's *ashram*." In her hand was the slip of paper Kamal had pressed into her palm before she had left his office. The receptionist's eyes widened.

"Bhavana Guruji is great man. He will help you, ma'am. He will help you understand, like he helps us all understand."

Later, with the help of a guide supplied by the hotel, Maria walked through the narrow streets to the *ashram*. The building was a nondescript white structure with several floors of windows looking out onto the street. Maria was disappointed. She had imagined finding an imposing temple. She rang the doorbell.

As she waited for a response, she heard faint voices chanting inside accompanied by the occasional chiming of bells or the soft clashing of cymbals.

The door creaked open at last and a man with a naked chest and wearing a saffron lunghi stood there. He stepped to the side, and with a silent *namaste* welcomed her in.

"Bhavana Guruji?"

He gestured her to follow him. They climbed a staircase, and as they crossed a few dimly lit passages Maria noticed the chanting becoming louder. Singing. She heard the regular rhythm of several bells and a deep occasional gong. The man ushered her into a huge hall. As Maria's eyes adjusted to the gloom, she saw several hundred people, young and old, kneeling on the floor. Their eyes closed, they were all swaying gently forwards and backwards as they chanted a single drawn-out sound that seemed to be coming from the depths of their bodies.

Maria found a space in the first row in front of a raised stage. As she was settling down cross-legged there was a commotion to one side and a door opened left of the stage. The chanting stopped and was replaced by excited murmurs of anticipation among the audience. A large man slowly made his way from the door to the centre of the stage, which was now illuminated brightly by spotlights. Maria knew this must be Bhavana Guruji.

An image flashed into her mind of the spartan church near the König department store, where most Sundays she, her brother and her parents had sat directly under the ornate wooden pulpit affixed to one of the large columns. She remembered feeling terrified as a young child by the stern-faced and black-robed pastor talking down at the congregation, usually about the terrible risks and dangers of sin they must avoid.

As the man came into the light she was taken aback. He was very tall with a long flowing white beard that stretched down to his waist. He was covered in long, flowing, gold silk and velvet capes that made him appear still more imposing. He emanated benevolence, gazing without any sense of urgency or concern at the audience in front of him. As Maria focused on his face, she saw a kind expression in his eyes and a gentle smile that played across his face. She could physically feel serenity flowing out from him into the hall. The excited murmurs in the audience subsided into a peaceful calm and silence.

"*Namaste, namaste.*"

His voice reverberated deeply from within his chest into the great hall. The voice was like no other she had heard before. It generated an immediate sense of release and trust and she felt herself relax.

Bhavana Guruji sat down in a large wide seating area on the stage covered in silk embroidered cushions, giving the impression of a floating throne. Then, he began to chant, and the audience joined him. Maria could feel the power of the sound vibrating through her body.

After several minutes of chanting, during which Bhavana Guruji had kept his eyes closed, he raised his arm and stopped. Almost immediately, except for a few isolated stragglers, the whole audience ceased as well. He opened his eyes, and a large gentle smile filled his face as he looked out at the devotees. Occasionally he seemed to connect with specific individuals, as his eyes and face would show signs of recognition, or seem to be communicating short wordless messages, before moving on. Maria felt his gaze linger on her for a moment, but she was still too intimidated to look back directly at him.

"Welcome. Welcome, my friends," he said in perfect English. "How can I help you?"

There were a few moments of silence. Hands were raised and an attendant passed a microphone to a woman.

"I have been trying to follow your advice for several months now, Guruji. But it is not …" The voice broke and paused.

"You want to say it is not working," Bhavana Guruji said with a chuckle. A few people tittered. Some laughed.

"When I relate to other people in my family I am quickly frustrated and get angry. What should I do?"

"What do you want to do?"

When there was no reply, Bhavana Guruji continued.

"See, you all come to me for answers. But I don't have the answers. You all have the answers. They are within you. You must learn to search inside yourself for the solutions you are seeking."

"But where should I look, Guruji?" another voice, this time a man's, sang out. I cannot find the answers on my own."

"It is not about looking for answers. It is about listening. Once you start to learn how to really hear what your true inner self tells you, and you have the courage to listen to that, and I mean really listen, you will find your way forward.

Some were nodding. All sat waiting for more.

"Everyone has a true inner self, a core, but we, … or you, because I have learnt already … "again, that charming chuckle, "… you are all used to not listening to that core, but instead listening to all the advice around you from your friends, family, society. See, the question is not what can you find in the world around you to satisfy your desires or goals, but what can you find inside yourself that offers the explanation and meaning to everything … to work, to life, to love, to death, to any and all questions you have."

The people sat rapt in silence, hungry for him to continue.

"Then one day you will discover you have no desires … you just have you … Then you have arrived … You will recognise that you are sufficient for everything in this life."

Maria was spellbound. She felt as if he was speaking directly to her and to her needs. The self-assurance with which he spoke combined with the tone of his voice persuaded her that she could believe him. After a few more questions from the audience, Maria tentatively raised her hand. The attendant passed her the microphone. She felt Bhavana Guruji's eyes resting on her and felt the warmth in his gaze. Maria was sure all around her could hear her heart thumping furiously as she struggled to keep her nervous voice calm and stable. She focused on her memory of the two tiny infants whimpering weakly in the burning hot sun on the causeway to help her concentrate.

"I am new to your country, Guruji," she began, remembering to use the title of respect that she had heard all the other questioners employ. "Why is there so much suffering here?"

"Is there no suffering in your country?"

"Yes, but …"

He looked directly into her eyes. "What is it in your life that is making you suffer?"

"Other people have always made me suffer."

"See, what is suffering for one person is something else for another person. You may feel suffering, I may feel satisfaction. To escape what we believe is suffering we must understand and recognise what it is in ourselves, in our core, that is making us believe we are suffering. It is not others that make us suffer, but we who make ourselves believe we are suffering."

Suddenly, in her mind image after image appeared. The babies on the caking hot causeway merged with a picture of Katrin Hudrich, the fellow pupil in her island school who had also been bullied, sitting cross-legged and with shaven head in the garden in front of her parents' home on the island. Suddenly the oak tree of her boarding school was here in the hall with her, and she could feel the rough bark on the back of her neck and the blood trickling down underneath her collar. Paulus Stockton seemed to be walking towards her holding a huge bouquet of roses but shaking his head vigorously from side to side. Then her mother materialized on the stage standing next to the guru but looking directly at her with that disapproving look into the distance that she knew so well. And then before any other images appeared tears welled up in her eyes. Sobs wracked her body as her shoulders shook, convulsing, and her mind went blank. She felt herself falling into a cushion of hands and then she fainted.

Around her there was silence and then, quickly, Bhavana Guruji directed a number of attendants to gather around her, lift her gently and carry her out of the hall.

Chapter 28

When she woke, she found herself in a bed with clean white sheets in a room she did not recognise. Her clothes had changed, and she was now wearing a white Indian *kurti* top and baggy white trousers that were bound with a simple cord around her waist. There was a plain table and chair in one corner, a small upright cupboard of light brown wood in the opposite corner, and directly above her a slowly spinning electric fan.

As she struggled to recall how she had got here, she saw the suitcase she had brought from Matheran to the hotel in Varanasi standing in a corner of the room. In the background she could hear the bells chiming again interspersed with the deep melancholy gong and with a rush she suddenly remembered the large hall and the rows of chanting devotees and the resplendent figure of Bhavana Guruji.

She sat up. There was a wash basin on one wall. She stood to wash her face. At that moment the door opened and a young Indian woman in clothing identical to Maria's entered. She was bearing a tray with some silver tin bowls of food, and a plate filled with *naan* bread.

"Good morning, Madam. Your breakfast."

"Good morning," Maria replied. "What time is it now?"

"It is 6 am, Madam."

"Where am I? Where are my clothes? How did …"

"Guruji arranged for it. He will come to meet you later only."

She placed the tray on the small bedside table and left the room soundlessly, her bare feet gliding effortlessly across the floor.

Maria moved to the window. Below in an open courtyard she saw a line of white-clad devotees carrying the same tin dishes she had been given for breakfast. They were waiting patiently to take their turn to rinse them at a long trough-like sink with water taps mounted at regular intervals before stacking them on a table nearby. There was complete silence with nobody speaking to each other and moving in some kind of reverie. In the distance, beyond the whitewashed walls of the compound, she could see the Ganges flowing majestically. Downriver, the light brown hues of the *ghats* of Varanasi were just visible. With a shock, Maria realised she was outside the city, no longer in the *ashram* with the hall, the chanting devotees and Bhavana Guruji.

After eating her breakfast and showering in a little alcove she discovered attached to her room and concealed with a full-length curtain the same colour as the pale green walls, Maria took her dishes and made her way down a staircase to the same courtyard she had seen from her window. It was now deserted. She washed her dishes in the long trough as the others had done and stacked them on the table. A number of open corridors led to and from the courtyard. Curious, she tip-toed down one of them, her bare feet noiseless on the clean stone floor. Through an open doorway, she spied some of the devotees sitting motionlessly in yoga poses, eyes closed in meditation.

'What is this place?' she wondered.

Not wanting to disturb them she found her way back to her room to wait for Bhavana Guruji to appear.

A few hours later, a loud knock startled her. The door opened, and Bhavana Guruji entered accompanied by a number of young attendees. His presence seemed overwhelming and to fill the small room, as she sat up on the bed.

Bhavana Guruji, signalling his followers to leave, sat on the only chair in the room and looked at her directly.

"How are you feeling today?"

"I … um … I feel fine … but …"

"You wonder where you are."

"Yes."

He chuckled disarmingly.

"This is the residential *ashram* my group runs in Varanasi. Where you came yesterday was the small day centre in the middle of the city. We were concerned for you yesterday at the meeting. I asked my attendants to bring you here. We took the liberty of arranging for your things to be picked up from your hotel and brought here. I hope you don't mind. It seemed clear to me that you needed some time in a place where you will not be disturbed and can find the answers you are looking for."

Maria looked at him in surprise "How do you know what I am looking for?" she said firmly.

"Your words about suffering and your reaction to my question were very clear. Something is disturbing you deeply. You are looking for an answer. But you are no different from others. We are all looking for answers or solutions to the challenges that perplex us." Bhavana Guruji gestured expansively. "Most people out there believe the world revolves around them. They think they can change the world, or people, around them and they only need to work out how to do that best. But that path is flawed. You cannot bend the world to your desires. You must enter a state of observation rather than one of direction. People and events around you are triggers for reflection and understanding, not for judgement and action. "We can only observe and wonder … and learn."

Maria felt herself calm. She felt safe. It was almost as if his voice was caressing her.

He paused, seeing she looked overwhelmed.

"I have spoken too much already. I would like to invite you to stay here for as long as you need. My only condition is that you commit to join the daily yoga and meditation routines and programmes of all devotees. I will also spend time daily with you to help you on your journey."

Maria did not respond immediately. Would this distract her from her purpose in coming to Varanasi? Her resolution in Matheran had not only given her direction but also such relief. She could not face losing that. Still, perhaps a time of reflection in this peaceful place would be good for her as preparation for her final journey.

"I will be free to leave whenever I want?"

"Of course, with our blessing."

"Then, I will be happy to stay. Thank you for your hospitality."

He smiled and rose. Putting his hands together in the namaste greeting, he left.

In the days that followed, she tried to settle into the daily routine of the *ashram*. But despite the peaceful atmosphere she found her sleeplessness returning. It became increasingly difficult for her to rise at 5 am when the sky was still pitch black, to join the other devotees filing from their rooms to the prayer hall with its life-size portrait of Bhavana Guruji. However, once kneeling amongst the others, she found the rhythmic chanting of mantras take control of her own breathing and give her relief from her growing anxiety.

As the sun's rays began to play through the leaves of the trees around the compound and shine through the dining hall's uppermost windows, the devotees finished their chanting and lined up to receive their food served from large simple cooking vats set up buffet style near the entrance. After months of isolation in Matheran, Maria recognised that she had missed talking to people. But all the others around her studiously avoided her attempts to establish eye contact or engage in conversation when she cautiously greeted them.

After yoga instruction, during which only the teacher spoke, came another silent meal. Afterwards many returned to their rooms. Some, wearing a saffron cloth, like the one she had found in the top shelf of the cupboard in her room, wrapped monk-like around their bodies, read under one of the trees within the walls. Maria and a few others met independently with Bhavana Guruji, or one of the other spiritual teachers who also lived in the *ashram*.

The more she met Bhavana Guruji, the more Maria felt she could trust him. Encouraged by his gentle eyes and clear, calm voice, she began to reveal almost everything about her past life. At times in tears, at others her voice raised in anger, she found his simple questions helpful in describing why she had felt or reacted in certain ways.

She told him of her mother's judgements, criticism and explosive outbursts. Of the fathomless pain she had felt in the train on the way back from Geneva after her visit to Paulus. Of her terrifying experience with the surfing instructor. Of her limitless happiness when she had first met Mischa. Of how she had failed to become pregnant. Of her love for Kanisha and her mother's refusal to accept the adoption. Of her escape from Bombay at the fear of disappointing too many people. All triggered the same warm smile, from Bhavana Guruji and, occasionally, the enigmatic Indian shake of his head.

"Do you think my mother was unfair to react the way she did and threaten to disinherit me for wanting to adopt an Indian child?" she asked one day through her tears.

"What I think is not important," he had said dispassionately. "What you think is important. Why does her reaction upset you so?"

"Because it was unfair after all the suffering I had experienced to hold me back in that way."

"But what was holding you back? Did you need an inheritance to live?"

"No. We had enough money. It was the feeling she would expel me from the family because I had displeased and disappointed my parents."

"How had you disappointed them?"

"By doing something they did not approve of, I guess?"

"But it seems as if you have done many things that did not meet with their approval."

"Yes, that's true. I went to Hong Kong without their approval and against their wishes. I married a man they were not in favour of. But this was different."

"Why was this different?"

"It was more important. It was keeping the family's legacy intact. The purity of the bloodline, about preserving what they had built in the way they believed was right ..."

"So, your children have to preserve your parent's legacy—is that how it works?"

His twinkling eyes waited for her answer.

"It's ... I don't know. It's complicated. I don't want to disappoint anyone."

Bhavana Guruji signalled that their time was up. But before he concluded, he repeated the same words he had at the end of every one of their sessions. Words she had by now memorized and could intone silently to herself before he even started.

"Remember, the answers to your questions and the solutions to your problems reside within you."

As the days became weeks Maria felt she was living in a cocoon, insulated from the world outside the *ashram* walls. She had no desire to leave the grounds. The daily routine was so comfortable and calming, she could probably stay there forever. After each of her sessions with Guruji she felt she was seeing things more clearly than ever before.

Her mind wandered less to painful memories, and past disappointments. When it did, more and more she found herself coming up with plausible explanations that replaced the spiralling vortex of self-doubt that had been her default way of interpreting unpleasant experiences throughout her life. At times, she felt almost as if she was standing outside her body, observing impartially the way she had behaved for so much of her life. It was as if she was a neutral observer, able to watch and understand the foibles of a well-meaning but imperfect person who overreacted when she felt criticized or rejected by others. She was unnecessarily prone to lose self-confidence whenever she faced a challenge. Her first preference was almost always to satisfy the wishes of others around her, without even considering her own needs.

Gradually she began to see that her interactions with people need not be a terrifying tightrope above an ocean of potential failure. Rather, they formed a map she could try to navigate as successfully as possible. As Bhavana Guruji said, "observing and wondering and learning."

But whenever she thought of her mother, the fragile edifice of self-confidence came crashing down. If she tried to imagine a conversation with her mother, she could immediately hear the voice full of judgement allowing her no room to observe and wonder. 'How could you even consider adopting a child from India? You don't understand what this means to us. How could you be so selfish?' Then Maria would spend a tormented night, blaming herself and only the morning chanting and yoga, followed by another conversation with Bhavana Guruji, would help her find peace again.

Occasionally she would remember the cremation pyres at Manikarnika Ghat and her agreement with Kamal. Although the longer she spent at the ashram, the more her plan had receded to the back of her mind, she hadn't completely forgotten.

She lost track of how many times she had met Bhavana Guruji. But one day one of the assistants came to her after lunch and asked her to meet him immediately. When she entered the simple room where they always met, he was already seated in the large wide low-backed chair he always used, his long train of saffron robes billowing over the chair and down to the ground.

"Please sit."

"Congratulations! You have made good progress. I think you have come a long way during your time here," he said.

She was taken aback. She was used to him taking a very passive and reactive role in their conversations and allowing her to drive the content and flow of their interactions.

"You have used the time here well, like a true *sannyasini*. It is time for you to consider your next step.

But before you do that, is there anything else you would like to tell me?" Bhavana Guruji asked.

She wasn't sure if it was her imagination, but she thought his eyes seemed to be watching her closely in a way he'd never done before. Suddenly she felt her pulse racing. Did he know her arrangement with Kamal for the Manikarnika Ghat?

She could feel the colour rising to her cheeks. She held her breath, unable to decide. Could she trust him so completely? If he asked again, she was sure she would reveal everything. But Bhavana Guruji did not ask again.

"The value of spiritual reflection is to clear your mind," he went on, "so that you alone can make the choices which are right for you. Once you are able to distinguish your choices from choices you think others want you to make, then you will be ready to take control of yourself and your *karma*."

"How will I know that I am making the right choice?"

"It will be your choice and that will make it right for you. You are ready for this step now, but it takes courage. A lot of courage. Do you have that courage? Are you ready for the final step of your journey? The step that will liberate you."

She couldn't believe her ears. Now she was convinced that Bhavana Guruji knew her plan. He was encouraging her to take the step of *mahasmadhi*. She need not have feared his disapproval. He'd been with her all along, helping her prepare for her final step. A wave of deep gratitude coursed through her. She was on the verge of jumping up and embracing him, but he signalled that their time was over and that she should leave.

"May your journey bring you peace," he said.

Maria now felt a renewed sense of urgency to complete her plan. Bhavana Guruji's tacit approval of her *mahasmadhi* plans inspired her. No one in her life had supported her in a major decision she made without judgement or disapproval. Bhavana Guruji was right. It was all about having the courage to accept her own path, her own convictions. She recognised now how her lack of courage had been holding her back throughout her life.

It was time to make her own choice and take the step that would finally liberate her.

Chapter 29

She sent Kamal the address where he would find her body. A small spartan apartment owned by her Mumbai friend Deepa Thani. Knowing Maria's fascination with Varanasi, she had once given her a second key to the flat, saying she could use it at any time since it had belonged to her deceased mother and she herself never used it. Maria hoped Deepa Thani wouldn't find out how she was going to use the apartment, but that if she did, she would understand.

The saffron cloth she had found in the top shelf of the cupboard in the *ashram* room would serve to wrap her body. She had already hand-washed the cloth and ironed it in the communal washing area on the ground floor. She would ask Bhavana Guruji to officiate as the priest. He was undoubtedly well-versed in all the Vedas scriptures, and the correct practices for cremations. Although she had not asked for his help, she was now sure he knew everything and was in effect giving her his blessing. She would leave a letter addressed to him at the *ashram* in the late afternoon. He would receive it the same evening, or latest the following morning. She planned to have her cremation with the rising sun, but later in the day would still be acceptable.

She wrote a short note explaining her plans and giving the apartment's address, while making clear the door would be open to allow easy access. She thanked him for all his care and left all her remaining cash in the envelope to cover the costs of her stay and as a donation to the ashram. As a special request, she asked him to grant her this one final measure of support to ensure her exit from this life into the next was smooth, and in accordance with the wishes she had set. To honour her pact with Kamal, she added Mischa's address and telephone number, explaining he should be informed that it was her wish he arrange funds for the college education of Kamal's two children. She began sealing the envelope then stopped, carefully eased open the back flap to take out the sheaf of paper and added a postscript: 'Please ask Kanisha to forgive me.'

She left the envelope addressed to Bhavana Guruji at the *ashram* reception and although it was quite a distance, walked to the city. She wanted to feel the earth under her feet and where the ground was paved and smooth removed her shoes and walked barefoot. It reminded her of how as a child she had loved to walk barefoot on the hardening sand of the island's beaches as the tide receded. How strange to think that her final steps would be on the other side of the world in a foreign country that then she had never heard of and could not have imagined.

Few of the people on the street paid her much attention, but occasionally the lively voices of children pealed through the air. "Hello Auntie!", "Was yer name?", "One rupee?" She remembered the orphanage and the sad girl with the braids among the lively children there. She shook her head to tear herself free from the claws of recollection. Mischa's comment that she did love children came into her mind. She always had. Their complete lack of any judgement before they grew up and were influenced. They really did represent the "observe and wonder" that Bhavana Guruji talked about.

As she walked, she wondered how to present her death as a natural one, not self-inflicted, to ensure she didn't break the rules for cremation. As her mind explored the possibilities, she wondered at her extreme, almost morbid calm. This was her own death she was planning, and yet she was approaching it as a mundane practical problem. A plastic bag around her head would be painless but would leave clear indications of a suicide. Alcohol and an overdose of sleeping pills, of which she had collected a large number, was probably the easiest as it would leave no trace but might not be reliable enough. If Bhavana Guruji was right and she had made significant progress in her spiritual development as a *sannyasini*, perhaps she could be true to the practice of *mahasmadhi* and simply will her spirit to leave her body and leave it lifeless behind? However, if she was honest, she wasn't confident she could manage that.

The sun was setting over the Ganges when she entered the small two-bedroom apartment overlooking the *ghats*. As she looked out the small window, she could see the priests gathering for the evening *aarti* ceremony to put the Ganga goddess to sleep. She would sleep her last night with the goddess, she thought with a short smile.

Maria had decided alcohol and sleeping pills would be the best and easiest combination, since she could remove all traces. She opened the bottle of Bombay Sapphire Indian gin. The sky-blue tinge of the bottle had attracted her in the small shop on the street below. She placed it on the table next to the small box containing her mother's pearl earrings, carefully poured the gin into a plastic water bottle she had brought with her, then took the gin bottle back down to the street and dropped it into a basket of refuse. Back in the apartment, she emptied the sleeping pills into a small heap on to the table.

What did one do at moments like this? Should she watch the sun set one last time? Or perhaps try and recall scenes from her life? Life seemed so fragile and lightweight when you were on the verge of ending it. She could see how leaving your body by choice could be the ultimate mastery of existence. Escaping the cycle of birth and death, where inexorably and repetitively children pass from the freedom of innocence to the chains of their own preferences and values and personalities, imposing those expectations on others and on themselves. Her mother had had very clear personality preferences and, without compunction or awareness imposed them on those around her. Mischa had as well. And no doubt, she had done the same with her own blind spots.

Through the window, she could see the sky was now pitch black. The tropical sunset was so short. She would swallow all the tablets with the first sips of gin, then drink the rest. She should still have enough time before oblivion set in to rinse the plastic bottle and stand it inconspicuously in a corner of the room.

She carefully opened the box with her mother's pearl earrings and fastened them to her ears. Although her mother had caused her so much pain, she had never managed to cut loose from that emotional bond. It was almost as if she had remained the child her mother wanted her to be, and her mother had remained the mother Maria wanted her to be. With the first pills in her hand, she stood once more looking through the window at the colourful and noisy riverbanks below. Finally, she closed her eyes.

"Forgive me, Kanisha. You did not deserve me," she whispered.

She sat down again heavily on the small divan she knew would serve as her final resting place. She placed the first six pills in her mouth and took a large swallow of the gin.

At that moment, the door to the apartment crashed open. Filling the doorway completely, so that she couldn't see past him, stood Bhavana Guruji. His normally serene face was agitated, his chest heaving heavily from the climb of the steep staircase. His eyes took in the pile of tablets on the table and the bottle standing next to them.

"You are making a mistake, Maria."

He had never called her by her name before.

"This is not your path. You have demonstrated great courage, but for the wrong step. This is not the next step I was encouraging you to take."

"It's the choice I have made," Maria said.

Guruji stepped toward the small table and scattered the pile of pills onto the floor. "This not a choice, but a needless waste."

He pulled her roughly off the divan. "Come with me."

She felt helpless to resist as he led her down the narrow staircase to a waiting car.

Chapter 30

On the drive through the dark streets back to the *ashram* Bhavana Guruji had said nothing, but repeatedly taken her hand lightly between his palms and raised their hands together in a prayer pose with his eyes closed. Once she thought she heard him chanting a short mantra under his breath, but she couldn't be sure because her head now felt very heavy.

Some of his assistants were waiting for them at the *ashram*. They helped her up the stairs and into her room and laid her down on the bed. Everything now appeared very blurred to her, but she sensed a hand massaging a cream with a sweet odour into her temples and scalp. She began to grow calm and soon fell asleep.

When she opened her eyes the next morning, the sun was glaring in through the window. Squinting against its piercing light, she noticed a young Indian woman sitting peacefully on the chair watching her. The woman who had brought her breakfast on her first day in the *ashram*.

"Good morning, Madam."

She rose to open the door, then spoke in a whisper to someone standing outside in the corridor. A few minutes later, Bhavana Guruji entered the room.

"We are getting quite good at saving and reviving you," he said with a chuckle. Maria couldn't but suppress a smile. He paused and looked at her, his eyes locked onto hers in such a way that she could not look away. She knew he could see into her soul. “I am impressed,” he continued. “You have demonstrated to me, and more importantly to yourself, that you have great courage.”

“I thought … I believed you wanted me to take this step,” she said haltingly. “I was ready. I still am.”

“I fear I inadvertently misled you,” Bhavana Guruji said quietly. “I apologize for that. As soon as I received your note, I rushed to prevent you from making a mistake.”

He shook his head and looked at her with such sadness, that Maria felt her own eyes welling up with tears.

“I couldn't have forgiven myself if I'd come too late. The step I was talking about, the one that takes great courage, is not to leave your body, but to live as your true authentic self. Once you have found your inner core, your inner self, you can find peace living as that person. Everything else is a lie, a lie that is most terrible because it is a lie to yourself. All those out there who tell themselves this lie and don't challenge it are searching for answers without finding inner peace.”

Maria had never heard him speak so directly to her, and she was transfixed. Every word seemed crystal clear to her, and she felt she had never understood what he was saying so completely until that moment.

“Living true to yourself will liberate you, but the path of liberation is not always easy. Those around you have become used to you as the person who has lived a lie. They may not recognise you once you liberate yourself from that lie and may not like the new person they are meeting for the first time."

Bhavana Guruji paused and looked at her thoughtfully for a few moments before continuing.

"And, even more, you may not like the people around you when you look at them through the eyes of your true self."

Again, he paused and for several moments appeared lost in thought with his eyes closed, but Maria could see from their tremors that he was not sleeping. With his eyes still closed he continued.

"I know you have understood what I am telling you, but understanding is not enough. If you want to complete your journey, you must also liberate your emotions. They are the only thing holding you back from taking the most important step in your life and achieving serenity. To free yourself, you must take a pilgrimage to a different and more challenging holy place. You have shown you have the courage, so I believe you are ready to face this challenge. Varanasi is the site to come to for death. You must visit the place for life, where you can discover your true self."

Chapter 31

Still half asleep, Maria heard the loud squeal of the train's brakes. She felt her body shoved hard against the narrow side-guard of the uppermost bunk bed on the overnight express from Varanasi to Gorakhpur. Beneath her in the bunk below, she heard the unabated snoring of the elderly, portly and kind gentleman who had offered her his top bunk and taken the middle bunk she had originally reserved.

"Much cooler on topside, Madam," he'd said calmly, waving away her half-hearted resistance. "Close to fan only, Madam," he insisted, pointing at the oscillating electric fan hanging from the ceiling. But given the oppressive heat in the compartment, even though it was close to midnight, she had thankfully decided not to demur. She was the only woman in the compartment and surmised that her benefactor's discomfort that a foreign woman should have to travel with five other men had triggered his chivalry.

The other passengers had ignored her and simply climbed into their bunks at the start of the journey before the evening express had even left Varanasi Junction station. As she lay and felt the rhythmic movements and sounds of the train slowly lulling her to sleep, she noticed how the passenger in the bunk opposite had unknotted a plastic bag and filled a small tin bowl with what looked and smelt like some kind of *biryani*. She could see from his long beard and *taqiyah* skull cap that he must be a Muslim.

At one point, through half-closed eyes, she also saw two hands from the outside gripping the iron grill that was fixed across the compartment's window. With a commotion of shouts and loud voices, arms reached down from the roof of the swaying carriage and pulled up an adolescent boy who must have run alongside the slow-moving train and jumped up to clasp the window grill.

She recalled the last few days at the *ashram*. She'd decided to follow Bhavana Guruji's suggestion immediately and to travel to Gorakhpur from where she could cross the road border to Nepal, the first stop on her way to Tibet. He'd warned her she would be ascending high in the Himalayas and would need warm clothing and time to acclimatize to the high altitude.

"Probably you will feel quite ill at first," he'd said. "Remember you are on a pilgrimage. This is not a holiday. You must open yourself to experiences beyond your body and its discomforts to go to a deeper level inside yourself."

The noise of the train's deceleration eased, and the acrid smell of burnt brakes gradually dissipated. Maria looked out of the compartment window and saw temporary wooden shacks, covered with tarpaulins or corrugated steel sheets. They were squeezed into the narrow area between the edge of the ballast under the rail tracks and the outer perimeter of the wall separating the railway from the streets of the city. Through the openings that served as windows or doors, she saw vignettes of lives. Babies being fed, mothers cooking, children watching simple black and white televisions, grandfathers sleeping. Their impoverished lives were also locked into interminable and repetitive cycles.

"This is your chance for liberation from the *samsara* of life, the cycle that most people never find an escape from," Bhavana Guruji had said in one of his final sessions with her. "Their lives are unchanging copies of the ones their parents lived before them, whether they realize it or not. They completely miss the wonderful uniqueness that each one of us is and instead choose the easier path and live on unquestioningly in the same way as the previous generation did."

Maria had never experienced Bhavana Guruji's face so focused almost unnaturally so. It was as if his body and eyes were emanating a kind of power so strong she could almost touch it.

"In each one of their lives, as they pass from birth to death and then are reincarnated, they complete the same cycle, never asking or challenging to find out who they truly are. They believe their lives are unique, but they don't see the lie they are telling themselves. Nor do they see how completely locked they are into the cycle. It is like sleepwalking through your life. The frustrations, the unhappiness, the despairs that many experience, show they are aware they are not happy, not fulfilled, but at the same time feel powerless to do anything about it. At some point they give up and accept that state of paralysis as reality and take it into their next life and the cycle is repeated.

"The pilgrimage you are about to take is your chance to break out of that cycle," Bhavana Guruji said to her almost fiercely and, most unusually for him, gripping her shoulders with both hands as she stood at the gate to the *ashram* compound waiting to take the small taxi to the train station. "It is a chance for you and a chance for your next generation and your reincarnation."

As he spoke, an image of Kanisha came to her mind. That could have been her next generation. She wondered how Mischa was coping with Kanisha on his own. She was sure he was. He was so well organized and disciplined that he would have found a way to arrange everything. She sensed a tinge of guilt and pushed hard against the feeling. What she was doing was more important.

The overnight train finally pulled into Gorakhpur Junction, and she managed to navigate her way through the teeming multitudes of shouting and jostling people on the platform. Once out of the distinctive red and white colonial-style station with its large-arched porticos, she found a taxi. She kept her only luggage, the small backpack she had purchased before leaving Varanasi, with her on the back seat. She'd discovered on the train that Bhavana Guruji had arranged for her envelope of cash from her letter with cremation instructions to be surreptitiously packed into her bag before she left and was unwilling to let it out of her sight.

"Where you go, Madam? To border crossing?"

"Yes please." Clearly this was a well-travelled route into Nepal and Kathmandu.

The border wasn't busy, and her Western passport ensured she was waved through without difficulty. Another taxi driver on the other side promised her a reasonable hotel located near the Tibetan embassy in Kathmandu and at dusk she was in the Nepalese capital.

The following morning the consular official seemed uninterested in why she wanted to travel to Tibet.

"How long you stay in Tibet, Madam?"

"About two weeks," she replied, following the advice Bhavana Guruji had given her.

The following morning, the visa for Tibet stamped into her passport, she was gripping the handrail of the seat in front of her as the heavily overloaded bus clawed its way up steep mountainside roads. She couldn't bear to look down at the precipitous drops literally inches from the bus's worn tires. A couple of times already the bus had come to a complete halt and only after a great clashing of metal parts, and with the engine racing loudly, had the driver managed to coax the bus back into continuing the climb. Once, he'd missed a gear and the bus had lurched backwards.

She screamed, sure they were plunging over the edge. But the driver had managed to halt the bus and then, after finding the correct gear, resumed the climb. The other passengers paid little attention to her and remained calm, either practiced travellers on this route or more fatalistic than she. Many were clearly Tibetans clad in bulky, padded clothes. The men wore felt cowboy-style hats and the women, colourful scarves or fur hats. Their faces were mostly deeply tanned, weather-beaten and wrinkled from the sun and wind. She surreptitiously watched a group of Buddhist monks at the back of the bus, noticing their shaven heads, saffron robes and open sandals. She shivered to see them wearing so little against the cold temperatures at the altitude they had now reached.

Despite Bhavana Guruji's warnings, she hadn't felt any discomfort from the high altitude. Only once, at one of the regular stops at a bus transit station, when she climbed a short staircase to the simple toilet block, had she felt her chest heaving and had to sit down on the short wall at the side unable to continue as her lungs strained for oxygen.

After she crossed the Tibetan border checkpoint, a guide and driver arranged by the *ashram* were waiting for her. The guide told her the trip would take fifteen hours. As the sun was beginning to set he suggested they should stay overnight in one of the small towns en route the main road and continue in the morning. But, anxious to reach her destination, she politely refused, promising them both a large tip if they went on through the dark. The driver agreed and, after refuelling, drove on. Thankfully, she noticed, they had no desire to talk and largely ignored her. After the terrifying ascent to the border from the day before, the journey was now on a tarmac road through a plain of gently undulating lush green hills on either side of the car.

Occasionally they would pass by a small *stupa*, that she recognised from a book she had read soon after arriving in Bombay. She recalled the typical whitewash base and main structure with the usually golden spire on top. Almost always there was a rainbow of Tibetan prayer flags fluttering in the wind and radiating out from the pinnacle of the stupa to the ground. As they drove past, the driver and guide would both briefly raise their hands in prayer and close their eyes for a short moment.

At one location, the road had been washed away by a flash flood. A queue of cars, buses and lorries was waiting, their drivers unwilling to ford the powerful stream of water swirling through a riverbed of rocks and tree branches. But again she egged their driver on, determined to lose no time in reaching her destination. The driver, pushed into the torrent of water. The car bounced and twisted. At one moment she felt it would tip over onto its side. But the guide opened his door and, balancing between door and frame, shifted his weight out. For a few moments the car hung in the balance, then at last sank back down heavily. The water level rose to the door handles. With a spurt of fear, she thought the stream was too deep, but then with a rush and roar of the engine they were through to the other side.

Beyond the hills in the distance, she could see the giant snow-capped peaks of the Himalayan range. She felt she was in the cradle of the world now, surrounded by huge rock formations, crushed into shape so many thousands of years earlier, and preventing the entry of any outside influences. She felt so small and immaterial in such a vast landscape, almost as if she was imprisoned by these gigantic peaks. No wonder this world was spiritual, she thought. No bustle of people, no distant horizon to wander beyond in exploration of new adventures. Here, the invitation to look inwards and search for the answers to your questions seemed the only available option.

The guide motioned ahead through the windscreen. Maria caught her breath. In the distance, shimmering in the midday sun, lay a vast stretch of water. Its deep blue hue nearly matched the cloudless cobalt blue sky.

"Lake Manasarovar, Madam!" the guide said excitedly.

And then beyond the lake, separating water and sky, almost like the broad sweep of a painter's brush, was a long range of brown mountains interspersed with still-higher snow-covered peaks. Stretching high above the other mountains and piercing into the sky stood one snowy peak shaped almost like a huge stupa.

"Mount Kailash, Madam. You see, Madam? Mount Kailash!"

Bhavana Guruji had given her instructions for her visit to Lake Manasarovar and Mount Kailash. She should bathe in the pure cold fresh water of the lake to purify and cleanse herself. This would wash away any thoughts or fears still holding her back. She must remain open and receptive, to think beyond the distracting physical discomforts of her body. Once she felt she was ready, she should then travel the short distance to Mount Kailash and complete the two- to three-day pilgrim's trek around the mountain.

"Be ready. If you touch your core, you will know immediately. The change you will experience will feel miraculous to you. Manasarovar and Mount Kailash are among the holiest of sites in the world, both for Hindus and Buddhists. For centuries pilgrims have visited. Thousands have come there seeking liberation from their *samsara* cycles of life."

She had listened carefully as he spoke.

"Very few succeed because they are unable to free themselves from their desires, and step outside their existing consciousness. They keep their self-perception and needs at the centre of everything they see, rather than searching for and finding something that is far larger and more significant.

"But some do and …" His voice had trailed off then and, wondering why he'd stopped, she'd met his warm gentle gaze and knew instantly he hoped she would succeed.

As soon as they arrived at the lake, she got out of the car. Ahead of her was a field of rough grass stretching to the water. Several large hairy Tibetan yaks with their sharp curved horns stood grazing, tethered to stakes in the ground.

While the driver and guide set up her tent and prepared for the late afternoon meal, she took off her shoes and walked gingerly down to the lakeside. Although the sun was still shining and warming her face, she could still feel the cold earth under her bare feet. She stood at the water's edge looking out across the lake. The water was crystal clear. She could see small fish darting between the fronds of the underwater plants, and stones scattered on the mud bottom. She was unsure where to begin, or how to follow Bhavana Guruji's guidance.

Raising her eyes she looked into the distance and saw the mountains. Then the view suddenly blurred, and it was as if she was looking at herself from a great distance away. She was suspended in the sky and could see herself standing as a tiny figure on the edge of this wide lake in the middle of a vast plateau surrounded by mountains and glaciers that had all been formed millennia earlier. Beyond that, a universe she could barely visualize nor understand. She felt suddenly insignificant, inconsequential. The disappointments, worries and anxieties she'd carried with her so long as inseparable baggage seemed small and meaningless from this perspective. Her mind was so remarkably clear in the cold air. Perhaps what she needed wasn't an escape but a new understanding. Slowly she returned to the small camp site.

Early the next morning, the glow of the rising sun not yet visible over the crests of the surrounding peaks, the guide woke her as she'd requested. She clasped her hands around the mug of hot tea he handed her and tried to warm her body beside the small campfire he'd prepared. When she felt she was ready, she walked down to a small area of hard dry ground with patchy grass near the water's edge. She sat in the cross-legged position of meditation facing the water and closed her eyes.

At first, she felt distracted by the hardness of the ground beneath her. Also, despite the thick clothes she was wearing, the gradual seeping in of the cold. In the distance she could make out sounds she couldn't decipher, and, closer by, the hushed voices of the guide and driver back at the campfire. Gradually, however, the sound of small waves lapping regularly and continuously against the shore, started to block out all other sounds. She felt a prickling of the skin on her cheeks, and a warmth began to radiate through her. She assumed the sun was at last rising above the mountains. But when she opened her eyes, to her surprise she saw it was still dark. She closed her eyes again, allowing the glowing warmth at the centre of her chest to gradually fill her body. She could feel her fingertips and her toes tingling as her face had earlier, with a radiating energy that gave her strength, and comfort.

Once again, she felt as if she was suspended above the lake, looking down at herself in a vast barren landscape. She rose to her feet. Removing her heavily padded jacket and trousers, she stood naked at the edge of the water. Without the slightest hesitation, she stepped forward into the lapping wavelets and felt how gentle and soothing the water was despite its cold temperature. She advanced further until the water was at her knees, then to her hips. As she moved calmly through the water, she felt the soft mud on the floor oozing between her toes. Cupping her hands, she filled them with water, then raised them to her lips and drank.

Suddenly, fleeting images of her past life began to rush through her mind like a film reel. Her escape from Bombay to Matheran. That last phone call with her parents. The children on the causeway to the mosque. The many IVF attempts, the wordless departure from her parents at the airport, Paulus' face as she entered the restaurant to see him with his partner. The surfing instructor. The earnest faces of the teachers as they discussed her school diploma. Blood trickling down the back of her neck as in tears she thumped her head against her boarding school tree. The taunting schoolchildren outside her parents' home. Her mother's stern, critical expression. And then, almost as if the reel had come to an end and spooled out, she suddenly saw herself very clearly in the gynaecologist's clinic with her mother waiting in the next room. The doctor was leaning over her with intense eyes asking, 'Miss König, are you completely sure you want to take this step? It is your choice, your choice alone and no one else's.'

At that moment, she became aware of shouts from the shore. The guide and the driver were standing at the water's edge, gesticulating and shouting. Suddenly she noticed she was now armpit deep in the water, and all at once like a knife piercing her flesh, she felt the cold. Her lips began to chatter uncontrollably. She saw her fingers were shrivelled and had turned a pale blue. She turned to make her way back to the shore, but her legs seemed held down by weights so that she could barely move them.

Inch by painful inch, she retraced her steps back through the water. It took all her remaining strength not to simply close her eyes and slip back into the water. Just as she felt she couldn't move any further, she felt the grip of strong hands on her arms, pulling her forward. The guide and driver half-carried her to land. They wrapped her in blankets, and supported her back to the tent, sat her in front of the now blazing campfire, and urged her to drink from a mug of warm tea.

As Maria's shivering subsided and the feeling re-turned to her fingers and toes, her mind cleared. She felt a sense of comfort, detached from her surroundings, a neutral observer of her life, intrigued but not disturbed by anything that had happened or would happen in the future. She felt keen to understand, and willing to be surprised. The radiating warmth returned, and with it a sense of inner peace that seemed to fit completely and appropriately into the stillness and calm of the vast surrounding plateau. A sudden tiredness came over her. She climbed into her heavy sleeping bag. As her eyes closed, she recalled the words of Bhavana Guruji. "We can only observe and wonder … and learn."

Chapter 32

She slept the whole day and night. When she awoke it was again dawn, the sun's first rays piercing the sky. She was hungry and saw thankfully that her guide was already warming some of the Tibetan *balep* barley bread in a frying pan, as well as some fried peas and cabbage. As she clambered out of the tent he smiled at her broadly. She liked his natural authentic friendliness. He had an unusually light-skinned complexion for a Tibetan, and prominent features. She had barely exchanged a word with him since their departure from the border. As she sat down on the small folding chair the driver had set up for her, he offered her a mug of hot tea.

"What is your name?" she asked him.

"I am Tenzin." the guide replied. And before she could speak again, he continued: "You feeling fine, Madam? We are worried for you yesterday."

"Yes, I am feeling fine now. I am feeling very good and very clean, very relaxed."

"Yes, Madam, Manasarovar is holy place. Can change your life."

She felt she had indeed changed but she wasn't sure exactly how. She certainly felt calmer and free of the anxiety she'd so long struggled with.

"Have you come here many times?" she asked.

"Come to help visitors, Madam. But first time I come to try and calm my inner spirit. Then I go to Kailash to pay respect to the god Demchok. Will you go for the Kailash *kora yatra*, Madam?"

Bhavana Guruji had described the fifty-kilometre pilgrims' trek around the base of the holy mountain.

"Yes, I will walk around Kailash."

"I come with you, Madam? I have experience. Walk is very tiring and dangerous."

She was grateful. Having a guide who spoke the local language and knew the route would be very helpful.

A little later, the driver and guide had packed the tent and other belongings into the car. Soon they were on the narrow road to Darchen, a small Tibetan village an hour's drive away. It was the starting point for the *kora yatra*. On the journey Maria continued the conversation she had begun with Tenzin.

"Where are you from?"

"I was born this region, Madam. My father was monk born in Darchen. The village name was Lhara before the Chinese communist, the Red Guard, come."

She had only a vague understanding of Tibetan history. But she did recall hearing of rampage and destruction by Chinese youths brandishing little red books filled with the thoughts of their revolutionary leader Mao Zedong. He was bent on destroying all traces of religion and idolatry in China. And in Tibet after Chinese troops occupied the country.

"I was very young. My mother tell me, Red Guards destroy many sacred sites and stupas. In Darchen, only one building left."

"Where is your father now?"

"My father die, Madam. Red Guards kill, Madam."

He paused, before adding, "But we are all Buddhists. We can all find harmony."

The village of Darchen was tucked in at the base of the foothills leading to Mt. Kailash, a peak so holy that no one had ever climbed to its summit, according to Tenzin. Apart from the occasional stupa, surrounded by colourful fluttering prayer flags, Darchen seemed like many of the other towns she'd passed. It consisted of two uneven side streets off the main road. What, she wondered, made this place so sacred?

When Tenzin left to organize a yak bull to carry their belongings and a few supplies, she looked down the gentle incline of the road. The simple row of buildings down either side of the street's uneven surface seemed either made of sun-dried mud or plastered bricks. The chimneys above each structure confirmed they were all heated with open fires, most likely burning yak dung. In the warmth of the bright early morning sun, heightened by the thin air and altitude, many of the people in the street were not heavily dressed, with some men wearing no more than a shirt, jacket and scarf above their dark trousers. Most of the women wore dark blouses but fringed with collars and sleeves in bright colours. They either covered their heads with colourful scarves or, if uncovered, had braided their long hair into two plaits with the ends fastened together behind their backs.

Two older women stood in the middle of the street facing the direction of Mt. Kailash. Each raised their clasped hands to their foreheads, then to just below their chins, and lastly to their waists, before gingerly kneeing on the ground and bending over to touch their foreheads to the rough stones and rubble. Then they stood again and repeated their worship. One of the women, her face weather-beaten and deeply furrowed, was clasping a string of beads in her right hand as she continued her tiring prayer ritual.

Around these two women, other people moved freely, not paying them any particular attention. Maria marvelled at how naturally spirituality fitted into the daily lives of the people here. Anyone who felt the need to reflect on their place in the world, and to give sense to their existence, could freely take the time to do so.

Tenzin returned, leading a large hairy black yak with sharp black and white horns behind him with a rough rope. Between the horns, the bull sported a colourful red headdress on its forehead, held in place by a dark brown leather strap with white crosses. On its back, Maria could make out a saddle with stirrups under a draped colourful rug. In front of the saddle, two large bulging saddle bags hung from the animal's shoulders. Strapped firmly onto its rear behind the saddle was a metal cylinder marked O2 with a mask attached.

"In case you tired, Madam, you sit on yak," Tenzin said. "Oxygen is for Dolma La pass, Madam. Very high. We start now, Madam. Long journey today."

"How long does it take to complete the journey?"

"For us can take three days to finish."

After she'd had paid off the driver, they were soon walking slowly along a dusty and stony path, passing through undulating barren plains. There were occasional stretches of grass where sheep and yaks and small horses grazed freely. In the distance, the blue waters of Lake Manasarovar glinted in the sun. As they made their way out of the village, Maria saw a Tibetan couple and recognised the elderly woman with the furrowed face she had noticed earlier in the street. They were walking ahead of them in the same direction. At a fork in the road the man and woman turned right to head in the opposite direction.

"Where are they going?"

"Bon people, Madam. Buddhists and Hindus follow *kora yatra* clockwise, Bon people anti-clockwise."

As the gradient began to rise, Maria found herself breathing heavily and moving more slowly with each step demanding increasing energy and strength. She began to worry whether she would be able to cope with the altitude and complete the trek.

Tenzin gestured for her to ride on the yak. But she shook her head, determined to complete the pilgrimage like any of the other pilgrims. Tenzing nodded and kept walking on ahead.

After another hour of walking she saw ahead of them, on the crest of a hill beside the path, a mound of stones draped in colourful prayer flags. Under the flags she could see the pinnacle of a small stupa. On the path beneath the mound two men were lying face down on the ground. As they drew closer, she saw one and then the other rise and stand, raise their arms, take one step forward, go down on their knees and then lie full stretch, face down, their foreheads on the cold dusty ground.

"*Chagtsal*, Madam. They purify themselves and show humility. They complete whole kora yatra this way."

She looked again at the two men. Both wore traditional Tibetan clothing, but without head cover or gloves. She shivered to think how cold they must be. But when they stood, their faces showed no discomfort at all. If anything, they seemed completely at peace, their eyes gazing upwards in awe at the pristine white slopes of Mt Kailash that was now visible above them.

She felt she must try to disregard her own tiredness. She recalled the advice of Bhavana Guruji to ignore the distraction of the discomforts of her body so that she could experience the pilgrimage fully. The freezing water of Lake Manasarovar had given her such clarity. Who was this person who had reacted and behaved in the way she had in all those different situations? What made her feel the unhappiness of people around her so deeply, and swallow the pain she experienced when others hurt her? Why did she prefer not to speak, rather than potentially disappoint someone? What stopped her from being firm and tough and untouched and able to manage her emotions in the way others around her did? As she let the scenes of her past play through her mind again, she recognised, regardless of which one she selected, she had always accepted blame. She might have been the one who suffered but she was invariably convinced she was the one at fault.

As she looked at the steep stone walls around her and ahead in the distance the glowing, towering white peak of Mt. Kailash, a voice in her head told her 'Strip everything as bare as those cliffs. Stop hiding, go to the centre of your being to find out who you really are.' Mt Kailash seemed to have taken on a golden tinge in the thin air and the rays of the bright sun. She felt the power of the sacred mountain that had drawn pilgrims to it over millennia. As she was struggling to circle the mountain, she felt as if she was also circling the terrain of her personality and emotions, trying to gain entry to her own inaccessible inner core. Bhavana Guruji had said, of those who tried only a few succeeded.

The incline of the path was rising again. She heard the loud rasping of her breath as she slowly put one foot in front of the next. But despite her growing exhaustion, she preferred to continue rather than rest. If she halted, she feared she might not have the energy to go on.

At a bend in the path ahead, Tenzin stopped next to a pile of coloured stones. He raised his hands in prayer, chanting quietly and monotonously. The stones were engraved with pictograms and text. She began to pass by the stones on the other side, but Tenzin motioned her to halt.

"Only clockwise, Madam. You must pass *mani* stones clockwise. Please come."

Tenzin led the yak and Maria around the mound. On top of it, a yak skull with horns was nestled between the stones. Once they had completed a full circle, Tenzin stopped again.

"Chant with me, Madam."

She followed his lead, clasping her hands in prayer while repeating over and over: "*Om mani padme hum, om mani padme hum, om mani padme hum.*"

Although she did not understand the words, their rhythmic repetition was soothing. She could almost hear them reverberating off the sides of the rocks, as they must have done for thousands of years.

"It is mantra for Tibet people," Tenzin said when they had finished. He pointed to one of the stones. "Chant written here. Give you blessing if you chant mantra. It is from Buddhist saint of compassion. He help all people who are suffering. Chant help you understand why you suffer and help you feel compassion for other people who suffering. If you feel compassion you are bodhisattva in our religion."

They continued upwards on the path, skirting a small river through a valley hemmed in by steep mountain peaks and rough cliffs. It looked as if a giant hand had carved a furrow in the earth. She continued to chant quietly under her breath, in rhythm with her breathing and her regular steps. She felt her mind becoming empty, focused only on the ground before her, the air rushing in and out of her lungs, and the pumping of her heart.

The sun had disappeared behind the tall ranges surrounding them, and although the sky was still blue the temperature had dropped sharply. She felt the chill on her skin and stopped to put on another jacket. Tenzin looked concerned.

"Must reach Drirapuk Gompa before darkness. Nighttime too cold and dark … very dangerous."

They renewed their trek, pausing only for another short break for water from one of the bottles in the saddlebags. Tenzin was now urging the yak on, in-creasing their pace. Gradually the gap between them lengthened until she could only just make out the yak and Tenzin's bobbing red brimmed hat against the grey colour of the mountainside. She resumed her quiet chanting of the mantra, struggling to keep her thoughts away from the discomforts of her body.

After a long stretch she looked up and could see the valley widening again. In the dying light, she could just make out a splash of white and red buildings hewn into the mountain side above the stream and valley floor. She could see lamps swaying in the breeze and could hear the deep reverberating sound of a gong. Tenzin came back to meet her.

"Drirapuk Gompa, Madam. We rest here."

Tenzin tethered the yak outside, then they climbed the large outer steps to the monastery entrance. Inside they were in a large room illuminated only by candlelight. A monk invited them to sit at a long table where a few other pilgrims were already eating. Almost immediately two bowls of steaming vegetable stew were placed in front of them. Tenzin and Maria ate in silence. When they had finished, he led her deeper into the monastery through a large hall to a small entrance to a shallow cave in the mountainside.

"Great Buddhist saint stayed here many hundred years ago," he said in a quiet, reverential whisper.

Looking into the dark interior, she could just make out a small statue of a monk in meditative pose on a large rock in the middle of the cave.

"Is that the saint?"

Tenzin nodded and clasped his hands in prayer.

When they returned to the main hall of the monastery, a maroon-robed monk was sitting in a small alcove at one end of the room. Two pilgrims sat in front of him, receiving his blessing. They were just rising to leave.

Tenzin's face showed a look of recognition, probably from previous visits. Maria was intrigued and moved closer. Tenzin hesitated.

"Late now, Madam. Maybe you like sleep now."

But she was already standing in front of the monk. He was old but with clear features and, like Tenzin, a lighter complexion compared with the dark weather-beaten skins of most of the Tibetans she had seen. His face was round but the nose, rather than flat and broad, was prominent and angular. His eyes seemed very alert.

"You want ask question? I translate," Tenzin said quietly as she settled down in front of the monk on the small rug. She thought she saw a look of disdain, almost contempt, flash briefly over the monk's face as he glanced at Tenzin, but she couldn't be sure.

Initially, her mind felt blank, and she was not sure what to ask. She looked at Tenzin.

"Please ask him how long he has been a monk at this monastery?"

Tenzin translated the question and then before the monk had a chance to reply gave her the answer.

"He has been a monk here all his life."

"Has he completed the *kora yatra*?"

She could see the monk had guessed what she'd asked because he started answering the question before Tenzin had finished translating. Tenzin raised his hand with four fingers outstretched confirming the number of completed pilgrimages. The monk was becoming bored. Could she ask him for help?

"How can I use the *kora yatra* to complete the journey to my inner core?" Maria asked and she saw from the brief hesitation before Tenzin began the translation and then from the sudden stiffening and straightening of the monk's posture, that he was now engaged.

Tenzin translated. The monk's reply was long. He spoke for several minutes. She could see he was clearly upset about something. Had she asked the wrong question? Tenzin looked disconsolate, peering down at the floor before him and barely moving his head as the monk spoke. When Tenzin finally translated, he said only, "You must try and be open and listen to mountain, open your heart to mountain."

"But did he say anything else?" she asked. "His answer was far longer than that."

"Time is finished," Tenzin said firmly. "Please leave donation," indicating with his hand the small basket with notes and coins on the rug in front of the monk.

Maria deposited the few coins she had in her pocket, then rose to follow Tenzin out of the hall and down the monastery steps. They crossed a narrow stretch of rock-strewn ground, like a lunar landscape under the pale moonlight, to the guesthouse where a monk showed them into a large communal dormitory with bunk beds and rough mattresses. Tenzin was silent and distracted. Exhausted by the long climb she fell immediately into a deep sleep.

The following morning a grey mist obscured the surrounding peaks. Tenzin had already prepared and loaded the yak and seemed impatient to leave. Maria could see he hadn't slept well, perhaps not at all.

"Would you like to wait until the weather clears?" she asked. She recalled that this day was the most physically demanding, as they needed to cross the Dolma La pass, the highest point of the *kora yatra*.

"No, we go now," Tenzin said abruptly, and turning started towards the path.

As she followed him, she wondered what had come over him. Until the meeting with the monk, Tenzin had been nothing but smiles and friendliness. Had her questions been so mistaken, or her donation too modest? Or was there something else she'd done wrong?

The path now became steeper. They left the monastery below them. There were patches of snow on the ground. The mist became thicker. Soon they were enveloped in a world of whiteness and could scarcely see anything. A whistling wind painfully chilled her face and still the mist didn't clear. The path was only visible a few paces ahead, and she had no idea where they were heading. Even Tenzin had stopped a few times, apparently himself struggling to keep to the path. Once they had to double back on their steps. On another occasion, they found themselves suddenly standing on the edge of a precipice where one more step would have seen them plunge down a long, steep slope of sharp loose rocks.

Gradually the gradient levelled, and through the swirling mist Maria saw what looked like a field of fluttering prayer flags. There were also items of clothing pinned to the ground with stones or fastened with strings. She looked at Tenzin.

"We reach top of Dolma La pass, Madam. Pilgrims leave personal offering for safe journey. We stay here now, wait for good weather. Wind too strong. Path down very steep, too dangerous."

He removed the coloured rug that was draped over the saddle and suspended it, forming a windbreaker from one side of the yak to the ground. He invited Maria to sit next to him. Immediately she felt a little warmer and more comfortable.

"I'm sorry if I asked the wrong question in the monastery yesterday. Or if my donation was too low."

Tenzin looked at her.

"No Madam. My mistake. Monk yesterday was my uncle. He is always very angry with me. He think I should follow my father, become monk. He always tell me I choose wrong life as guide. Yesterday, he say why foreign woman can ask good spiritual question on meaning of *kora yatra* and I am only guide. He say he embarrassed for me that foreign woman know more than me about Kailash *kora yatra*."

Tenzin's voice was sad and tired. "My father was famous monk, and my uncle say my responsibility to family to also become monk. Say I cannot choose my own way because duty to family. But I am proud of my work. I like to show foreign people my country and culture and tell them about Buddhism and spiritual experience." Suddenly, he looked energized again. "It is good for foreign people to learn and understand. But my family treat me like I am child. Say I don't understand life and responsibility."

"Why don't you simply tell them what you want?"

"I cannot, I don't know how. It's better stay quiet otherwise my uncle more angry."

She listened silently. Now she understood the critical glances and the treatment Tenzin had received the evening before and she felt as hurt as he did for the lack of understanding, for the rigid control, for the unwillingness to allow him to develop in the way he wished and for the forlorn manner in which he saw no alternative but to accept.

An image of her mother floated into her mind. Almost instantly, she felt a flash of clarity pass like a bolt through her. Her life was no different. She was also controlled, not free to develop as she wished. She was the child in the relationship with her mother, always being told why she was wrong and not meeting her mother's expectations of responsibility and obligation. Her mother had discouraged her from developing as she wished, just as Tenzin's father had him. And, like Tenzin, she had bowed her head and accepted.

At that moment the mist and clouds around them suddenly, almost miraculously, cleared. Before them lay a vista so beautiful that Maria gasped. Above them the sky was completely clear, while just below them the cloud was thick and impenetrable, concealing everything. It felt as if they were floating on a carpet of white, almost as if they had entered another world. But more than that, what took her breath away was some trick of light that projected a glorious golden reflection of Mount Kailash, not visible directly from the pass, on the carpet of cloud at their feet. It was a picture of purity free of any distractions. A unique moment of unmitigated beauty and peacefulness that she wished would never end. Tenzin too was overcome, his eyes brimming with tears.

"Madam, Madam, Kailash come to us. The god, Demchog, he bless you and he bless me."

Yes, she did feel she'd been blessed, with a clarity in herself that she had never experienced before. She felt she had at last looked into her core. Bhavana Guruji's prediction about the power of Kailash was fulfilled.

But gradually the clouds whipped up again in the wind, and the sight was gone. Tenzin stood, his eyes still closed in adoration. Just as he stepped clear of the windbreaker as if his movements were in slow motion, a sudden powerful squall knocked him off balance, forcing him to lunge backwards to stay upright. His foot came down on the side of a large rock by the path and turned outwards at a completely unnatural angle. Above the roaring wind, she heard a loud crack. Tenzin crumpled to the ground and stared in wordless bewilderment at his left leg, twisted and broken below the knee. He turned to look at her with an expression of astonishment before his face suddenly contorted and he screamed out in pain.

She didn't know what to do. She couldn't bear to look at the broken leg, but also couldn't stop herself. Something sharp and white was protruding through a tear in Tenzin's trousers. It was the sharp edge of splintered bone. She tried to ease the leg from its unnatural angle, but Tenzin yelled in such agony she stopped.

"Tell me what to do. What can I do?" she begged. "What should I do?"

Between deep gasps for air and cries of pain, Tenzin managed to point at the heavy rug he'd used as a windbreaker. She understood and covered him with it, being careful not to touch or move his leg. She found a sleeping bag in one of the saddle bags and put it under his head. Tenzin was now moaning loudly at regular intervals, his eyes clenched shut. She tried to offer him some water to drink from one of the bottles, but he barely opened his lips. Without the protection of the windbreaker, she felt the icy cold. Suddenly she realized they couldn't stay here much longer. She was no mountaineer, but she knew the freezing temperature and windchill were too dangerous. But equally it was clear Tenzin needed urgent medical care and couldn't walk. They were on their own. Yesterday they'd seen a few other pilgrims trekking in both directions. But today they'd seen no one, probably because of the bad weather.

"Madam … Madam …," he said weakly, between gasps and moans. "You must go. Wind too strong. Too cold. You die if you stay here. You take steep path down to Gaurikund lake. Only one hour, Madam."

"No, I will stay here with you. We will be fine. The wind will pass. I am sure someone will come by soon." She was almost shouting now, so strong had the wind become.

"No, no Madam. No one come on path today. Weather too dangerous. Other pilgrims at guest-house tell me this morning not walk because weather so bad, but I so angry with my uncle I walk anyway. I am very sorry, Madam. I should keep calm, should have no desire, but I so angry. I want to show my uncle I am good guide. I want him to be proud of me."

His words seared into her. She understood so clearly what he was saying. She knew she would have said the same herself. Her desire for her mother to be proud of her had burnt inside her as long as she could remember. She knew before she spoke.

"Tenzin, I am staying with you. I will not leave you here."

Tenzin looked at her for a moment, then glanced away in despair.

"Madam, I can die here, but you die I am responsible."

"I understand Tenzin, but if I leave you here, I am responsible."

Despite the pain in his face, Maria thought she detected the faintest of smiles flit over his features. She replaced the sleeping bag under Tenzin's head with one of the saddlebags and then unzipped the sleeping bag and wrapped his body as best she could in the howling wind to try and retain warmth. Maria could feel her own body getting very cold, and she tried to wrap the second sleeping bag around herself, using one of the saddlebag straps to hold it in place. Tenzin's face and hands already felt icily cold to her touch, and he seemed to be slipping in and out of consciousness. With a sudden flash she remembered the oxygen flask Tenzin had bought with them from Darchen. She fought her way through the freezing wind to the yak which was standing still seemingly unperturbed by the weather and managed to release the flask from its harness at the rear of the animal. Then she remembered the oxygen mask in the saddle bag under Tenzin's head. He was now moaning quietly in a regular rhythm with his eyes closed. Without disturbing him she managed to pull out the face mask with an attached tube and valve unit that she could see needed to be screwed onto the top of the flask before she could release the oxygen. She placed the face mask over Tenzin's nose and mouth and with her other hand turned the small release lever. The oxygen hissed into his face, then after a few seconds he opened his eyes and turned his head towards her and smiled weakly.

He motioned her closer and, holding the mask aside for a moment, she leant towards him to catch his hoarse voice.

"Flare, Madam. In other bag. Signal flare, Madam."

Leaving him holding the oxygen mask to his face, she returned to the yak. She found the other saddlebag, mustering all her strength not to be blown against the animal's flank. She needed to remove one of her gloves to unfasten the buckle of the bag. As she did, she lost grip of it and the glove whipped up into the wind, but then extraordinarily caught itself on the spike of the yak's horn. the wind itself holding it firmly in place. Maria retrieved the glove and stuffed it between her legs, then opened the bag. Inside she found a long red and yellow plastic tube with the words 'Rocket Signal Flare' written on its side.

She returned to Tenzin. The oxygen mask had slipped from his face, and he was lying without moving. Maria fixed the mask straps round the back of his head so that he wouldn't need to hold it in place. His eyelids flickered faintly. The instructions on the flare said to unscrew the bottom, hold it above her head, point away from the wind and pull the trigger string. Initially, she could not get the bottom to budge as it kept slipping between her gloved fingers. She did not want to risk losing her glove again. Finally, the base gave way, and she was able to unscrew it. She held the flare above her head, having no idea which way the wind was blowing—it seemed to be blowing everywhere at once. She struggled to catch the cord as it whipped in the wind. At last, she caught it and pulled down sharply. The flare kicked in her hand and with a loud hiss the rocket shot into the sky. She was just able to see the glowing exhaust disappear into the cloud and mist. A few seconds later, the heavens seemed to take on a red tinge for what felt like a minute before disappearing again.

She decided to lie down next to Tenzin on the far side from his injured leg, to try and give him some of her body warmth. She unfastened the sleeping bag from around her chest, and somehow managed to wrap it over him as well as she clasped him close to her. As she lay there, images of rescuers finding their frozen bodies appeared in her mind. And suddenly she saw her mother's stony look, the rigid line of her mouth and heard the tone of voice she knew so well admonishing her that it was all her own fault. Angrily, she shook her head. 'This is not my fault. This is my life and the way I wanted it,' she thought. She wondered if Mt. Kailash, after teasing them with the miracle of sudden beauty, was now punishing one or both of them for some misstep.

"*Om mani padme hum, om mani padme hum, om mani padme hum ...*"

She started chanting quietly to herself, so quietly she wasn't sure if it was only in her head or actually coming out of her mouth. She continued and then after a few minutes heard ever so faintly Tenzin's voice in chorus with hers from behind his mask.

"*Om mani padme hum, om mani padme hum, om mani padme hum ...*"

Chapter 33

When she opened her eyes, she had no idea where she was. Above her, she saw dark wooden timber beams below an angled ceiling. She was lying in a small bed on a thin mattress covered by a heavy blanket. She could see a clear blue sky and bright sunshine through the wooden-framed window on the other side of the room.

She tried to lift her bed covering up, but her hands had been swathed in bandages so that she couldn't move her fingers to grasp the covers. She struggled to sit up and then shift her legs over the side of the bed to put her feet on the ground. They too were wrapped in bandages. When she stood up, she felt a numb pain in her feet. She was dressed in rough Tibetan clothing with a heavy woollen waistcoat over a pink blouse and a heavy cloth dress. She needed to know where she was and moved gingerly in her foot-bandages to the window. From there she looked out from an upper floor of a large building over an arid, brown earth and stone valley through which a river was flowing. Several monks were busy in the open space below. The resonant sound of a gong broke the silence followed by the accompanying repetitive choral chant of many voices. She realised she was in a monastery.

She limped across the room and opened the small wooden door. Two young novice monks passing by looked at her, whispered urgently between themselves, then one rushed off. Leaning on the doorway, she heard shouts and excited voices, and the slap of running feet. Two older monks hurried to her and, each taking an arm, helped her along the corridor, down a staircase to a lower floor, then into another room.

Tenzin was lying in a bed. He turned his head. His face broke into a beautiful broad smile. Suddenly she recalled the wind and the cold, his horrific injury. Her legs weakened. The monks swiftly brought a wooden chair for her to sit on.

"How are you, Madam?"

"I am fine. How is your leg?"

Tenzin lifted his bedclothes to show his leg strapped straight to a wooden splint and wrapped in bandages. His hands and feet were swaddled like hers.

"Much better. My uncle monastery see flare and send rescue party. They find us just in time. Yak was gone. But oxygen and your body heat keep me alive. Madam, you save my life."

At that moment, the bedroom door opened, and Tenzin's uncle entered. Unlike the stern expression she recalled from their previous meeting, his face was beaming.

He bowed to her, then sat on another chair that was drawn up alongside Tenzin's bed. Gently taking her bandaged hands into his, he started to speak without waiting for Tenzin to translate.

When he was finished, he let go of her hands.

"My uncle thank you for self-sacrifice you make to save my life," Tenzin translated slowly. "He remember your question in his monastery and he say you have listened to Mt. Kailash very carefully. You have show great compassion, like a bodhisattva of compassion, to save my life. He say you must have very pure compassion to risk your life. He think you have no personal desire, only compassion."

After Tenzin finished translating the last words, his uncle turned to her and looked deeply into her eyes.

"Thank you. Thank you," he said quietly in English, then bowed his head low to her and was silent for several minutes before standing and leaving the room.

Later, back in her own room, she gazed out of her window at the serene view of Mt Kailash towering over the valley and the other mountains. She felt calm and at peace. Tenzin's uncle had given her the final piece of the puzzle. It was her compassion that was the key to her core. Her compassion was her strength, and whenever she lived it she was calm and at peace. When she felt compassion in others, mostly by searching through their eyes, she sensed meaning. An openness to give and to take, to learn. But where there was no compassion, only rigidity or no understanding of her emotion, it was as if a door had slammed shut inside her and left her confused and unsure.

She understood now, in a way she hadn't before, the serene closeness between her and Mischa, despite their differences. She also saw clearly how her mother didn't share her compassion. The harsh and violent outbursts of Johanna had, since her childhood, closed the door on emotional understanding or openness between them, and left her perpetually insecure. And it had continued throughout her life with others, as well, often leaving her crushed and silenced by their harshness. She realized now that her most important choice was to live her compassion.

And even if the door to her mother was closed, it could still be opened. Perhaps only from her own side, and perhaps only the smallest of cracks to start with. But to live compassion truly she could never abandon her mother, or anyone else. It was wrong of her to expect more. It was wrong of her to impose on others. Even if her mother didn't have her compassion, it wasn't a fault, simply a difference. Maria could only "observe and wonder … and learn."

As pictures from her childhood coursed through her mind, and she recalled her mother's judgemental expressions and loud angry voice, the images began to blur. Now she saw her mother as a young girl, scarred by the brutality of war, petrified at the threatened violence of Soviet troops, terrified of her own father's fierce authority, and desperate to rebuild her parents' lost social status and respectability. Her mother had never had the desire or, perhaps even the freedom, to search for her core in the way she herself had. For the first time, she felt sympathy for her mother, the sympathy of equals. Not that of a child worried about the unhappiness of its mother, but the sympathy of one adult for another.

She knew she was now a *sannyasini*, no longer weighed down by the burning unfulfilled desire to win her mother's approval or love. She felt a kind of invulnerability she had never experienced before. By embracing compassion, she could escape the cycle of *samsara* and free herself from her past. She could avoid living the same life her mother had lived in her cycle, imprisoned in a world of expectations and desires, failing to discover the real person within. She could see now that she was also to blame for her own long unhappiness. The expectations her mother had imposed on her had simply been a perpetuation of the cycle. Now she had found herself and could step out of the cycle.

As she gazed out in wonderment at Mt. Kailash, the white snow glistened and shone like a jewel illuminated from within. Somewhere close by in the monastery, she heard the slap of running feet on a stone floor. In her ear she heard the patter of Kanisha's feet. She knew that now she was ready.

Chapter 34

She left the monastery and Tibet a few days after it was safe to remove the swathes of bandages on her raw hands and feet. Since Tenzin was still recovering, his uncle arranged for a car to take her to Lhasa, the capital from which she could take a sequence of flights to Bombay. The route into Tibet via the road crossing from Kathmandu was preferred by pilgrims, but departure was easier from the capital city.

Tenzin had been sad to see her leave. His leg was still in a splint when the car arrived to take her to the airport. He prevailed on a group of young monks to carry him down to the forecourt in a stretcher so that he could see her off.

"I not forget you, Madam. Thank you. Thank you," he had said, clasping her hands gingerly in his own raw hands. "I not forget your compassion, Madam."

"Thank you, Tensing. You have helped me find my way."

At the airport, where she found a flight to Bombay via Delhi, she had found a small shop offering long-distance calling and Internet services and sent Mischa a fax from a small shop offering long-distance calling and Internet services. She could have called but felt she wouldn't know what to say, how to find appropriate words. The office clerk had looked up in surprise at the short text on the sheet she handed over the counter. But after a moment's hesitation, he dialled the number and, following the shrill tone of connection, waited until the sheet sputtered through before handing it back to Maria. She looked at the two short lines again before folding the paper and placing it in her inside jacket pocket.

> *I am sorry if I have hurt you, but I am now ready and able to return. I very much want to. Would you like me to come back? Love M.*

As the taxi drove through the streets of Mumbai from the airport, she grew increasingly tense. Would Mischa accept her back? Would Kanisha remember who she was after five months of absence? As those thoughts swirled through her mind, she wondered how she would feel when she saw them again.

The same watchman, who had seen her leave months ago, saluted smartly when she entered the building compound. He did not show any surprise at her return.

"Welcome back, Madam," he said, rushing ahead to press the elevator button.

She exhaled deeply as she stood in front of the door, but before she could ring the bell one of the maids, still clad in the uniforms Maria had designed for them, opened it and couldn't stifle a cry before rushing to take her bags.

As she stepped into the bright living-room she had fled so unhappily from months before, Mischa entered from the other side of the room.

"I am back," she said quietly, feeling powerless to move.

Mischa walked across the room towards her and between her sobs of relief, as he took her in his arms and clasped her painfully close, she heard a muffled "Yes, yes, I would like you to come back."

She didn't want to let go, but she heard the maid whispering from the far side of the room. She opened her eyes. Over Mischa's shoulder she saw a small figure unsteadily holding onto the maid's hand. She sank to her knees, tears running down her cheeks.

"Hello Kanisha."

The little girl was staring seriously at her across the room. She felt a surge of panic rising in her stomach. Would Kanisha not accept her? Had she been gone too long? Had she forgotten her? But then she gingerly edged one foot forward, and then another, until she was moving so fast that she was at risk of stumbling. She reached out her arms, Kanisha fell into them and laid her head on her shoulder. After a few moments, she lifted her head, looked into Maria's eyes and there it was: the trusting look, free of judgement and the beautiful smile she remembered so well.

For some days, she luxuriated in the warmth of her return. At every chance, Kanisha would clamber into her lap, clasp one of her fingers in her own tiny hand—just as she had back at the orphanage—and rest her small head just under Maria's chin, as if trying to hear her heart.

She knew Mischa wanted to give her time and space to choose her own moment to explain her absence.

"I feel so much calmer, serene, in a way I have never felt before," she tried to explain one evening over dinner. "I was so full of doubt, sure I was doing so many things wrong. I was almost always terrified before."

"Terrified of what …?"

"Terrified of disappointing you, disappointing my mother and others around me," she said slowly, trying to find the right words. "I felt I was always failing to meet the expectations of other people. I couldn't face disappointing others around me, whether it was you, Kanisha, parents or friends. For me it was a question of survival. The idea of disappointing or hurting someone was so painful to me I couldn't face it. So I avoided it whenever possible until I was avoiding it unthinkingly and automatically. I assumed everyone's disappointment was my fault and that I myself had no value. In the end the burden of that was too great for me to bear."

"What made you change your mind?"

"When I realised that my compassion for people is what makes me unique. It's why people like me, it's why I like myself."

"It's why I love you," Mischa said, leaning over to kiss her on the lips.

"And what about your mother? Do you have compassion for her?"

She paused, realising she hadn't thought of her mother since leaving Mt Kailash and the monastery. Was this the final stepping stone on her journey?

She felt a sudden dull ache in her stomach. The last challenge she needed to face?

"Yes, I think I need to see her."

"Do you want me to come with you?"

"No. I need to do this on my own."

Chapter 35

Several weeks later, she stood at the door of her parents' home on the island. She had decided to come unannounced. She was nervous. She pressed the doorbell. It was late morning, and through the frosted glass she could see the shape of her mother coming closer.

The door swung open.

"Hello Mother."

Johanna stared at her. "What ... what do you ... what are you doing here?" she stammered. "Why didn't you call?"

"I thought I should come so that we can talk in person. It's easier than over the phone."

Johanna led her to the study, closing the door behind them. They sat opposite each other. "When did you arrive? Have you come on your own?" She looked nervous, uneasy, which she'd never been before "Or is your husband here with you?"

"No. I came alone."

"Why?"

"The past months have been very difficult for me", she said after a long pause. "I was very unhappy after our last phone call. I didn't know what to do. I had to leave and live on my own in Matheran and then in an ashram in Varanasi. I almost ... died there ... and then I went to Tibet on a pilgrimage."

The words came out in a torrent. She knew her mother couldn't understand what she was talking about.

"But ... but ... Mischa said you ... We called so many times. Why didn't he tell us, ... Why didn't you?" That familiar angry tone rose at the end of her question.

"I asked him not to tell you", she lied. "Something very important has happened to me over the last five or six months. I've come because I wanted to explain it to you. I hope you'll understand."

"What happened? Why couldn't you tell us earlier?"

"I think I learned ... I discovered more about ... well, I understand myself and who I am much better now." Somehow the words wouldn't come out in the way she wanted. It had felt so clear in her mind when she had described her feelings to Mischa a week ago over dinner in Bombay, but now she knew that whatever she said would sound far-fetched and exaggerated to her mother.

"I realised I am a different person from the one I thought I was before," she tried again.

"Well, alright. Who are you?"

"I suppose I'm still discovering that, but I am different from the child who grew up here with you. I don't belong here. People don't understand me and what is more important for me ... maybe you don't either."

"What do you mean I don't understand you? I know you better than you think. You've always put yourself and your own concerns first. Have you ever thought of me and what I need? Have you ever put the family first?"

While in the past her mother's loud bitter voice would have struck a paralysing bolt of fear into her, she now found herself calm and confident.

"Why did you not support our adoption of Kanisha?"

Her mother, who had seemed ready to launch into further accusations, fell suddenly silent. Then, after a long pause. "Why did you have to adopt a child from India?" she asked. "Not everyone has to have children. Childless couples can also be happy."

"Kanisha makes me very happy. She doesn't demand anything from me or have any expectations and all I want to do is give her everything she needs to become the person she wants to become—not the person I want her to become."

"And you believe I haven't let you become the person you want to be?" Her voice was quiet now, no longer threatening.

"No, … you have not." She felt her body tense. This was the line she had to cross … You never did," she said calmly and firmly. She saw her mother look away, that long faraway look in her eyes that she'd seen so often as a child. But this time it seemed tinged with sadness rather than determination.

"It was difficult … we had lost everything in the War when we came here," her mother said. "We were outcasts. The one thing my parents wanted to save us from was scorn and contempt. They taught me the only way to survive is if you have the respect of people around you …," her voice tailed off. "Without that we are nothing."

How many times had her mother told her that in the years of her childhood and adolescence? But now her voice sounded empty, almost sad.

"Did you disinherit me for that reason," she asked quietly.

Her mother's eyes widened in genuine surprise. “Disinherit? Whatever made you think we'd disinherited you? We would never have done that!”

Maria believed her. Perhaps she'd only imagined they'd disinherited her? Bhavana Guruji's understanding and smiling eyes came into her mind. ‘We can only observe and wonder … and learn.’ She'd come such a long way, but the journey wasn't over yet. Probably it never would be. For the first time in her life she was able to look her mother in the eye. And she saw anxiety, even fear.

“I know I was sometimes harsh … you probably thought … you must have believed I didn't love you. But I do, I did … but you were so different, so different from me in so many ways. It's hard, very hard to love someone who's so different to you … particularly if she's your own child. It forces you to ask yourself who you yourself are, who you really are. And that can be a very uncomfortable question. And I thought then … I still do think it's better to avoid those uncomfortable questions. They don't lead anywhere, except to confusion.” Her voice was suddenly firm again, her eyes determined.

Maria felt the tension leaving her body. She couldn't blame her mother for not wanting to face those questions even though she herself had done so. Neither could she blame her for not understanding what her daughter had experienced. She'd never had the opportunity to seek and find her core. Maybe she'd sensed there was more to life, perhaps at some moment in time she'd decide to look. But only she could decide when that moment had come.

She knew now that her mother wasn't at peace in the way she herself was. She had broken the *samsara* cycle with her mother. She was free, liberated from the endless wait for her mother's trust, for her mother's permission before she dared trust herself, for her mother's love … Yes, she had lost her mother, but at the same time she had found her again.

Then

"When can I see my granddaughter?" her mother asked in a calm gentle voice.

Selected Books from PalmArtPress

Martina J. Kohl
FAMILY MATTERS – *Of Life in Two Worlds*
ISBN: 978-3-96258-143-5
244 Pages, Novel, Softcover/Flaps, English

Kevin McAleer
L.A. KID
ISBN: 978-3-96258-193-0
316 Pages, Novel, Softcover/Flaps, English

Dennis McCort
The Golden Pot – *A Fairytale for Our Time*
ISBN: 978-3-96258-109-1
300 Pages, Softcover/Flaps, English

Patricia Paweletz
Tracing the Past in the Present – *En Route to Gaby Glückselig in New York*
ISBN: 978-3-96258-169-5
180 Pages, Non-Fiction, English

YoYo
One Man's Decision to Become a Tree
ISBN: 978-3-96258-136-7
268 Pages, Four Novellas, Softcover/Flaps, English

Rüdiger Görner
The Marble Song
ISBN: 978-3-96258-079-7
280 Pages, Softcover/Flaps, English

Robert Brandts
As We Drifted – *Als wir dahin trieben*
ISBN: 978-3-96258-056-8
Translation: Mitch Cohen, Wolfgang Heyder
100 Pages, Poetry, English/German

Peter Wortsman
The Tattooed Man Tells All – *Der Tätowierte Mann*
ISBN: 978-3-96258-164-0
134 pages, Theater Play, Softcover/Flaps, English/German

Sophia Alexandra
Summer on the Subway
ISBN: 978-3-96258-152-7
118 Pages, Poetry, English

Carmen-Francesca Banciu
Fleeing Father
ISBN: 978-3-96258-083-4
152 Pages, English

Sibylle Prinzessin v. Preussen, Friedrich Wilhelm Prinz v. Preussen
The King's Love – *Frederick the Great, His Gentle Dogs and Other Passions*
ISBN: 978-3-96258-047-6
Translation: Dennis McCort
160 Pages, Biography, Softcover/Flaps, English

Matéi Visniec
MIGRAAAAANTS! – *There's Too Many People on This Damn Boat*
ISBN: 978-3-96258-002-5
220 Pages, Theater Play, English/German

Michael Hampe
The Wilderness. The Soul. Nothingness – *About the Real Life*
ISBN: 978-3-96258-150-3
390 Pages, Phil. Novel, English

Reinhard Knodt
Pain – Schmerz
ISBN: 978-3-941524-77-4
200 Pages, Short Prose, Softcover/Flaps, English/German

John Berger
garden on my cheek
ISBN: 978-3-941524-77-4
Paintings by Liane Birnberg
60 Pages, Poetry/Art, Softcover/Flaps, English

Wolfsmehl
An Unsurpassed Age
ISBN: 978-3-96258-138-1
94 Pages, Theater Play, English

Mitya New was born in Indonesia to an Austrian Jewish mother and a British father. He grew up in Hong Kong and has lived and worked there, as well as in India and Japan, for the past 30 years. He began his career as a foreign correspondent in Hong Kong and China and later in Switzerland and Hungary. He is currently a professor of management and leadership in Hong Kong and India, with a particular interest in the influence of personality on individual behaviour and personal fulfilment. Mitya New is also a trained and certified coach, who is in highly sought after by people seeking a deeper understanding of how their personality, emotional needs, and cultural values influence their behaviour. "Beyond Mount Kailash" is his debut novel. Mitya New currently lives in Bangkok, Hong Kong, and Hamburg.